CHOSEN TO FALL

EMMIE HAMILTON

CHOSEN
TO
FALL

Emmie Hamilton

For Oliver, the foundation of all I am.

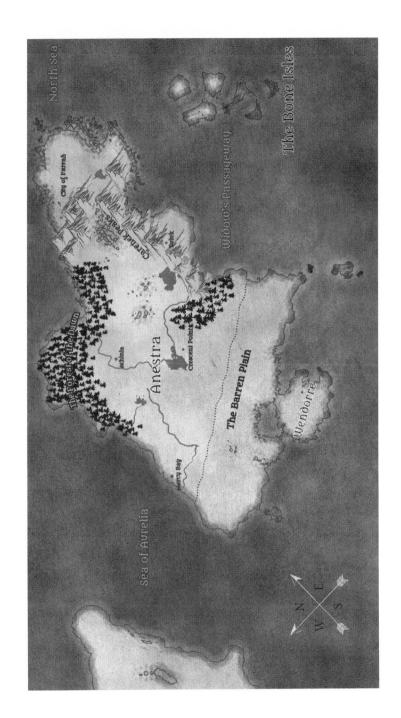

NOTE TO THE READER

Dear Reader,

Thank you so much for purchasing a copy of Chosen to Fall. Countless months and endless hours have been devoted to creating a world worthy of escaping to. As such, I feel it is not only my desire, but my responsibility as an author to make you aware of what you are about to read.

While this book features young characters, there are very adult situations that occur. As such, some of what you can expect are violence, adult language, and sexual content, the importance of consent, a brief childbirth scene, and death. This story, and the series as a whole, may not be suitable for anyone under the age of sixteen.

I would never wish to lead you astray or cause unwanted triggering effects based on the story I created. Please consider this information before you proceed with reading.

Thank you, once again, for your interest in my book. It means the absolute world to me to provide time away from reality. I hope this story and the others to come fill you with joy, gratitude, and resilience.

Yours always,

Emmie

PRINCESS ALENA

CIRCA 50 YEARS AFTER THE GREAT WAR
✦ STORED IN THE ROYAL ARCHIVES ✦

My Dearest Daughter,

Back before the world almost cleaved in two, before the destruction brought about The Great War, before the Val so valiantly fought and sacrificed themselves for us, the Fates visited me in the Dreaming.

I was terribly frightened as voices resonated around me in a darkness so thick, it felt as if I were unmade. Time and reason had no place there. I thought I had Faded and that was what waited for me in the Beyond.

They told me of our family history, how we are direct descendants of the Originals. Of course, I already knew that. My great-grandmother lived until I was five and I remembered how she glowed like the Originals did, and the stories she would tell of our three goddesses.

They said our line was Chosen, that it was predetermined, that They alone sought out which descendants of the Originals were brave enough to take on the responsibility of saving the world.

That cursed darkness swallowed my laughter. The Fates were displeased by my reaction. They flooded me with images—such horrible images of what was to come, up until I Faded into the Beyond. They gave me a choice. The only choice, They said, that I would ever truly be given. If I felt I could take on the horrors of my future, knowing I would not be able to change my destiny, I could begin the trials to become Queen. I would be given one chance to say no.

We know the story of the Prophecy. The one that will bring upon or save us from the End of All. I do not know when it will come to pass. I do not know if it is you it speaks of or your daughter, or her daughter after that, but I do know one thing.

We are alone, Alena. Utterly alone in this world. The Val are no longer here to protect us. The Fae, wicked as they are, abandoned us. I do not know how long their magic will remain in this realm. The warlocks are all but finished, and those who remain hate us. I do not know where the King of Wendorre went or what his fate is. I fear we have not heard the last of him. I worry about the future of our line, especially with this curse in place. Though we won the War, we are still failing.

I did what I could with the peace treaty and again with the blood contract. I used the last of my knowledge of the Old Magic of the land to ensure peace and prosperity so no one could use their power against another should they choose to live here. You must uphold this pact. I believe it will work.

The Fates visited me again last night. They said there is more work to be done through you and all who come after you. They are not finished with us. They are mighty and unforgiving. Do not cross Them. I do not know whether it is an honor that they chose our line or a curse, but there is nothing to be done about it. I accepted on all of our behalf.

Be better than me, Alena. Do not rule with fear in your heart. Be benevolent. Forgive. Allow those who are different a chance to thrive. Raise your daughter with kindness. Love fiercely with abandon.

You are my brightest star and my eternal flame. We shall see each other again.

Yours forever,

Memi

ONE

FARIA

There were times in her life when Faria Agostonna was composed. Calm. Collected. Confident, even, in her ability to maintain constant control.

This was not one of those times.

Blood pounded in her ears as she pumped her legs faster, muscles aching with every step. The ground provided her stability, a way of keeping her in the present.

Instead of stuck in her nightmares, again.

Night blanketed the grassy field, its inky darkness preparing to give way to dawn's first light. The stars dimmed, mocking her, saying, *Our turn for sleep now.* The princess had lost count of the miles she'd run around *Mentage,* just as she lost herself to the night in an effort to release the lingering fear of her dreams that yet again woke her from a restless sleep. The nightmares were getting worse, turning prophetic in nature, though they made no sense to her. She hardly remembered them now, though she still tasted the sharp tang of blood, felt the caress of shadows against her skin—remnants of her dreams. She longed to go back to how it used to be, before she started the Change. Before her abilities manifested. Life was so simple and carefree then.

It would never be the same again.

Distraction was a necessity, and running gave her a sense of control over her life, something she seemed to have very little of as heir to the Elven Royal Bloodline and future Queen of Anestra.

Few people stirred this early; the cooks in the kitchens were preparing breakfast, the smoke from the kitchen's fire bringing with it the scent of fresh-baked bread. Young stablemen saddled the horses for those whose turn it was to patrol the winding roads leading to Athinia, the capital of Anestra, and beyond. A smattering of guards sparred with wooden swords in the practice arena, squeezing in a session before their watch on the walls.

The long grass felt supple and dewy as it brushed against her bare ankles, and the crisp air burned in her lungs as she ran mile after mile around *Mentage*, the prestigious home of the Agostonna Royal Family. Faria was hardly winded—a gift of her elven ancestry.

The cold air prickled against the sheen of sweat on her cheeks, though she knew it would be short lived. The end of summer was just as hot as the beginning, and soon the air would be thick, oppressive, and unforgiving, despite how far north they were.

She slowed her pace as she ran alongside the Forest of the Dawn, its magic sending fluttering waves of awareness down her spine. It called to her, as it did to most Anestrians who were of magical descent, and she welcomed the feeling as she would a hug from an old friend. The Forest was enchanted by the same three goddesses who had gifted magic to the inhabitants of the land long ago. Fae used to live among its trees before they disappeared, though the Gate of All Realms still resided within its shadowy depths. Ancient, gnarled red oaks towered from within, their leaves changing from crimson to gold, depending on the season. The Forest's beauty brought Faria comfort, and it was one of the only constants in her life. Its stability was reliable, safe, and often felt more like home than *Mentage* itself.

The ground crunched beneath her as she took care to avoid thick roots peeking through the tall grass. She glanced over at the sprawling mansion that lay beyond orderly farms and sloping hills. To strangers, *Mentage* appeared to be little more than an elaborate log cabin, sitting nonchalantly outside the gates of Athinia. Anestrians, however, saw a fortress in its place, with tall parapets and a stone wall protecting it. Once inside, the cabin transformed into a white mansion with dozens of rooms, equipped with its own farms, stables, and apothecary. It also housed the main barracks for most of Anestra's army along with a practice ring. Fae magic was sprinkled throughout the property—remnants from when Fae had lived among the Anestrians—allowing the mansion to change according to the peoples' needs. Often, the queen would allow newcomers or struggling families to stay within the Agostonna mansion. The royal family ruled the way they lived: in harmony, for the people, and with mercy.

Faria stopped outside the barracks, dreading the start to her day. She knew the conversation her mother wanted to have after her practice and she was not ready for it. She was never ready for it.

The stars faded as she contemplated her upcoming session with the weapons master. She trained with him or one of the Elven Royal Guard every morning before starting her duties around *Mentage*. Though she would never admit it, her daily training was the only time that Faria truly enjoyed herself. She knew she could never show any sign of discontent to her people; being a princess obligated her to perform her duties without complaint.

Soft grunting and noises of exertion reached her ears. The breeze shifted and with it came the scent of sweat, earth, and spice. The weapons master, Hunter d'Valero, appeared to be getting his workout in early as well.

She sighed to herself and entered the practice ring. She had hoped she would train with Endo, the weapons master's assistant, or even one of the newer guards. She wasn't sure if she had the energy for Hunter. She often found that having witty comebacks to his snark was difficult to come by after a sleepless night.

The practice ring was bare except for a few targets at the far end and a large wooden rack filled with swords, various knives, bows and other weapons. She recognized a few guards yawning to themselves while they stretched making sure to smile at them when they bowed their heads. Even after all this time, their reverence made her uncomfortable. Most days she wanted to be nothing more than a normal person like everyone else and had the mind to ignore them. She acknowledged more people she didn't recognize who were scattered throughout the ring. She had seen many new faces who came to train with Hunter in the past several weeks thanks to rumors of a warlock uprising.

She felt limber, her muscles warm and achy from her run. She'd purposely come here early, hoping to have a few moments to prepare before subjecting herself to Hunter's keen eye. She didn't want him to notice that she was out of sorts. She didn't need to give him fodder for his ridicule; his arrogance did that enough for him. She stopped a few yards away from him, half hidden in the shadow of a target, and watched as he went through his own set of warm-ups.

Faria marveled at his control as he swerved and slashed at an invisible enemy with a wooden practice sword. She couldn't help but admire his strong form, the muscles of his biceps shifting as he moved, a thin sheen of sweat glistening from the first rays of the morning sun. She let in a small intake of breath as it glinted off his brown hair, shining with gold in the light, his already tan skin brightening. She watched the sun reflect off his deep green eyes streaked with gold. Everything about him seemed to shine, as if he were a mythical warrior or even a god come to life.

It infuriated her.

Even if he weren't the most arrogant human she'd had the displeasure of meeting, she wouldn't have liked him anyway. His skills—though impressive—irritated her, the way he seemed to best her every time they practiced, and the way his endless knowledge of weaponry surpassed her own. For a human barely older than herself, he had reflexes like an elf, and he had quickly proven himself as an asset to their community. Anestrians far and wide came to *Mentage* to train with him, and they were the better for it—but unfortunately for her, it meant she was subjected to his near perfection each morning, making her feel inadequate.

Okay, so she was a little insecure, but she liked to excel—at being what everyone wanted and expected her to be. To be as worthy a queen as her mother.

And she was a sore loser.

He paused in his warm-up, watching the sunrise crest over the horizon. He lifted his shirt to wipe his face, his lower back muscles curving out from his spine. She swallowed against the dryness in her throat.

She especially hated how attracted she was to him and the constant reminder of the things she couldn't have.

"You're early, my lady."

His deep voice melted into the space between them, tucking into all the bends and curves of her, nestling against her skin. She snorted, ignoring the feeling it gave her. Of course he knew she watched him. "You're observant," she replied.

He smirked at her over his shoulder. "Like what you see?"

She did. "Nope."

He raised his brow, cocking a half smile as he turned to face her. He recently began antagonizing her when no one else was around. She wondered why he decided to cross the line, to act so familiar with her and how bold it was of him to do so. No one else would dare speak to her in such a way. It sent a thrill through her just as quickly as it doused her. There was no point in dwelling on it for too long. She had to choose a bonding partner soon, and a human was off limits.

Not that she wanted that from him. At all.

"I already warmed up," she said.

Hunter gave her a once over then returned the practice sword to the weapons rack. He walked back over to her, stopping a polite distance away, taking her in more thoroughly this time, observing everything from her sleeveless tunic to her crossed arms. He took his time and she felt a not so uncomfortable flutter below her navel. She hated how much she responded to him without him having to do anything. His eyes met hers, trapping her in place. She thought of turning away but she lifted her chin higher, feeling her shoulders tense. It irked her that he seemed so completely unaffected by her. She hated it even more when his half-smirk returned, as if he knew exactly what she felt.

"I'm ready for you."

Arrogance dripped from him, cooling her down. She thought about telling him how she was ready to set him on fire but thought better of it. Her elven abilities had been developing at a rapid pace, and she wasn't sure if it was something she could actually do. Better to not tempt the Fates.

She veered off toward the weapons rack and selected a cache of daggers, placing them in the sheaths attached to her belt. She faced him, annoyed to see a smile still on his face, a stupid dimple blessing her with its presence.

"What?" she asked, contemplating the punishment she would receive for throwing a dagger at him.

"Nothing."

She went back to the targets, lining up in front of the one farthest away. She cracked her neck and twitched her fingers, calming herself before she started.

"I want to try something new," he said. She suppressed a jolt. She hadn't heard him sneak up on her. She watched warily as Hunter made his way to the target, stopping just in front of the painted bullseye. "Hit me."

Maybe it was the lack of sleep, or perhaps the remnants of her nightmares still haunted her, but she was certain she hadn't heard right. "Excuse me?"

"Anyone can hit a stationary target. Chances are that any potential enemies you come across will not stay in one place, waiting for you to hit them. No one else is around so it'll be safe when you miss." Anger surged at his subtle taunt. She never missed. "This is the perfect time to practice."

"I know you're excellent at what you do," she said, immediately regretting the way he winked at her, "but I am a Royal. I have heightened senses and incredible accuracy."

"Someone's feeling themselves this morning," he teased her.

"You are a human," she continued. "I don't want to hurt you."

"Ye of little faith," he said. "You won't hurt me, Princess, but I'm flattered you care."

She felt her blood heat. She hated that name, even if it was her official title.

"Don't call me Princess," she said. She rubbed the hilt, searching for the perfect grip and prepared herself to launch the dagger.

"Do something about it."

She didn't know what put him in such a playful mood. It used to be that he hardly spoke to her outside of correcting her stance or pushing her harder as she tried to master the fighting styles of other realms he seemed to know. She missed those days. She accepted his challenge, however, figuring that the healer was close enough to help if she severely maimed him.

Faria faced him, unmoving, a smile playing on her lips as she watched Hunter dart from side to side in front of the target. Even if he wasn't slow enough for her to envision where he would be for the proper aim, the shuffling of his boots against the dirt gave him away. She took aim and threw. And missed.

Her eyes narrowed as she reached for another dagger, flipping it so she felt the cool edge of the blade. She waited a moment and predicted the path Hunter would take as he rolled on the ground and jumped back and forth. She took a deep breath, exhaled, then threw the dagger straight for where his stomach would be.

And missed. Again.

"You aren't trying hard enough!" he called out to her. "You need to picture me as the target. You have to really want to hit me. Focus, Princess."

"I always imagine hitting you," she grumbled to herself. He let out a short burst of laughter. She whipped her head around, surprised that he heard what she said. Though they shared the same rounded ears, humans didn't have the same heightened sense of hearing as elves.

She cracked her neck again and turned to face him, two daggers in her right hand this time. She didn't want to hold back, but maybe she did have reservations about stabbing a human. She really didn't want to face the queen if she learned her daughter had maimed the weapons master.

Faria inhaled deeply, blocking out any noise other than those Hunter made as he ran through the sandy pitch. She closed her eyes, picturing his heart, listening for its steady beating. Well, just to the right of his heart. No need to actually do any lasting damage. She flicked one dagger, then the other in quick succession.

Hushed gasps surrounded her as she opened her eyes to a crowd of people standing in a circle around them. She recognized some warlock guards whispering in low voices to each other. A few city dwellers preparing to start their daily practice eyed her curiously. Her cheeks flushed in embarrassment. Though she was used to the attention, she didn't realize how many were there to witness her practice. He must have planned it that way on purpose. His taunting her was really starting to grate on her nerves.

Her eyes swept over to the weapons master, almost scared of the amount of blood that surely poured from his body. He stood halfway down the practice arena, barely visible through the hazy morning fog. She cautiously approached, disbelief spreading through her.

She found one dagger casually hanging from his left hand, his fingertips barely grasping the handle. His other hand held the remaining dagger at his heart. Even from this distance she could see a droplet of blood drip from his chest, staining the front of his sleeveless tunic.

Impossible. No one had the amount of control or discipline it would take to stop a dagger from entering their heart. Not at the speed she threw it.

But he did. An unfamiliar thrill passed through her.

"How did you do that?" she demanded, careful not to allow her eyes to linger at the blood trickling down his front.

His chest rose slow and even as he stared down at her. His breath cooled her face with each exhale. His expression held the faint echoes of laughter, though a muscle in his jaw flexed.

"That's all for today," he said.

"Wait, what?"

He handed the daggers back to her before he turned around, walking off the pitch. She was dumbfounded. She couldn't remember the last time he ended a session early.

Keeping her chin held high and ignoring the whispers in her wake, Faria made for the weapons rack. She stopped short at the sight of the queen standing on a hill in the distance. Queen Amira wore a dress of crimson, her white antler crown stark against her dark hair. She looked formidable, and Faria knew how deadly her mother could be. She was as good a warrior as the best of their army, though she hadn't been on a battlefield in decades. The queen nodded at Faria, indicating the need to speak with her. Faria's heart plummeted.

She sighed deeply, leaving the arena. At least she'd forgotten about her nightmares—or the visions, whatever they were—for a short time. Faria glanced back up to the top of the hill but found it empty, the queen already departed. Faria veered toward *Mentage*, knowing her mother would want to meet in the Council Room, the only place they had discussions as of late.

As if she were one of the queen's subjects rather than her daughter.

She crossed the lush lawns before entering the Spring Garden. It was her favorite short-cut to other parts of the mansion. Black roses with purple veins greeted her as she walked along the path that would lead her to the atrium. A dull ache throbbed just behind her right eye and she wondered if she would have time for a quick nap before her lessons with Faline. She was exhausted after the lack of sleep and she still had a full day of lessons and chores ahead of her.

A wave of dizziness crushed Faria and the scent of sweet jasmine flooding her senses was the last she remembered before she blacked out.

TWO

FARIA

It happened because of the secrets she kept. The visions. They always started the same.

A dark cavern, its walls soaked with seawater and the smell of decaying moss. A faint blue orb glowing in the distance. Flashes of light. Fire, searing pain, dead bodies piled in mounds, realms colliding. A baby, lying on a set of golden scales, the other side weighed down by a darkness. Evil claws extending to reach her, choking her, piercing her with its daggers. Then, light. The ocean. The sun. A new beginning. A face, too blurry to see, but familiar all the same, deep jade green eyes staring into her mind, searing their image there.

Strong hands grasped her shoulders as Faria came to consciousness. Her head pounded as the images leaked away, leaving a roll of nausea behind. She shook her head, raven curls bouncing as the dizziness dispelled. Her sight focused on two familiar faces.

"Wilhelm," she said, slightly out of breath. "Reed." Two of the Elven Royal Guard stood by her, each mirroring a look of concern.

"Are you alright, lady?" Wilhelm said. He removed his hand from her shoulder as she straightened her tunic. The rustle of fabric was the only sound in the hallway.

She blinked up at them and took in her surroundings, noting the ornately carved double doors towering behind the two guards. She stood outside the Council Chamber of *Mentage* but had no recollection of getting there.

"Of course," she wiped the sweat from her neck. "And call me Faria, Wil. We have known each other our whole lives."

Wil shifted on his feet, peering behind him at the chamber door, as if he could feel the queen's glare on him.

"T'isn't right, Lady Faria," he mumbled.

She raised a brow at the two guards now standing rigidly beside the door, one on each side. Their bows were at ease with a quiver of arrows slung across their backs and simple daggers and a sword on their waistbands. Each wore thick leather garb, traditional for members of the Elven Royal Guard, the supple material bent and cracked in places. Reed was tall, thin, and had slightly protruding teeth. He shifted under her gaze, calling attention to the limping gait Faria would recognize anywhere—an old injury from Wilhelm when they were younger. Wilhelm stood tall next to Reed, though was much stockier and built more like the dwarves who lived deep in the Caranek Peaks rather than an elf. His prominent brow did little to ease his hardened features.

"You know the last time you said that to me was when I tried playing with you. When we were eleven. Nearly seven years ago."

The memory appeared before her, that distant sun warming her face, the grass feather soft between her bare toes.

"T'isn't right, Lady Faria," Wilhelm had said. *"We come from different families."*

"We're children! We can be friends if we want to."

Both Wilhelm and Reed shifted uncomfortably. *Sweat dripped down their faces despite the chill in the air, and dirt stained their pants from the wrestling she just interrupted. They stared hard at her dress made of fine Elven silk then back up at her face, as if she were too dim to understand their rejection. They were right; she didn't understand.*

"We don't live like the others," she insisted. *She just wanted them to notice her for who she was: a normal girl who wanted to play with someone her own age, for once.* *"We can be friends! There is no real hierarchy in Anestra, you know. We are all equals at* Mentage."

"Says you, the one in silk layers while we are shivering our bottoms in our threadbare tunics," Reed *had responded, shrugging his shoulders as he turned away.*

She had never hated her clothes, her beautiful rare fabrics brought over from distant human lands, her polished shoes, her jewelry, more than she did in that moment.

A snort escaped her at the memory. Threadbare, indeed. They never let their people go without. All were dressed as finely as the next. Only the women of the royal household had any different fabric to set them apart.

Faria's father, King Dennison, refused to wear fancy garb unless they were entertaining guests, and even then, he usually put up a fight.

Wil looked at her, biting his lip. "You are the future queen."

"Right you are," she said easily to hide the hurt she felt at the distance they maintained, especially after she had played matchmaker between Wil and Reed months ago. "Decades from now, and even then, I will insist you call me Faria. Might as well start now."

"Heard you attacked Hunter this morning," Reed said.

She was grateful for the quick change in subject, though she would rather talk about anything else. She looked him in the eye, careful to keep a straight face. "Just practicing."

She smiled and walked toward the door, away from her disappointment lingering in the air. She shook it off. She had more important things to worry about than her lack of friends, such as why she was having blackout visions and more importantly, the conversation she was about to have.

Her nerves calmed with the soothing scent that washed over her as she entered the Council Room. It smelled of the land. Rocky dirt floors, stone walls, the fire endlessly burning with and the faint scent of spiced bark that hung in the air. The rest of the house was modern; polished wood and glass made up most of their home. Here, though, this room felt as though it hadn't been touched since the Ancients Originals ruled millennia ago. She felt the buzz of something powerful humming through the walls. It was a special magic, one no creature had anymore.

In the middle of the room lay an ornate wooden table with the entirety of the Elven history carved into it featuring the Originals— direct descendants of the Fae who came to rule the Elven realm. Carved deep into the oak was the outline of the three Goddesses and what they promised to provide; lasting life, fruitful labors, and unending wonders of the lands they came from. Around the table were six chairs, one for each of the Queen's Royal Guard and one for the queen herself.

The king and queen occupied two of those chairs, determination searing their faces. The tension in the air was palpable. Faria didn't bother sitting down.

The queen shifted, her thick crimson gown rustling with the movement. She was dressed for a festive occasion, though no such affair was to take place; gowns and shimmering slippers were her usual garments these days. She used to dress more sensibly in the same tunic and pants as everyone else, when she was more involved with the people of Anestra. Faria wasn't sure when she changed and she resented it. Her father, on the other hand, was dressed similarly to Faria; worn leather tunic and pants with a belt of various weapons hanging from his waist.

To a human eye, the king and queen appeared to be in their early thirties but they were over a century old and wrinkles had started to line their faces. Where the king's were laugh lines, the queen's were from years of frowning and displeasure.

The king opened his mouth to speak, but Faria interrupted him before he could.

"I know what you're going to say," she said, holding her hand up. "I've already told you at the Harvesting that I simply am not interested in anyone right now."

"We have been through this, Faria." The king took a deep breath while her mother gazed at the empty stone wall behind her. Faria clenched her fists.

"I know," she replied trying to keep her annoyance in check. It took all of her energy not to roll her eyes. "We come from the Ancient Originals. We are the leaders. As heir and only female, I am the next ruler of Anestra and it is my duty to make babies." She blew a stray curl from her eyes and could barely keep from tapping her foot with impatience. "I'm just not ready to find someone to procreate with! I'm hardly eighteen. I still have two whole years left to worry about the curse." She tried and failed to keep the whine from her voice.

The dreaded curse—the one the Warlock King had put on the Agostonna bloodline after the Great War one thousand years ago; it was the reason for all Faria's problems. Though elves had expanded bloodlines, this curse made it nearly impossible to procreate after the age of twenty—barely old enough for the Change to settle into their bones.

Queen Amira was an anomaly. She had Faria when she was over a century old, and Faria couldn't help but wonder if the fear of losing the bloodline contributed to their urgency to have her breed.

The crackling of the fire was the only sound in the room as her father considered her, tapping his fingers on the wooden arm of his chair—the only indication of his budding annoyance. "If you don't take your responsibilities seriously, we will be forced to take matters into our own hands."

Heat seared Faria's face. Did he mean to say that *he* would choose her life partner for her?

"Please, make haste. There are plenty out there worthy of you." His eyes begged her to agree with him, to ease the tension in the room that ratcheted with every passing second.

"You know this is an archaic tradition. Some might even say *barbaric!*" Faria's words echoed off the walls and bounced into the fire where they burned away, along with her temper. She knew she shouldn't have shouted, knew it wouldn't amount to anything. This was her duty, after all.

The temperature plummeted, Faria's breath whisping in the suddenly frigid air—a chilling reminder of her mother's displeasure.

"You will do this, my child." Her father's eyes shone with love. He could never stay angry with her for long. "The Goddesses will it of you. Do not try to run from Fate."

She swallowed. That was the second time today she had thought about those infuriating Fates.

"And Faria," the queen's voice was soft as she finally turned her icy gaze upon her daughter, "we do have an alternate plan, should you keep postponing the inevitable." Her frozen azure stare ripped into Faria's soul, as if attempting to reveal the secrets she kept hidden. "You have two months before he arrives."

She tightened her fists to stop their shaking. Faria held her mother's eyes for a long moment, focusing on her breathing and racing heartbeat, before giving a quick nod and leaving the room.

She kept her head down, careful to avoid any sympathetic looks from Wil and Reed, and collided with something very solid—something that smelled of cinnamon and the ocean breeze. She reverberated off the strength of it.

"My apologies, Princess." Dark green eyes stared down at her.

"Hunter." She didn't try to hide her contempt as she took a step back.

The weapons master stood a foot taller than her, but seemed even larger with his overwhelming ability to take up more space than necessary, as if his shadow were sentient too.

"I did not mean to run into you," he said, focusing his gaze past Faria's shoulder. "Please, forgive me." He bowed at the waist, his dark hair falling over the rest of his face.

Faria crossed her arms and gave a tight smile that didn't quite reach her eyes. "No need, I wasn't watching where I was going. Please, excuse me."

She made to leave as he straightened and stepped closer into her space. Everything about him unnerved her, though she couldn't quite place why. Not for the first time, she wondered where he came from and why he had no family in Anestra. She frowned; she'd half-expected a snarky remark or cocky smile and she found his formality discomfiting. She held his stare for a moment longer than necessary before turning on her heel and walking away.

Faria rounded the corner but peered back in time to see Hunter walk into the Council Chamber. Was Hunter who her parents meant to set her up with? Her chest tightened at the thought. No, it couldn't be since he was human. Though as weapons master he brought much value to their lands, he would never make a suitable partner for her. He would never be able to provide what she needed. A bloodline.

Faria escaped into the garden, craving the illusion of freedom the open air gave her. She walked along a broken stone path and stopped by an elaborate jade fountain that depicted majestic beasts of the human realm; a Stag, a Lion, a Bear, and the fabled Phoenix all stood guard at north, south, east, and west, water erupting from their mighty roars. Such animals did not exist in Anestra.

When she was young, King Dennison would wake Faria before the sunrise and they would sit by the fountain in the chilled morning air, sipping from mugs of steaming melted chocolate. They would talk about what life might be like in other realms, and what mystical creatures might lurk in the shadowy corners of the land. The king always promised to take her on adventures outside of their borders but when his military duties called him to the Caranek Peaks or the Barren Plain, he left her behind. He did whatever he could to not only lead their army, but to do the hard work with them. It was no surprise that he never had time to take her anywhere.

"I thought I would find you here."

The king's shadow cast a chill along her skin, as if she summoned him from her thoughts.

"Do you really intend to marry me off to a stranger?" she asked, not turning around. She was afraid to hear his answer.

The mid-morning sun shimmered off the surface of the fountain, casting rainbows along the water as it rose higher in the cerulean sky. He sighed. "You know that was never our intention, Faria. You also know what has been expected of you."

"Do you not think it a strange practice, Father? To sell me to the highest bidder?"

"It is nothing like that," he said, placing his arm around her shoulders. "And you know as well as I do what is at stake. We cannot risk the Agostonna bloodline, especially not with such unrest in our lands."

Faria had heard rumors of small groups of warlocks protesting and starting fires in a few villages she hadn't visited before. "Is it really that serious? Do you think we have true cause to worry?"

King Dennison's eyebrows knitted together. "I think any time we hear of our people being unhappy, it is cause to worry. Besides, they are at risk of breaking their Contract."

"And you're worried that the warlocks will rally together to overthrow us if I don't produce an heir? Their powers that remain are because they live in this land. Isn't Wendorre all but a wasteland? Who would fight with them? Who would risk breaking the Contract and having what magic they have left torn from them?"

"I don't know, my darling, but we must take every precaution. Is there no one that has caught your eye?"

Faria snorted. "Honestly, Father, I have hardly been paying attention. Between my training, learning my abilities, helping around *Mentage* and then volunteering in Athinia, I don't think about it. And who knows— perhaps my life partner is someone I haven't met yet. It isn't like I have seen much of Anestra."

She almost felt guilty at the crestfallen look on his face, but it was the truth. Did they expect someone worthy of her power and intelligence to appear on their doorstep?

"I know I haven't taken you out as much as either of us would have liked. I apologize, Faria. I'll see if we can work something out in the coming days."

He turned to leave, but she put a hand on his arm to stop him. "Will you speak to her? Please? Make her change her mind?"

The king swept her into his arms and kissed her forehead. "You know as well as I that no one can make the queen change her mind, but I shall speak to her."

He left Faria at the fountain, lost in her thoughts.

I suppose we are at the edge of peace, Faria reasoned with herself. *Or war.* It explained why Hunter worked her so hard on the practice field. She just wished she knew what she was training *for*.

A sudden shuffle in the hedge garden behind her interrupted Faria's thoughts. Glancing over her shoulder, she spotted a giant blue eye staring back at her from between the leaves, framed by wispy blonde bangs.

"I see you, Nellie," Faria said, smiling in welcome to the young girl.

"You only see me because I *let* you see me, Fifi."

Faria warmed at the nickname. "I can smell you from a mile away," she said. Dirt streaked along the girl's clothes and mud lined her shoulders where her dark blond hair fell. Actually, Faria couldn't smell her at all, which was odd given how dirty she was. "What in Aurelia's Garden have you been doing, young lady?"

"Aw, nothing really, Fifi." She kicked the ground as her chubby cheeks bloomed scarlet. "Anyways, Mother sent me to get you. You're late for your lessons again."

"Well, we mustn't keep her waiting." Faria linked arms with Nellie and guided her to the East Entrance of the garden, treading lightly over the loose stone gravel beneath their booted feet.

The pair walked in amicable silence, enjoying the fragrance of wildflowers dispersed throughout the wide arched halls. For such a young human who had nothing in common with elves, Nellie brought Faria a sense of kinship that she craved.

Nellie leaned closer to her and whispered, "Fifi, if you want to talk to someone, you know you can talk to me, right?"

Faria glanced down at the tiny girl who seemed wise beyond her thirteen years. Fondness for her bloomed as if Nellie were her own blood. "I love you as a sister, Nellie, but sometimes things will happen here that young humans can't understand."

"Well, I can try!" Nellie put her hands on her hips. She was the spitting image of her adoptive mother Faline, Faria's tutor, who had claimed Nellie for her own when they'd found her wandering through the Forest five years ago.

"Don't chastise me like your mother, little one," Faria said, swatting her on the nose. She continued down the hallway without her, watching the shadows shift along the wall, the pitter patter of Nellie's steps hurrying to keep up.

"Well, look who it is!" Faline stepped from around the corner. She kept her graying hair in a tight bun, and though she frowned at Faria, light danced in her russet eyes.

"Apologies, Faline," Faria said as she curtseyed. It was important in Elven culture to respect their elders. No one was above curtseying or bowing to them, not even the queen.

"Run along, Nellie." Those sharp eyes turned to her adoptive daughter. "We have elf business to discuss that little humans don't need to mind themselves with."

Nellie shrugged and winked at Faria as she walked away, a little swagger to her step.

"Will you finally be teaching me something useful, Faline?" Faria waggled her eyebrows at her, attempting to charm her into submission. "A little magic, perhaps?"

Faline's mouth hung open. "Absolutely not! You know that is not my place. Anyways, we are due for more fun than that!" Her triumphant tone filled Faria with dread. None of their lessons were what Faria would exactly describe as fun. She hoped they would at least distract her from the way her thoughts kept straying back to Hunter, or the ultimatum presented to her earlier. Not that the two were connected. Because they weren't. And she couldn't stand him.

Faline threw open the door to her library. A blazing fire crackled in the hearth, illuminating the outline of a person. The shadows were too deep for Faria to recognize who it was. Faline entered with a certain gusto Faria failed to muster, her arms spread wide, the sleeves of her emerald dress hanging straight down to her waist. Her voice boomed, "Today we will learn how to entertain your foreign guests!"

"Perfect," Faria mumbled as she entered her personal library, the heady scent of spice and ocean breeze going straight to her head.

Her mouth tightened to a slim line.

"Hunter."

THREE

NELLIE

S he wore the cocky grin as a mask, careful to hold it in place as she rounded the corner. Swagger was all she had to keep her ruse as a confident, annoying, thirteen-year-old human going. Faria didn't know who she really was. *What* she really was. She wasn't supposed to know until it was time.

It was safer that way.

Turning the corner of the large Agostonna home, Nellie approached a large tapestry that depicted the mighty Val—the fierce protectors of the Originals who were neither elf nor Fae. The scene before her was of Val's sacrifice for the elves, their soldiers surrounded by pools of blood, and bodies littered among the ground. Their prince stood at the forefront, arms open wide, a brilliant white light emanating around him. Nellie once remarked that he looked like an angel, servants of one of the humans' many gods.

She glanced side to side, then slipped behind the tapestry.

As far as she knew, only she and Faline were aware of the hidden door and the passageway underneath the tapestry. It was a blank wall before Faria had hung it up, but one day Nellie thought to hide from Faline to avoid her chores by sliding behind the thick tapestry, only to discover a door suddenly behind it. She jumped as the door closed with a soft *whump* behind her.

The passageway was silent, save for a faraway sound of trickling water. A long dirt hallway patched tightly together with rocks lay before her. It was a crude space, one that smelled as though it had been there since the Ancients, or maybe when gods still walked the land. Being from Earth and having only been in the human realm before arriving in Anestra, Nellie didn't have the best sense of "old," but what she did know was that nothing in America compared to the ancientness of this place. Though it was dark, it had an ethereal blue glow, lighting the way for her.

She followed the passage for about half a mile or so before it abruptly ended in a mossy rock wall, its stones tinged black from age. Two years ago, it had been sheer luck to discover that the rock wall turned into a one-way mirror to any room in *Mentage* she wished to see.

Nellie didn't know how it worked. It must have been Fae magic of some sort, left over from when the Ancient Originals built this home. She knew the magic wasn't one that she possessed, but it worked for her every time. All she had to do was think of a room and its image appeared on the stone wall, as if she were glimpsing mirrors of time. It was awesome.

She wouldn't have become an exceptional sneak without its discovery. It also became a safe haven for Nellie when she felt an uncontrollable urge to shift.

Nellie thought of where she wanted to see. The rock wall shimmered before her as she looked down on the king and queen in the Council Room. She could smell the spiced fire burning in the hearth.

The king rubbed his wife's hands, his thumbs massaging circles into the soft padding. Their faces were tense. She held her breath as the royals spoke, fearful of making any noise, though she knew they couldn't hear her. She stomped down on the guilt she felt and instead focused on what they had to say; perhaps she could figure out what was bothering Faria. Nellie heard them as if she were listening through headphones.

"I don't know why you can't be warmer toward her," the king said, peering intently at the queen. The wrinkles on his forehead deepened with his frown. "Tell me, Amira, please. What is bothering you? It feels like every year that passes you are weighed down with another unknown burden."

"I'm the queen of Anestra, of course I'm burdened." The queen waved the king off as if it were nothing. "I can't be warmer toward her, not now. There is something she must soon do and she won't if she is attached to me."

"A thing she must do? Amira, that makes no sense." The king dropped her hands. Nellie had the impression they'd had this conversation more than once. "I've tried to listen to you, my love. When you tell me to give you space, when you tell me to trust you. But I am your king. I am head of our army. You might control the realm, but we lead it together as we have for decades. Help me to understand. Let me lighten your burden."

Queen Amira stood abruptly, the swish of her skirts scratching over the popping of the fire. She glanced down at the king.

"It is almost time, anyway." Her voice was sad, her shoulders drooped in resignation. "There are things you must know, love, but not here. These walls have ears." Her eyes shifted toward the fireplace, then above, where Nellie listened.

"This is one of the most heavily warded rooms in all of *Mentage*," the king reasoned. "Your secret is safe here."

The queen pursed her lips. "Wards and enchantments mean nothing when it comes to what I have to say. Even the Fates have ears." She frowned and started to pace. Seconds passed before she stopped and faced her husband. "I will tell you, but only because soon it will be time. It will all come to pass."

She lowered her voice to a whisper as Nellie squeezed in closer to the image and willed the queen's voice to rise. "You know, of course, of the Prophecy."

"Of course," the king replied. "It is the most famous story in all of Anestra. More than that, across the realms. The final battle will commence once the tides of good mix with the forces of evil."

"Almost." The queen's skin paled in the flickering firelight. "You know when queens are chosen, they must undergo the trials."

"Yes," the king said, shifting uncomfortably. "I am not to know about them, Amira. No one is."

"During one of those trials," she pressed on, ignoring him, "I glimpsed pieces of the future. I had to choose—was forced—to accept my Fate to become queen, though I knew what was to come."

"What are you saying?" the king asked. "Were you shown the truth of the Prophecy?"

"I know who it directly involves, but I do not know how it will come to be."

King Dennison took a deep breath, trying to keep his patience under control. "You're speaking in riddles, *indira*. Please, speak plainly."

"I believe, though I do not have proof that I can supply, that Faria is the good the Prophecy talks about."

"But how will she mix with the forces of evil? She may be meddlesome and stubborn, but in no way would she ever choose a path that contained evil."

"As if she has a choice," the queen huffed, bitterness dripping from her words. "As if the Fates let us really *choose* anything."

"Amira! You must be careful," the king said. "You don't want to anger the gods."

"The gods have abandoned us," she spat. "If I anger them then all the better. Perhaps they will show themselves once again and side with us." She waited a moment, staring deep into the fire. "I don't know how the final battle will come to pass. I was...unable to see it. But I do know the warlocks are involved. I petitioned Wendorre to send a representative to Anestra."

Nellie gasped. During her five years in Anestra, she had never heard of Queen Amira petitioning another country for help. She didn't need to; Anestra was a peaceful land and as far as she knew, no one in Athinia, let alone all of Anestra, was so displeased that they would cause problems enough for the queen to become directly involved. Even the small fires and protests on the outskirts of Athinia were the work of what she believed to be teenagers, rebelling against whatever bothered them that week. Nellie hadn't realized it was serious enough to call in reinforcements, especially not from Wendorre. The warlock country was falling to pieces, almost completely destitute.

"Without consulting me?" the king asked, his voice quiet. Nellie shuddered. She felt the deadly calm rush over her and was grateful to not be on the receiving end of his inquiry. "The safety of our land and people is my job. They could now be in jeopardy."

"I finally received word back," the queen replied. "Darroc L'Azare, liaison between the fallen royal line and other nations, said he would personally come to attend to the situation."

"We hardly know anything about him," King Dennison replied. "Darroc has not been to Anestra the entire time we have ruled, and my people haven't seen nor heard of any movement coming from Wendorre. We don't know what he looks like, if he is who he says he is. What if it's a trick?"

"He will be here in two months' time," the queen finished.

King Dennison stood, fists clenched. "Is that who you plan on pairing with Faria? Is he the evil you speak of?"

Amira hugged herself. "I do not know, but the final battle will occur soon, no matter what we try to do to stop it. The Fates have decided."

"You should have told me. Given me warning."

"It does not matter. It is done."

"It does not matter?" The king turned and made his way to the door. "I must gather our forces. I must send lookouts and spies. I must strengthen our defenses around all major ports and cities. You are deeply out of touch, *indira*, if you think I should not have known about this."

The king stormed out, silence ringing in his wake.

Nellie sat back on her haunches, breath whooshing out of her. She had heard of the Prophecy, or most of it anyway. It was an old fairy tale; the one humans retold over and over. The ultimate battle of good versus evil. Most humans called it their apocalypse, a fable in many of their minds. Since jumping realms, Nellie had learned that all races she encountered had a similar story.

The End of Times. It was enough to make her eyes roll. Nellie hated apocalypse stories and preferred to live in the here and now, but she couldn't shake the sense of foreboding at the queen's words.

Queen Amira tilted her head, as if listening to some unknown noise. She looked directly at the wall through which Nellie viewed the room and said, "She must be protected. At all costs. To whatever end. She must be saved."

Her breathing stuttered. *Did she just say that to me?*

The queen held direct eye contact with Nellie, or as direct as one can be when staring through a wall. "Do you hear me?" the queen said again. "To whatever end. She must be saved."

Well, that has never happened before.

Nellie backed away, her mind reeling with information she wasn't prepared to process. Why did she have to eavesdrop? Why couldn't she have minded her business, just this once? Trouble always seemed to find her. She ran back down the hall and listened closely to the door for any sounds before slipping back out from behind the tapestry, waiting for her pulse to return to normal.

Nellie peered closer at the tapestry of the Val as she rubbed her chest. They stood at attention upon a battlefield, waiting for the prince to sacrifice himself so they could follow. Even the oldest shapeshifters in the human realm had heard of the Val. They had been gone for a thousand years, but as she stared harder, she couldn't help but feel that they were familiar somehow. They were clad in thick armor, their weapons made up of bows and swords, black daggers and lances. They looked every bit the hero that Faria needed to protect her. Were they still alive or were they gone, like the Fae? If they knew that Faria needed help, would they come? Did they even care?

There was little sense in thinking about the *what ifs*. No one really knew the truth and there were none who would know how to contact them. *Mentage* had several libraries, but none that held scrolls filled with precious secrets and—

Scrolls!

Faline rented a room at the Athinian Athenaeum deep in the heart of the city. Nellie went there once, after Faline came back from a trip to Mercy Bay, on the edge of the Sea of Aurelia. The two of them headed into the city and dropped off golden scrolls in one of many locked cabinets that lined the room. Nellie didn't know what those scrolls were, but maybe they contained some information on the Prophecy. She had to find out.

Nellie scrambled back through the hidden door, nearly tearing her face open on a loose stone as she rushed back to the mossy rock wall. She needed to make sure Faline was fully occupied with Faria before she crept through her things. If she were a better, less impulsive person, she would have waited and asked permission, but that was never really her style. Staring at the wall ahead of her, she thought of Faria's library where she left them and waited for the image to appear before her.

She exploded in a babble of laughter at what she saw.

Faria and Hunter danced awkwardly in the middle of a cozy circular room. Actually, that was an understatement. One could hardly call it dancing, and it was certainly more than awkward. Nellie could have comfortably stood between them and there would still be room. The fact that she knew Faria would rather stick a fire poker through her eye than touch Hunter made it even more comical.

And Faline said she wanted to teach Faria about diplomacy or whatever it was? What was she playing at? Everyone knew those two had an unspoken rivalry. Sometimes Wil, Reed, and Nellie would place bets on who would lash out on who first. She had meant to ask Faria about throwing a dagger at Hunter that morning. She lost three gold marks over it.

Faria stared hard at Hunter's shoulder and he kept his eyes dead above her, burning holes in the clock over the large oak mantle. Nellie peeked at Faline. A bemused expression lit the shadows dancing on her face.

Nellie watched as Faria took in the planes of Hunter's angular face then quickly averted her eyes before he did the same. Nellie wondered if Faria felt weird because Hunter was a total babe. Maybe he had the hots for her because when he looked at her, he struggled to look away.

Okay, Nellie thought. *Maybe I'm confusing awkward for serious sexual chemistry.* Hunter shifted his eyes back to the clock on the opposite end of the room before Faria looked back at him.

Reel it in Nells. Thirteen. She was supposed to be thirteen, not a seventeen-year-old shapeshifter from the human realm of Earth who got thrown into this world as banishment from her clan. The thought sobered her. The last thing she needed was to risk discovery.

The bangs on Nellie's forehead shifted as a breeze gushed through the dark passageway. Strange. The cavern was completely encased in dirt and reinforced by thick stone on all sides. There was no room for wind, let alone enough of it to be so noticeable. Goosebumps rose down her back and a tremor tickled her spine. She didn't know much about this hidden spot in *Mentage*, but she was certain she had never felt a magical, preternatural wind in there before.

Peering back into the room, Nellie saw where the strange source of power was coming from but had no explanation for it. Faria had caught Hunter's eye and as soon as she did, the library had come to life. Books left open on the table next to them danced in frantic delight, their pages a flurry of fingers eager to tear themselves from the prisons that bound them.

The crackling fire drew Nellie's attention. Changing colors reflected against the shadows on the walls of the room.

Orange, green, blue, then a brilliant violet, strong enough for her to need to shade her eyes—which was insane, Nellie realized, since she watched them through a rock wall! Faline stood in the doorway, same serene expression as before, as if the entire room weren't coming to life.

Nellie had seen enough. She needed to do research, immediately. Before anything stranger happened, she ran back to the end of the passageway, listening at the doorway for any movement. Reassured no one was out there, she pictured her real self and began the shift.

A cool tremble passed under her bones and a sharp burning pierced her limbs as she grew several inches. Her scalp itched as curly hair sprouted, changing from dirty blonde to honey brown. Freckles appeared all over her darkened skin. Her body was much lither like this and she groaned a bit as her muscles stretched out and bones hardened. Her eyes changed to a bright hazel and a slight gap in her teeth appeared. Her clothes were suddenly too small, and she cursed herself for making a rookie mistake of shifting while still clothed. She ripped off her shoes that were now pinching her toes and slunk out into the hall. It was still empty. She thanked the goddesses and universe for such good luck and she ran down the hall, veering toward the suite she shared with Faline. She tore the door open, shivering as she entered the dark entryway.

She didn't bother turning on lamps as she made her way to her bedroom. She grabbed a stash of leggings and a long tunic. As she pulled on dark slippers, she caught a glimpse herself in the full-length mirror and nodded. No one in *Mentage* knew her true form, so she would be able to leave without question. As long as she didn't run into Faline, who might murder her if she saw Nellie taking such a huge risk.

She snatched a purse with spare coins and left her rooms, cutting through the Autumn Garden before she crossed the sloping lawn to the front gates. A few guards watched her as she went under the stone archway, but they didn't call out to her. The magic the Fae put on *Mentage* centuries ago prevented intruders. They would assume she was an invited guest.

The walk to Athinia was a short one. She followed the river along the dusty, forested road until a bridge appeared. On the other side of the river, large stone walls flanked the entryway to the bustle of Anestra's capital city. More guards stood watch here, though they were hardly ever needed. They tended to sort out drunks more often than villains. She could already hear the murmur of voices and clomping of horses within the city walls.

As she enjoyed her walk, she thought of all she learned. The End of Times was apparently nigh, and Nellie couldn't help but wonder what that meant for her former clan in the human realm, or even what it meant for all creatures in every realm tied to theirs. She hadn't learned enough of the clan lore, hadn't been alive even a fraction of the amount of time she needed to obtain all the stories and legends of all known races. She had only just discovered what she truly was before she'd been banished.

If Nellie was supposed to protect Faria "at all costs" then she needed to know exactly what she was dealing with.

Before it was too late.

FOUR

FARIA

There was little in her privileged life that Faria thought could be worse to endure, than having to embarrass herself in front of someone she found so repugnant. She gave Faline her best withering stare, begging to be freed from this special kind of hell she was thrown into. Faline ignored her, amusement in her eyes. Her fingers tapped on her crossed arms to the song playing from the large music box that lay on the table next to them. Hunter looked as uncomfortable as Faria felt, his fingers barely grasping hers while they swayed in front of the library's fireplace. Faline's idea of enhancing foreign relations was, of all things, dancing. Apparently, Faline believed that dancing was a skilled artform and essential to diplomacy. *"You never know when you might be dancing with the enemy!"* Faline had said.

Before they started, Faline had asked Faria to come up with a scenario to negotiate with Hunter. To role play. This was a chance for Faria to get under his skin just as much as he got under hers and the thought sent a jolt of excitement through her. She could use the time to find out how a human knew so much about weapons and why his skills were still so much better than hers even though she had the advantage of being an elf.

Instead, they swayed to the music, barely shuffling their feet along the braided carpet, for an uncomfortably long while.

"Look," Faria finally said, speaking to a spot over his shoulder. "I don't want you here any longer than you want to be here. Let's just pretend and get it over with."

"Is that how you plan on winning over any suitors, my lady?"

She snorted. "What suitors? There are none here worthy of me." The arrogance with which she said that made her cringe inside, and she hoped he wouldn't say anything about it.

"Ah," Hunter replied. She risked a quick glance at him, noticing the easy smile spreading across his face. "I'll have to remember that."

Faria didn't know what he meant by that, nor did she want to think about it. She quickly said the first thing that came to her mind. "You seem to know your way around the Forest of the Dawn."

"That was abrupt, suspicious, and rude, Faria," Faline chastised.

Faria could not have rolled her eyes any harder. She wasn't even sure why she had blurted that out. It wasn't often she found herself lacking basic communication skills. "Tell me, Hunter, what do you find most enjoyable about your daily walks through the Forest?"

"Still a little rough."

"How do you know I take daily walks through the Forest?" he asked in a voice low enough for only her to hear. "Are you watching me, Princess?"

Refusing to rise to the bait, she smiled sweetly and said, "What about the Forest inspires you to keep going back?" She found herself holding her breath, surprisingly eager to hear his response.

He quickly scanned her face. "I'm drawn to nature, its beauty, and how people of every race seem to be affected by its power."

Faria stilled for a moment. *Unexpected from such a brute on the field.*

Hunter's mouth tightened as she paused, but still, he did not look at her. She watched as his jaw clenched, the sun-darkened planes of his face unmoving under her scrutiny. What was it that made him different from everyone else? It was infuriating. She subtly scented him, trying to detect something different about him, but nothing beyond the peppery taste of mild irritation and his normal smell of spice and ocean radiated from him.

"I see. What does it inspire you to do?" She was jealous of his freedom, at how he was able to wander as he pleased, at how he could survive whatever obstacles came his way. She wanted to be on that level, too. She could swallow her pride and ask for his help if it came to it.

"To protect." Jade eyes met hers, locking them in place. She was reminded of all the colors she saw earlier that morning, the greens and yellows interlocking and the way they glowed. Predatory. Beautiful, even.

Faria's body thrummed with the intensity of his stare. Goosebumps erupted across her flesh, though she felt sweat trickle under her tunic. Her breath stuttered.

They interacted every day on the practice field, but this was something different. Intimate. It felt like he saw who she was and understood her true nature more than she did herself.

Faria noticed wind playing with the chestnut strands sweeping across his forehead, though she couldn't figure where it came from in a windowless room. Hunter's eyes were emerald fire as the flames in the hearth grew and cast shadows against his face.

She didn't dare breathe, for fear that slight movement would tear him away before she was ready.

Hunter's grip tightened on Faria's waist, and if she said she didn't like it, she would be lying. She hated him, she reminded herself. Hated how he frequently made her feel insecure and insignificant, like this morning. What was she doing?

They were no longer dancing or pretending to dance, or even looking at each other with their usual hostility. Time was an illusion. How long had they been standing like this? A few seconds? An hour? Faria would die of embarrassment if he wasn't feeling at all what she felt.

As if sensing her thoughts, small lines of tension formed around his mouth and he looked away. The energy erupting from them drained in the movement. How he was able to let go, Faria didn't know, because her entire body locked down from the moment his gaze met hers. Her knees shook either from him or the sudden fatigue that weighed her body down. He annoyingly seemed unaffected, other than his slightly quickened breath and the tinge of rouge that touched his cheeks. He kept his composure, while she did everything she could to not melt into the floor. Only he could make her feel so out of control.

It made her seethe.

"Hunter!" Faria jerked as Faline's voice broke her trance. "You are dismissed. Thank you!" She held the door open for him, waving her hand to shoo him out.

Talk about abrupt.

A sudden emptiness consumed Faria as he dropped his hold on her, briskly walking out of the room. His shoulders were stiff, his gait militant in its swiftness.

Faline turned narrowed eyes to Faria, a thoughtful look on her face.

"Did you see that?" Faria said. "Did you *feel* that?" The heat on her cheeks flushed her skin and from the looks of Faline, she wasn't the only one.

"Yes. A human, Faria?" She tutted. "The only race you cannot do the bonding ceremony with. Your mother won't be pleased."

Faria frowned. "Hardly. I can't stand him."

"I'm sure," Faline said, giving her a knowing look. She paused a moment. "Have you thought about it? The bonding ceremony?"

Faria snorted. Had she thought about it? It seemed it was all she could do to *not* think about it. "Some," she replied. Faline stayed quiet, which Faria was grateful for. She didn't want to think about anything she had no control over.

Faria glanced at the fire, which was rapidly changing color from violet to blue, green to orange. She couldn't remember if it had been doing that the whole time and if it was, then *how*. Surprisingly, Faline didn't mention anything about it so neither would she. Instead, she tucked that information aside for later contemplation.

"We have something to discuss." Faline's eyebrows knitted, her hand shaking slightly as she guided Faria to a chair. She was more of a mother to Faria than her own, and the tone in her voice put her on edge as she sat at the worn oak table, the chair groaning as she settled in.

"There is a darkness that I can see; oil smudging the land. More of it every day." Faline's ability was to see that which was not there, intangible objects, like feelings. She once described it as reading a person's aura, only this worked for all living things including land and water. Faria knew she meant it quite literally when she said oil smudged the land.

"It covers the grounds, the trees, the animals fear it. It started off small, but its presence is starting to make itself known even to humans." Her musical voice shook, revealing to Faria how unnerved the normally collected elf was. "I was in Athinia this morning, and the owner of The Phoenix Fire—that human, Desmond—he was out front sweeping a completely empty entryway. His eyebrows were furrowed and he looked angry, so I asked him if something was the matter. He said he felt as if the stones wouldn't come clean and sure enough, I looked down and saw an inky smudge. I asked if he could see anything on the stone and he said no, but he could feel it."

That was certainly cause for concern. Faria knew for a fact that Des had no magical abilities, which meant that whatever the darkness was, it was extremely potent.

"Nellie?" Faria asked. "Does she feel it as well?"

"Oh, yes. She picked up on it rather quickly, actually."

That didn't surprise her; the girl was extremely perceptive. Almost on par with the elves.

"I admit, I have felt something strange, too…" Faria shook off a sudden chill. Her nightmares and visions had been increasing and she didn't doubt this dark presence had something to do with it.

"What do you know, Faria? What is it you aren't saying?" The fierce way Faline looked at Faria told her that she suspected her powers were more than she let on, but still, Faria hesitated. Putting it out in the open proved there was something wrong with her. Something she wasn't ready to admit yet.

"I know it isn't my place, child, but war is coming. I've lived long enough to know what that feels like. Do you know that? Evil is already corrupting this land. If something is happening here—with you—please, we all must know."

War. *Because of me? My abilities?* The thought of such violence when they had been at peace for centuries was unimaginable. Surely, the rumors of the warlock uprisings would not give way to such a harsh outcome.

Faria wanted to tell her everything she knew, that something was happening to her. The way her strength increased, the suddenness of her visions, even the ability to change her appearance; it was unusual for elves to have more than one gift and she was working on seven. She wanted to tell her that she was worried she was turning into something else entirely, that perhaps she wasn't really an elf at all, but she couldn't voice those thoughts. She was still the future queen and she couldn't lay her burdens on everyone else. There were some things she needed to learn to keep to herself, to work through as a queen would. Wasn't that what Faline was trying to teach her anyway?

She sat up straighter, desperate to relieve the tension between her shoulders. The ache behind her eyes increased and she wondered if she would be able to get any sleep that night.

"No, Faline." Disappointment met Faria's eyes. "I'll let you know if something changes."

She was silent for a beat and Faria wondered if her face reflected the overwhelming guilt she felt from lying, or if her mask of neutrality was firmly in place.

"Before it's too late, Fifi."

Her words were an omen, echoing in her mind.

FIVE

NELLIE

Mid-afternoon sunlight glinted off the wet cobblestones as Nellie made her way through the crowded streets of Athinia. The first time she had set eyes on this city, if it could be called that, she fell in love. Nellie was used to the vastness of iron jungles, the intrusive scent of pollution and endless sounds of horns honking their right of way. To her, Athinia felt more like a bustling town filled with restaurants, shops, bars, and two different inns. It was home to museums, art galleries, and even a university of sorts, where scholars come from all over the continent to study whatever they desired—alchemy, the properties of magic, botany.

The streets were made of dirt and stone, and horses were the main mode of transportation. There were no streetlights but rather street lamps, though some businesses had floating orbs thanks to the elemental elves who could manipulate light. Though many places in Athinia did have electricity powered by water, most preferred the gentle glow of a lamp or torch. She had felt like she entered a medieval TV show the first time she had visited, except here there was indoor plumbing.

She weaved her way around sellers with outdoor carts hawking their wares and street vendors roasting meats. Her stomach grumbled at the luscious scent. It had been a while since she last ate and switching forms always made her extra hungry, but it would have to wait.

Athinia wasn't large, but as the capital of Anestra, it was home to more temples and shrines for the many various gods they worshipped than any other town on the continent. It had a massive library containing more books than Nellie had ever seen in her entire life. Faline once told her there was a place beyond Caranek Peaks, way to the north, that held the secrets to all realms. It supposedly housed more books than could fit in all of Athinia, but she found that hard to believe.

Her pace quickened, urged by the thought of Faline discovering her missing, but she couldn't help but take in the fresh air, the wonderful smells, and the happy feeling she had whenever she was around this much vibrancy. It used to make her homesick for her life on Earth, but she soon realized that this new life could be even better. It was a shock to end up in a realm that seemed centuries behind the human realm, especially with the lack of technology, but the magic that hummed throughout the land of Anestra more than made up for it. Something about it made her feel like she was finally home.

A warm body collided with hers, sending Nellie to the ground, her lower back hitting against stone. "I'm sorry," she said, shielding her eyes against the sun to see who she bumped into. The barking pain was soon forgotten once she heard who replied.

"Oh, no, that was my fault," a deep voice answered back. Strong hands reached down to help her stand. "I wasn't paying attention."

Nellie's mouth dried and she swayed as the blood rushed back to her head. Her heart fluttered for a moment before she remembered how to speak. "Endo!" she exclaimed, recognizing the jet-black hair and blue eyes belonging to the warlock who often stayed at *Mentage* and worked as Hunter's second in command. He wore a tunic of rich green and dark pants, his black boots scuffed and well worn. A gold belt adorned his waist and Nellie had the absurd thought for a moment that he looked a bit like a pirate.

"Do I know you?" he asked, the crease in his eybrows letting Nellie know that he didn't recognize her.

Right, I don't look like me. "Oh, I've seen you around *Mentage*. You help train the younger ones in archery, right?"

"That's right," he said, flashing her a smile. "I'm sorry, I don't recognize you. Are you new to Anestra?"

"Yes," Nellie said, the lie rolling off her tongue. "My family and I came upon this realm the way most others seem to, by accidentally crossing through a Gate. We just signed the Contract the other day, but we're non-magical so it was fairly straightforward. Queen Amira is so nice!" She couldn't stop babbling no matter how much she tried to bite her tongue. "She is letting us stay with her at *Mentage* until we find housing we like. I can't wait to start working around the city! It's so lovely here. We are fortunate we ended up here instead of any other realm. Everyone has been so welcoming."

"Yes, quite lucky," Endo said, staring at her. Nellie had the sudden impression she had said too much and raised his suspicions. She licked her lips and smiled at him, hoping to appear at ease. Endo shook his head and looked at the shops around them. "I'm sorry, I don't mean to stare. You just remind me of a young human I know. Where are you headed?"

Nellie nearly choked. She knew she reminded Endo of herself. She always blabbered on like that whenever she saw him in her child form as well. "The Athenaeum. I heard it's filled with more books than any other city."

"That's mostly true, from what we know," Endo said. He considered her a moment. "Would you like company? I would be happy to show you around."

Nellie felt an ache in her chest. She'd had a crush on Endo for almost as long as she had been in Anestra. He reminded her so much of the mate she left back in the human realm. She desperately wanted to spend time with him, especially in the body that belonged to her and not to the child she normally represented. But she couldn't risk it. She knew Endo had an added ability that warlocks didn't normally have: the ability to detect illusions. Having extra abilities like that meant someone in his family must have been an elf. She had no idea if him detecting illusions meant he could detect shapeshifters. The last thing she needed was to be crucified, or worse, for being discovered.

"Actually, I was hoping to have a bit of alone time. I hardly ever get time to myself." She bit her lip, knowing she didn't need to try hard to give him a look of regret.

"I understand," he said. "It was nice to meet you…what is your name?"

"Maggie," she blurted, giving him her mother's name. She extended her hand to shake. "You can call me Maggie."

"Well, Maggie, I hope we can run into each other again," he said as he bent over her knuckles and brushed a soft kiss against them.

Melting. She was melting inside. She gave an awkward chuckle and turned the corner, breathing heavily. There was almost nothing she wanted more than to finally flirt with people her own age again and be carefree like she used to be on Earth, but she had to stay focused. She looked to the sky, guessing she had an hour before she needed to head back, and crossed the winding road leading to the Athenaeum.

It was as grand a building as *Mentage*, and impossibly larger. Standing seven stories tall and made of white stone, it resembled a church more than anything else. Its dome-shaped roof was built of glass, and the sun reflected off it like a beacon, beckoning all to its doors. It was a formidable building, the type one would want to be in if there were a siege, for surely it could withstand whatever was thrown at it. Like most places in Anestra, it was protected by magic, though not the Fae kind. Warlocks, though their powers waned, warded the building, and elves fortified it. It housed some of the most ancient scrolls and texts known to both warlocks and elves, and it even contained important human documents that were thought to be lost to time and space.

Which, of course, they were.

Nellie climbed the steps leading to the entrance, its shadow causing a chill in the sudden coolness. It took a moment for her eyes to adjust as she entered the darkened space, and just as every other time before her, she was lost for words at what she saw.

Her eyes were first drawn to the wide, circular area in the middle, scattered with large tables. Her gaze shifted to the glass dome ceiling, the sunny afternoon giving it the appearance of opening to the heavens. It was the only natural light penetrating all seven stories. Each level, rotund in nature, contained floor to ceiling shelves, and she knew from her many wanderings that the dark corners held shadowed alcoves filled with old artifacts of the land. There were countless hidden nooks to read by lamp light and desks for studying. The Athenaeum was attached to their version of a university, and as such, classrooms and private studies were available for rent.

Nellie walked along the darkened rows of books, breathing in the scent of dusty pages and old leather bindings. Soft murmurs and the rustling of pages were a melody all its own. She sighed. There was nothing like being in the cozy darkness surrounded by endless stories of love, heartbreak, history, and war.

She strolled along the farthest wall, lined with at least twenty doors leading to different rooms for rent. The first half of the doors were available for everyday use. She walked past those and paused in front of the thick oak door she recognized as the one Faline permanently rented.

She reached for the handle but stopped short. There was no handle. Only the smooth expanse of a solid door lay in front of her, the lamp light casting shadows in its deep grooves. She glanced at the other doors to see if they were the same, but was dismayed to see they were not. Each one of those had brass handles, ready to be used.

She was stumped. The last time she was here with Faline, the door just seemed to open, but she couldn't recall how. Was there a special keyhole? A word she had to say?

Nellie nudged the door, hoping it would budge. It didn't.

"Open Sesame?" she whispered. Nothing happened.

"I wish to enter the room." Still nothing.

She rubbed her hand up and down the front, looking for a hidden latch or something to give her a clue.

"Excuse me," a shrill voice said. Nellie whirled around and saw the small body of an elven woman in a simple pink frock, glasses balanced on the edge of her nose. Nellie almost snorted. She knew the glasses were for show; elves never lost their eyesight. "Are you the owner to that door?"

"No," Nellie said. "But the owner is my mother. I'm supposed to check on something for her."

Shrewd eyes looked back at her. "It is spelled. If you don't know how to open it, then I cannot help you." She gave Nellie a piercing stare before turning around, leaving her alone again.

Nellie groaned. It would be pointless to attempt to enter without Faline. If it was spelled then she was the only one who could open the door. Determined not to make her trip a complete waste of time, she wandered in the darkness until she reached a section of human literature and browsed the shelves. Titles both familiar and not jumped out at her. She ran her fingers along the spines, tracing the letters. She often wondered how Anestra came to be filled with human artifacts, but she found that she didn't really want to know. It was a blessing to have a piece of home, should she wish.

She meant to turn a shadowy corner but stopped at the sound of furious whispering. She backed up a step and waited, listening. She peered in between the stacks and the broad shoulders of a human came into view. Standing next to him was a tall, thin warlock dressed in fine silks of purple and blue. Around his cuff he wore a gold bangle, one that Nellie immediately recognized as belonging to Crispin Jakfour, the slimiest warlock she had ever come across.

"...can make her suffer, if I wish," Crispin was saying to the human.

"N-no, you can't. The Contract binds you." Nellie recognized the voice belonging to Callum, a human teen who lived at *Mentage* and often worked in the stables.

"There are ways around the Contract," Crispin sneered. "You will do this for us."

The Contract referred to the magic binding all who wished to live in Anestra. It was old magic, one that ensured that each resident of the land follow the rules set forth by Queen Amira—otherwise their magic would cease and they would be forced off the land. It was one of the most powerful ways in which peace was enforced, to ensure another war would not break out among their lands. That Crispin claimed ways to go around that was terrifying to think about. Who would risk the consequences it would take to find out?

Callum trembled. "What do you want a human for? I have no qualms here. I am happy with the Agostonnas."

"You are nothing but a pawn in their game," Crispin said. "We all are." He picked a piece of lint off his sleeve. "I would tell you to think on it, but I know you will come to see reason soon enough." He turned on his heel and walked away, arrogance marking his every step.

Nellie left her hiding place and approached Callum, who stared at the book titles before him with tears in his eyes. She liked him; he was always kind. She reached out her hand to comfort him but noticed the different shade of her skin, the long nails she gave herself. Once again, she forgot she did not look like the disguise she usually portrayed. She let out a breath.

Callum jumped, frightened from what hid in the shadows. Nellie cleared her throat. "I'm sorry, I didn't mean to frighten you. I—Are you okay?"

He nodded, scanning her face. "Who are you?"

"I'm new to Anestra. I found myself missing a bit of home." She looked at the human literature surrounding them. "Who was that?"

"Just a warlock you don't want to mess with." He shifted uncomfortably. "I have to go, sorry."

Callum practically ran away from her, bumping into the shelves as he went. Nellie stood there a moment longer, heart racing. What did Crispin want him to do? Why was he threatening him?

The rumbling of her stomach reminded Nellie she needed to eat something before she passed out. Cursing herself at wasting so much time, she found her way back to the entrance and out into the winding streets. She paused at a vendor and bought some type of spiced grilled chicken on a stick, which she ate as she practically ran down the main road. If she wasn't back for dinner then Faline would become suspicious and she could hardly tell her she just tried breaking into her spelled room, although she was certain Faline would be interested to hear what Crispin had to say.

Nellie burned her throat as she wolfed down her food, eager to regain some energy. She gazed through the shop windows, pining after the fine silks and jewels on display. She never had much money growing up and still didn't have anything to trade or barter, but it didn't stop her from wanting to own something more lavish. It was pointless, however. Jewels and silks meant nothing to her when she already had everything she could possibly want with the royal family.

She paused outside another window as her eyes rested on the Blacksmith's display. Weapons she didn't have the name for were lined up on a dark velvet cloth. She peered closer at a set of daggers that seemed to be made completely of black metal, its blade shining with a deep crimson sheen. They were beautiful, and would make the perfect gift for Faria's eighteenth birthday. The tag next to them read, *Val, dipped in the blood of a Drogosterra.* The price tag was exorbitant, surely far beyond what anyone in Athinia could afford.

She sighed to herself, wondering how the shopkeeper could have gotten his hands on such a rare weapon. Any relics belonging to the ancient Val were either locked away or else unaccounted for.

Nellie started to peel her eyes away but did a double-take. Someone stared back at her through the window. A male with broad, muscular shoulders and golden skin stood next to the counter inside the store, his deep green eyes boring into her.

Hunter.

She thought about waving at him but stopped, remembering once again that the appearance she wore was that of a stranger. He had no idea it was her. She glowed for a moment, excited that she'd caught his eye. Perhaps he found this body attractive. Honestly, if he wanted a go at her, she would not say no.

Her smile faltered when she noticed his mouth was set in a straight line and his eyes were like chips of ice. She didn't know why, but he seemed angry with her. He nodded his head once in her direction, maintaining eye contact.

Her heart pounded and sweat trickled down her neck. She felt as though he recognized her but that would be impossible. Nellie turned around and walked quickly back to the edge of the city and into the darkening line of trees. She crossed the small bridge over the river that separated *Mentage* grounds with the rest of Athinia, and walked along the winding path in the growing darkness.

Night fell by the time she got back to the suite she shared with Faline. She was surprised to find it empty. They usually went down to the Great Hall for dinner together, though if Faline wasn't there, it meant that she was tied up in a meeting with the queen.

Nellie sat on the edge of her bed and warmed her toes by the fire. She wanted to tell Faria everything she had learned, but it would be too difficult without explaining what she really was. She could go straight to the queen, but she would ask too many questions. No, she had to wait for Faline—had to tell her that a final battle was imminent and that the queen wanted Nellie to protect Faria, though from whom or how, she had no idea.

She wondered if she should also tell Faline about that weird moment with Hunter. Did he recognize her? He seemed angry *with* her, not his general moodiness. She wasn't looking forward to the next time she saw him. Something about the way he looked at her as if he knew exactly who she was unnerved her.

Nellie stretched her arms, working the kinks out of her body. She'd have to attend an early morning yoga session with Josephine, another human who lived at *Mentage*. Perhaps she would catch a glimpse of Endo in his morning practice. Gods, what she wouldn't give to have a moment alone with him.

Guilt overcame her. Even after five long years, she was still broken-hearted and empty inside over leaving her mate. The space he used to occupy was cold and hardened, the pain of it spearing her every so often. She wished she could, for once, have a day as herself and do the things she wanted to do. The things any normal teenager on the cusp of adulthood would want to do.

Nellie walked around the common room of her suite, her eyes snagging on a golden chest in the corner beneath the window. The key stuck out of the lock. If Faline didn't want her to go through it, *surely* she wouldn't have left the key, right? She ran to the door and peeked out, making sure the coast was clear. She eased her way back inside and skipped to the chest, heart racing. Perhaps the day wouldn't be a complete bust after all. She felt bad for snooping, but curiosity got the best of her. There was a wealth of secrets she had yet to uncover, and she needed to start somewhere.

IT HAD CLICKED OPEN THE moment Nellie turned the key, and the smell of old vellum and dust crept up her nose. Each document felt delicate to the touch, as if the gentlest breeze would disintegrate them. Countless parchments and books lay scattered around her, though she couldn't make rhyme nor reason of them. Nellie suppressed a shudder as she reached for one book in particular whose oily and stretched cover felt grossly like human skin.

The door to her suite creaked open and Nellie dove on top of the mess surrounding her. Faline entered, giving Nellie a particularly pointed look at the pile of ash that was once a black scroll.

"What are you doing?" Faline didn't sound the least bit surprised at catching Nellie with her private chest broken into.

Nellie had the good grace to be embarrassed. "I'm sorry, Faline. It's such a long story." She took a breath to explain but then remembered what she saw earlier. "Wait! What was going on with Faria and Hunter? Did you see that fire?"

"Yes, and I felt it long after, too." Indeed, her cheeks were still rosy.

"What's going on?"

"Seems like you have some idea if you're looking at those." Faline glanced down at the paper currently in Nellie's hand.

"I have no idea what any of this stuff says," Nellie admitted. "I barely needed to turn the key and it opened, I swear. I'm sorry," she added.

"Only those of honest blood can open it," Faline said, then paused, weighing her next words carefully. "What you're sifting through is over one thousand prophecies, told by many races, over many centuries, in countless languages. One of which might be true."

Prophecies. Nellie knew these papers had something to do with what the queen said. "What do you mean *might* be true?"

"Those are ancient. Beyond ancient. I have no idea how old, maybe a millennium, probably more. And, as it was told to me, one of those prophecies may be true while the rest are not. We aren't meant to know. The Ancient Ones had a weird sense of humor."

But Nellie knew what was true now, thanks to Queen Amira. Or rather, what the queen believed to be true.

She cleared her throat, staring holes into the floor beneath her. "So, I should probably tell you that the queen caught me spying on her," she blurted out.

Faline stilled, her face inscrutable. Nellie explained what she had overheard. Crossing the queen would be enough for banishment at best, execution at worse. For both of them.

"I mean, not *caught me* caught me, but I was in that hallway creeping on her and the king and she looked right at me through the wall, I swear it! She was telling the king about the Prophecy, the *true* Prophecy, according to her. Something about how the final battle is approaching. I didn't hear all of it, but I think it is the right one. She certainly seemed sure of it."

Nellie paced the room, carefully avoiding the ancient texts scattered about her. "She must know somehow. And I can't be sure that she definitely saw me, but she looked right at me while she said that Faria must be protected at all costs."

Faline took a deep breath, measuring her words before responding. "She knows what you are, Nellie."

"Impossible." Nellie shook her head. "You said yourself that I smell human and I haven't been anything but a thirteen-year-old for the most part. And I certainly haven't changed outside of these rooms or in the Forest, except for a little while ago when I knew there was no one around," she rambled. "I mean, how could she know about the hallway? About the wall? And even if she did know, how did she know I was there, or that it was even me?"

"Take a breath, child. I was with Amira this evening. She knew what you were from the moment you arrived." She gave Nellie a look. "Of course, it was silly to think she doesn't know about everything that happens on her lands." She paced back and forth with Nellie, the candles sputtering in their wake. "She would have banished us by now if she felt the need to."

Nellie felt the blood drain from her face. "Banished?" Where would she go from here, when she was already banished from Earth? She didn't want to think of the horrible possibilities that could come from that.

"She revealed little to me, other than you were kept here for a reason." Faline bit her lip as she worried a hole in the floor. "I suspect that reason has everything to do with the Prophecy, the final battle, and keeping the princess safe."

"What am I to do? I've only been here for a few years. I barely understand the politics of this place, I'm hardly fluent in your language even after all the studying I've done, and there has been nothing weird happening until recently." Nellie's voice worked into a frenzy as she continued. "I have no magic ability outside of shifting. What am I supposed to protect her from? This evil is spreading." The words wouldn't stop tumbling out as Nellie rubbed her hands up and down her arms at the sudden chill taking over her body. "Whatever it is festers in the ground. It's messing with nature. The magic I have as a shapeshifter pushes against it. I don't want to go anywhere near it, and I don't have the ability to take it on anyway."

"I know, I feel it, too." Faline turned concerned eyes to Nellie. "We will know what to do when the time comes."

Something else nagged at Nellie. "And can we just rewind for a second? What the heck is going on with her and Hunter? That was seriously powerful magic. Does it have anything to do with the Prophecy?"

Faline paused to consider her words before responding. "I studied the lore when I was much younger, years and years ago. There are thousands of prophecies, several hundred of which say that she will fall in love with something more ancient than all the realms. But can we take that to mean a person? An object? A feeling? We don't know. There are more that suggest a human is her mate, or rather, that with no power is her true half. Yet more say that she will bear a male child, of all things. I can't see how that one is true, but you never know. I don't know what the power between Faria and Hunter means but the strength of it that I feel when those two are around each other…he must be involved somehow. I think he is meant to be in her life. I just don't know what it means."

Faline furrowed her brow. "There is one thing we are sure of: everyone who has studied this Prophecy—those who truly believe, who have spent their life poring over these scrolls and more—know without a doubt that it is Faria they speak of. That she must bear the weight of all evil. That she will change the fabric of what is." Faline rubbed her tired eyes. "What's more, she has developed abilities that she is hiding from everyone, and I think she has started to realize that Hunter is different. It's a pull she can't escape." She let out a deep sigh. "She will be blessed and cursed with these abilities. And she will determine the fate of all beings, in *all* realms."

"You mean the apocalypse." Nellie whispered the words, not daring to believe the truth of them. That it was real and happening in her lifetime, that she was friends with the person who was meant to cause it, or prevent it.

"That is the human name for part of it, yes."

Part of it? "I overheard Crispin talking to Callum earlier." Faline whipped her eyes to Nellie's face. "I didn't understand most of it, but it sounded like he was threatening Callum. Claims there is a way around the Contract."

Faline blanched. "I will have to seek an audience with Amira again, I think." She worried her lip. "Perhaps this is where you come in. You have an incredible knack for snooping. Maybe you help Faria by finding information as you can. Until then, stay as young Nellie. Keep teaching Faria your silly Earthen colloquialisms, follow her around. Be your usual self. See if anyone appears unusual around her. And until *then*—" she grabbed the parchment from Nellie's hand. "We keep searching."

For the next few hours, Faline taught Nellie a few key symbols to look for among the texts. Candles died down and true night fell, but they were still no closer to figuring out the truth. Not even with the clues Nellie had picked up during the day.

The apocalypse was coming, and Nellie had no idea how to protect Faria or try to stop it.

Cripes.

SIX

FARIA

The scent of fire and burnt ash seared her senses as she bit through the pain coursing through her wrecked body. The world was silent.

She was alone.

Seconds passed as her Fae-blessed senses returned to her broken elven form. Sound, then feeling. Her body burned from the blast and cracked ribs stabbed as every inhale pierced her sides. Slowly, she peeked open her eyes, expecting red light from the blood moon to penetrate through, but there was nothing.

Jolting upright, she felt her blood pound to the beat of her heart as awareness fully returned to her.

Alone. She shouldn't be alone.

She breathed deeply and, ignoring the pain in her side, dove into her well of power, willing its forces to help strengthen her. Goosebumps shot down her arms and nausea threatened her as the power rose too quickly—higher and higher, until a violet light shot out her hands, only to be swallowed by the darkness surrounding her.

She looked for any signs of life, but the warlock's magic had destroyed everything. Where there was once a rushing vitality in the Forest of the Dawn, now there was nothing.

Leather boots crunched on dead leaves and broken twigs beneath her as she tried to rise, but she fell to her knees, still too weak to stand. Panic set in.

Her eyes adjusted to her surroundings, and she was grateful for the low-light vision elves were gifted with. She found herself in her secret glen. Once filled with bright energy and love, it was now a graveyard of dark magic.

Scorched earth surrounded her, all traces of grass and flora crisped. It extended to the trees, their usual rich tones of gold and brown replaced with scorched black. Their branches held upright in a silent scream and the smell of charred decay permeated everything.

"Ander?" Her voice cracked in the silence of the dense night. No response. "Ander, please, are you there?"

Nothing returned her plea. He was gone.

Bile seared her throat, leaving the tang of denial creeping in its path.

Find Ander. Find Ander.

She swallowed down the panic threatening to overtake her, counting to ten to clear her head. Panic led to mistakes.

She steadied herself and leapt to her feet, taking stock of the injuries that remained. Her advanced healing had taken care of most of them.

She had only started to run for a moment before she stumbled over something hard a few yards away.

Something solid that didn't belong there.

Her knees skinned against rocks in the path, and suddenly her face was inches away from a male body. It took her eyes a moment to adjust, or maybe she just didn't want to believe what she saw. She didn't want to think that his neck was broken in an impossible way, or that his skin was burnt straight to the bone, or that his body laid lifeless before her. But staring into those glassy green eyes confirmed what she so desperately tried to reject.

He was dead.

The pit in her stomach expanded through her heart and overwhelming grief joined her panic. She screamed into the night until her lungs gave out, though she knew it would do no good. She dug her knees farther into the torn earth and pounded the cold ground, willing it to crack under her anguish. Time stood still as tears flowed down her cheeks.

She screamed, and screamed, and screamed—

FARIA'S BREATH CAME IN HUFFS as she ran laps around the practice field—more laps than she cared to keep count. She hadn't been able to go back to sleep. The nightmares were getting clearer and more confusing still.

Who is Ander?

Jitters kept her moving. She was unable to release the nerves she felt about being near Hunter again. When her lungs burned holes through her chest and breathing became nearly impossible, she stretched her muscles and sat in the middle of the pitch, focusing on meditation to quiet her mind. It was a sticky morning, the last of summer staking its claim while a cool breeze soothed the sweat off her back.

Meditation did nothing. Her thoughts drifted endlessly back to Hunter and what had happened between them the day before. The way he held her. The way his stare threatened to lay her bare, as if he could strip her of all her secrets. As if she wanted to let him. It irritated her to no end, and goddess forbid she ever let a male get under skin like that. Yet, he did, and she was moments away from seeing him again and it was all she could do to not vomit with anticipation.

Taking a long gulp of water did nothing to cool her down, so Faria reached for a practice sword. She gripped the pommel tight, hardly noticing the rough splinters piercing her calloused hands. She slashed and swung, warming up her arm, then switched to the other side.

A shadow caught her attention and her breath hitched at the sight of him, observing her with that penetrating stare she hated. He uncrossed his arms and casually made his way over to the weapons rack, nodding his head in greeting to a few Anestrians getting their practice in early as well. Though she heard their grunts of effort, Faria lost sense of her surroundings as Hunter chose his sword and made his way toward her. They stood inches from each other. Like her, he breathed heavily, though she didn't see anything that warranted his exertion. After taking a moment to size each other up, they began their dance of swords.

For every parry she gave, he blocked. For his every slash, she avoided.

The *thunk* of swords echoed in the field, their focus solely on anticipating what the other might do. Birds sang in the distance, their morning song adding to the melody of clashing weapons. Murmurs rose from the crowd around them. She distantly noticed that there were more elves and humans there than usual, but she hardly paid attention.

They turned, keeping each other at arm's length, reading every signal and tell they gave off. Faria had practiced with Hunter for a few years now, and though she never showed any signs of besting him, she resolved to make it happen. Her muscles strained with the thought of enduring much longer, but fierce determination brought forth renewed effort. She needed to show him that she could beat him, more so than any other day. Before, she needed to prove it to herself. Now she was doing it for him. She hated it, yet it gave her motivation to keep going.

He struck a hard blow that normally would have had her on her back but she blocked it in time—barely. Her teeth clacked with the effort of staying upright.

Sweat glistened on his forehead and dripped down his neck. The sun made its appearance over the horizon and once again reflected in his eyes, highlighting the unusual golden halo she'd noticed the day before. Their eyes locked together and all thought left her. She felt as though she were drowning in his stare, felt as though that golden halo could provide the answers she sought if only she looked hard enough. She dropped from her stance, leaning in closer to him, desperate to figure out what it was that pulled her to him, what made her feel so frustratingly crazed around him.

"What are you?" she whispered, her breath stirring his hair around his neck.

A beat passed. He withdrew, abruptly turning his back to her and walking away. She caught herself from falling, aware almost too late that she leaned fully toward him, expecting the weight of his presence to keep her afloat. She suddenly felt cold without him. Her stomach sank, wondering what it was that caused him to walk away this time. Had she gotten too close? Or was it because she questioned what he was?

Whatever it was, it wouldn't go unnoticed that their practice was cut short again.

Remembering she wasn't alone, Faria glanced around at the onlookers but no one moved, save Hunter. She watched as he threw his sword back on the rack and peeled off his gloves. She shook herself, ignoring the hurt of his sudden rejection. That was the second time in as many days that she watched his retreating back and, once again, she was angry. Angry that she let herself feel anything at all toward such an impossible person, angry that he once again was in control. She was so tired of it. Just once, *she* wanted to be in control. She wanted to be the one to rile him up. She wanted to be the one to walk away and smile at the victory of it.

Faria wiped her face. Her own juvenile thoughts disgusted her, but she couldn't keep them at bay. She looked up to the stands at the crowd moving on to their own weapons practice and caught sight of the queen. Grim-faced, she wore a fitted black jumpsuit and clutched a bow and quiver at her side. She nodded slightly at Faria, the only indication she had seen and heard everything.

Faria broke eye contact first and walked away.

DAYS HAD PASSED SINCE FARIA'S last practice with Hunter. She wasn't complaining; she didn't think she could handle any more frustration. Besides, she needed to focus on her people and the danger posed by the dissenting warlocks. She spent her time volunteering in Athinia, mostly in shops and taverns that needed an extra hand.

One morning, Faria had the rare opportunity to have breakfast with her parents after helping the healer restock his linens and tonics. Without the excuse of training with Hunter, she found herself suddenly free and wanting to see them. Well, her father, at least. She hadn't had a proper conversation with him since their chat by the fountain.

The Great Hall was a large circular room with a ceiling made entirely of glass. It was big enough to host hundreds of people and, during mealtimes, long tables were laid out for any who wished to join them. There was one wall built entirely of windows, which overlooked a large stone patio with a sloped lawn peeking through behind it. Grand wooden archways crisscrossed along the ceiling, and banners with the Agostonna royal crest hung on the walls. Faria glimpsed at the image of the ivory antler crown backlit by flame. She had never asked the meaning of it before.

"Mother," Faria said, sipping on raspberry juice. "Why does our family crest have a flame? The gifts that have passed on from mother to daughter are typically those of water, are they not?"

Queen Amira chewed slowly on a grape before turning her eyes to her daughter. "The first of the Agostonnas was a direct descendent of both an Original and Fae. Her gift was that of flame."

Faria considered that. It surprised her that after a few thousand years they hadn't changed the crest. "Why haven't we changed it? In a millennium, we have evolved, have we not?"

"The power of the flame still resides in us and it shall return when the Fates deign it necessary. Wouldn't you agree?" The queen looked at her and Faria had the feeling she was asking an entirely different question.

"Of course," she responded.

"Faria, darling," King Dennison said, "would you like to go riding with me today? I must meet with some of the soldiers patrolling the roads between here and Mercy Bay."

"Yes, absolutely, if Faline will let me skip out on lessons today."

"Speaking of lessons," the queen said, "why were you not with Hunter this morning?"

Faria suddenly found her food very interesting. "Oh, I was feeling unwell. Upset stomach."

The queen looked down at Faria's plate and pursed her lips. "Did you see a healer, then?"

"Feeling better now," she said around a mouthful of pastry.

The king looked between the two of them, probably wondering if they were going to start arguing in front of everyone. He didn't need to worry, though. While Faria had quite the temper, she wouldn't make a scene in front of their people. She hated being the center of attention, anyway.

One of the glass doors leading out to the fields banged open and Enis, a member of the Queen's Royal Guard, stalked her way to their table. Her short black hair swished against her leather armor and sunlight glinted off a sword at her waist. The murmurs of the hall quieted to hear what she had to say.

"My Queen." Enis crossed one arm over her chest and bowed. "We just received word of a skirmish in Athinia involving some warlocks." She lowered her voice. "It appears there was a protest of sorts and someone set one of the barns on fire. Warlocks fought off those who tried to put it out. There were some injuries."

"Gods, whatever could be the reason for the destruction?" the queen wondered. "I must go at once."

"You stay here, Amira. I was going to head out that way, anyway." The king wiped his mouth then stood, readjusting his short swords.

"I'll come too, Father," Faria said.

Her parents exchanged a look. Faria watched them have a wordless conversation before her father said, "I need you to stay here, my darling. You can come with us next time."

"But I can help! It's rare that there's actually a chance at talking to someone angry enough to cause a problem. As future queen, shouldn't I learn how to deal with these situations?"

"In due time," the king said. "Word will spread quickly enough and there may be some at *Mentage* who are worried. You can help keep them calm, as a queen must do."

He smiled at her as he hurried off. Faria drummed her fingers on the table. "There must be something I can do, Mother. What good is there to talk about my duties and responsibilities if I can't act on them?"

The queen stood, smoothing the wrinkles from the jumpsuit she wore. Her hair was pulled back with tiny braids peeking through her ponytail. Faria studied her mother's high cheekbones and the slight upward slant to her ice-blue eyes. There were times, such as that moment, when Faria was in awe at her mother's beauty. She felt a painfully empty feeling in her chest at how much she wished they could have a close relationship.

"You will be needed here, I'm sure. Perhaps you can use this time to entertain your undoubtedly many suitors." The queen gave her a pointed stare and walked away.

Faria played with the food on her plate, her appetite having turned to ash. Entertain suitors? That was what her mother wanted her to do? Flirt while pieces of property were set on fire for some unknown reason? She scoffed to herself. Even if she wanted to, who was there to choose from?

It wasn't as if she never looked for a life partner. She had several times, but her thoughts were always preoccupied. The first time Faria had snuck out of *Mentage* to roam around Athinia was after a particularly disturbing nightmare. Her hair was a different color and texture—she'd almost looked like a different person. That night, she had changed into a loose pair of pants and a tunic that barely covered her skin. She had wrapped a gauzy shawl around her, ready for a night of fun. She ended up at one of the taverns and sat in the corner, admiring how *normal* life was for anyone who wasn't a Royal. She certainly flirted that night, and even shared kisses with a stranger.

It wasn't forbidden for her to do so, necessarily, but it was dangerous for her to be out without anyone knowing where she was. She hadn't cared in that moment, though. No one had recognized her and she finally had that taste of freedom she had been craving. Though she had to admit, she hadn't come across any serious contenders for a life partner.

Perhaps she would sneak out again. If she was going to be forced into an arranged marriage, then she wanted to at least do some of what she wanted before then. Before her obligations caged her.

Faria sighed as she rose from the table. She would at least head out to the fields to see if they needed help with the final harvest before frost struck. It might be a good way to get information from some of the warlocks there. Perhaps they would feel more comfortable opening up to her.

She stopped short on her way to the door, distracted by a buzzing feeling in her stomach. She waited a moment, wondering if karma struck her and she actually was going to be sick. Moments later, Hunter walked in. He wore all black with a dark brown harness to fit his usual assortment of weapons. His hair brushed the collar of his tunic, a stray piece falling across his forehead. The buzzing turned to butterflies and Faria wondered if her body was aware of Hunter's presence before she was. He scanned the room, his eyes brushing over everyone until they met hers and filled with something like a challenge. Faria's breath staggered.

Until she remembered that he had embarrassed her twice in two days and therefore was not worthy of her lack of oxygen.

He stopped in front of Faria, mere inches away, his body heat seeping into her. Goosebumps snaked down her back.

"You didn't practice this morning."

"Look at that, you're still observant," she said.

His lips twitched, though he didn't smile. "Why not?"

"Maybe I got tired of your disappearing act."

"Miss me?" This time he cocked a half smile, which only served to infuriate her more.

She swallowed hard, desperate to wet her suddenly dry mouth. "Never."

He smiled wider, his teeth biting his lower lip. Gods, that was distracting. The pull in her stomach dipped a bit lower. "Whatever you say, Princess."

She stepped around him, intending to leave, but he reached out a hand to stop her. It landed on her waist and she heard a collective gasp from those who watched, their breakfasts long forgotten. Her heart echoed in her ears as fire filled her veins. It was all she could do to remain still.

He quickly removed his hand but the feeling remained as a brand. He leaned in closer, dropping his voice. The scent of spice and ocean made her lightheaded. "Where are you off to?" The words were a musical caress in her ear. She closed her eyes and breathed him in deeper.

It took her a moment to regain control of herself but it was too late. He saw the way he affected her. His smile changed to one that promised forbidden things. She took a steadying breath before leaning in closer to him, their lips almost touching. It was dangerous to put herself in this position. So dangerous, but she couldn't help it. She wanted to affect him as much as he affected her.

"I'm doing what you do best," she said. Their breath mingled and she was almost surprised to see that he didn't pull away.

"And what is that?"

She smiled and licked her bottom lip. His eyes zeroed in on the act and for a moment she detected another scent mingled in with his own. Something spicy on her tongue.

"Leaving."

She stepped around him and this time he didn't stop her as she walked away. She felt his eyes on her long after she was no longer in his sight. She couldn't help but think that the victory she wanted to feel didn't feel much like a victory at all.

FARIA SPENT AS MUCH TIME as she could out on the grounds, attempting to get information about any discontent among the workers at *Mentage*. It proved unsuccessful.

She couldn't tell if they were scared to express their discontent or if there was nothing to be aggrieved about. She always believed her mother ran a fair and empathetic Queendom. In the past there were many meetings held at *Mentage* to listen to the complaints and there was always a swift and fair solution. When did that change? Perhaps she was yet too inexperienced to see what might have been right in front of her for years.

The weather this far north had changed from oppressive to downright chilly. Frost covered the crops overnight, so Faria worked with the others to bring in as much bounty as they could. The leaves on the trees within the Forest were beginning their switch from deep red to burnished gold, and the feeling of a harvest holiday was in the air. Because Anestra was filled with many different races who all practiced their own religion, they didn't celebrate religious holidays widely. Those were kept more private. Faria knew her mother would be found at a temple devoted to the three goddesses in Athinia to give thanks for the bountiful harvest. As a country, however, they always celebrated the two solstices. Though winter solstice was still a few weeks away, the preparations for both that and her birthday had already begun.

After Faria had done all she could—including teaching the children how to make elven flatbread—she locked herself in her room, wanting to test the limits of her abilities. Those that were expected of her—the low light vision, the exceptional hearing, her speed—were common in all elves. It was the visions, the ability to see through glamour, the scenting of those around her, and the manipulation of elements, that made her different. Seeing through glamour, or illusions of magic, was uncommon among elves. Many could sense magic, but Faria could see a shimmer where a spell lay.

Scenting was something else quite uncommon to elves. She knew of a few warlocks who were able to scent people. It went far beyond smelling them. It was like breathing in their essence. There were some elves, such as Faline, who could sense the emotions of others, including guilt if they were lying. Faria had first noticed a nearly a year ago that she was more than sensing the emotions of people, but rather tasting what they felt. Anger was like breathing in a fire, lust was spicy on the back of her tongue.

She never expected to harbor all of those abilities.

The only ability expected of her was an affinity for manipulating the elements, specifically water, the way her mother could. The way all Royal female elves could. Twice she was able to call upon mere droplets of water out in the fields, and once she had ripped the oxygen from the air during a small barn fire. An older stableman named Smyth witnessed that, and he had looked at Faria as if she'd grown the wings of a *Drogosterra*. She never told anyone what happened, nor did she try to do anything like that again. She wasn't sure how she would explain it, anyway, only that she was scared the fire would spread to the animals and it was her fright that had brought about her power.

More recently, she felt an ember burning beneath her skin. It seemed more than coincidence that her mother had mentioned a flame returning to their line when the Fates deemed it necessary. She could feel the press of the burn, feel it as if she could summon fire to her hand, on her skin, manifest it in a tangible way. She felt it most when she was with Hunter. At first, she thought it was the bloodthirsty nature of her irritation with him that brought about the desire to set things on fire. But it was more than that. As if he ignited the passion necessary to wield a flame.

One thought repeated in her mind.

Hunter is not human.

Never before had she questioned his humanity the way she had the past week. She knew he wasn't using a masking spell or some sort of illusion, but something was different about him. He smelled human, but not. That was nothing new, but Faria had never thought anything of it before.

Until now, she hadn't cared.

Humans tended to smell quite plain to elves, mostly of the earth, sometimes a spice or two depending on how inherently good or evil they were. Humans didn't normally smell of elderberries and the *palodun*, the oldest flower of Anestra, or of the ocean breeze and fresh rain. Of spices long since forgotten in this land.

None, but Hunter.

Still, there was that underlying scent all humans had; equal parts desperation and hope. Mortality.

Faria gazed out the window and thought of him. Of the feelings he awoke in her. Her face flushed as the blood rushed through her veins and the burn beneath her skin licked her fingertips.

A small flame danced on her hand.

Her heart raced, wondering what it meant that the Fates allowed flame back into their bloodline. That it was her they chose to bestow it upon. She flicked it between her fingers, getting a handle on its energy, the way it pulsed at attention, waiting for her command. She felt something click and settle in her, as if there were a piece of her she forgot was missing.

Nellie barged into Faria's room and the flame flickered out. "I'm not going anywhere," she said without preamble. "I need to know you're okay, Fifi. I left you alone for a full day and not once have you come to find me. Enough is enough." Her blue eyes stared deep at Faria as she puckered her lip, begging to stay.

That wasn't necessary, though. Faria would do whatever she could to keep Nellie happy.

"Of course you can stay," Faria said. "Why don't you teach me more of your human slang? I love learning your language."

"Sure, if you answer one thing first." A coy smile spread across the girl's face.

"I'm not sure I want to know the question," Faria said, reaching for a goblet of water on her console table.

"Why didn't you tell me you have a thing going with Hunter?"

Faria spit out the sip of water, spluttering as she choked. "What are you talking about?" She wiped the water running down her chin.

"All of *Mentage* is talking about how close you guys were and the way he touched you. I can't believe it."

"It was nothing," Faria said. "We were just messing with each other.

Now, about that slang..." she trailed off, hoping Nellie would change the subject.

"Hunk," Nellie grinned. "Say it with me now."

Faria hesitated a moment. "Say it in a sentence, please."

"Hunter is a major hunk." She cackled her head off as Faria tried to shove her out the door. The kid made her crazy sometimes, but she did love her dearly.

Distant shouts interrupted them. Faria ran across her common room to the balcony overlooking the Spring Garden and listened.

The commotion came from the other side of *Mentage*, difficult to hear from so far away. Taking deep breaths, Faria focused her energy, allowing vibrations to caress her whole body as she focused on listening harder. A gush of warm air surrounded her then lifted away, and suddenly she could hear as clearly as if she were in the middle of the chaos.

Shouts of fire. Of blackened Earth. Trees dying.

Trees? *Impossible.* The only trees on that side were from the enchanted Forest. Fae magic protected it as well as what surrounded it for miles. It was infallible.

And yet, shouts of alarm. Of people needing the queen.

Needing *her*.

Faria threw on a fresh tunic and boots and pulled her ebony hair back, a vain attempt at keeping her wild curls tamed. She almost collided with Nellie whose eyes were frantic.

"Fifi, something is wrong!" she said.

"I know Nells. Stay here." Faria raced out of her bedroom and down the hallway, narrowly avoiding cleaners in the hall, but soon heard the patter of feet following her.

"Like heck am I missing out on this. Are you crazy?" Her breaths came in pants as she tried to keep up with Faria's speed.

"Just stay out of trouble," Faria yelled as she ran faster. There was no point in trying to convince her to stay, knowing she would likely end up in the thick of it anyway.

Faria rounded the corner and flew past the Great Hall, Council Room, and the Atrium, exiting through the Autumn Garden on the southern edge of her home. The smell of blossom and cardamom should have hit her, but instead there was only the stench of rotting soil, nauseating in the dense air.

Faria leapt over the stone wall that separated the garden and fields. Farmers watched in confusion while others tried to jump into action, though it seemed their efforts were wasted.

Black flames consumed the Forest and the darkness spread deeper into the dirt, branching out like wicked fingers grasping at whatever life it could find.

Faria ran as close as she could get to the edge of the Forest, sure she could do something about the fire. She had to.

An arm reached out and grabbed Faria's waist, snatching her out of the air.

"Don't get any closer, lady." Hunter's voice whispered against her. "It isn't a normal fire."

Faria looked up at his towering frame, noticing his arms now crossed over his chest. His strong forearms were bare, save for leather bracers, the hint of metal flashing against the light of the flames. A sense of power surrounded him.

He was right about it not being a normal fire. No smoke left in its wake, just the stench of decay. It neither gained power nor died down. It simply burned.

Faria felt an overwhelming presence beside her, one that cut through the panicked energy she felt from the onlookers. The queen had arrived, and though she was dressed for battle in a fitted combat pantsuit that undoubtedly had weapons hidden all over her body, she made no further move. Her stance was rigid, ready for a fight.

"What do you need me to do, Mother?" Faria asked, forcing herself to make eye contact. Her body jittered from pent up adrenaline and the intense need to protect her people. Faria's blood turned cold at the look she found on the queen's face, pouring from her essence.

Fear.

"What can you do, Faria?" The queen grabbed her arm, squeezing as her eyes searched Faria's face, looking for the secrets she knew she was holding onto. "Tell me now, quick."

The queen's fear stirred an urgency in her, a need to not hide the extent of her abilities anymore and to do whatever was necessary. Faria took a deep breath, centering herself, wondering what she could use to fight the abomination ruining her land.

She focused inward, allowing her power to take over. Her muscles relaxed and a cool breeze tickled her face. Her body hummed, priming her for what she knew she needed to do. She glanced to her right and ripped a dagger free from Hunter's belt. She distantly noticed its beauty—pure black with a bloodred sheen on the blade. Before either of them could stop her, Faria slashed her palm and held it to the earth.

The power locked deep within now flowed freely through every molecule, starting as a kernel of warmth she felt in the pit of her core. She silently coaxed more out, allowing it to take over her body. Blood dripped into the ground as Faria maintained even breaths, but soon she felt something slide between her fingers.

Water.

Droplets at first but then more, puddles soaking under her feet. She heard gasps from around her. Sweat pooled down past her ears as Faria willed the water toward the fire. It hissed as it made contact but still, it was not enough to douse the flame.

Come on, come on.

Desperate for her lungs to take in precious oxygen, the blood pounded behind her closed eyes and she reached farther *there*. A new well of power she hadn't yet disturbed appeared. Lightheaded from expending too much energy too soon, Faria didn't dare waste time wondering how it was possible. She couldn't stop now. Something told her to keep going.

This new source- of power was not the same type of flame dancing on her finger tips moments ago, but deeper, hotter, and unnatural, burning tiny as an ember, barely light enough to pierce through the darkness of the inner chamber it was harnessed in. *Release me*, it seemed to say.

Instinct took over. She reached her other hand to the queen, silently asking her to slice her other palm. The queen shook her head, face pale with shock as she looked at Hunter. Faria felt him hesitate before he heeded her silent command, the sting of the blade reaching through the fog gathering in her mind. Faria channeled the pain into more focused energy and slammed that hand to the ground as well. She might have considered it strange that her body called for blood magic, which was more typical of warlocks or gifted humans, but in that moment she hardly cared.

Faria's legs gave out. She kneeled in the mud, coldness seeping through her pants as the blood rushed out of her. She stoked that inner ember until it burned brighter. Energy gathered in her as she shot the power toward the flames devouring the forest. A scream pierced through her concentration and it took her a minute to realize it was coming from her.

She squinted against the tears rushing from her eyes. A fire appeared, hovering over the stream of water still flowing to the Forest, one that changed from blue, to red, to violet. It looked vaguely familiar, those flames. A light flashed and flared a brilliant emerald green. Her whole body shook with effort and bile crept up her throat but still, she kept going.

"Enough." Hunter's voice cut through her concentration. His hand squeezed her shoulder and it became her lifeline. "That is enough."

She didn't listen. She wasn't sure she could stop. Once the power was let out of its cage, she lost all control. She had to follow what it wanted her to do.

"Release the power, Faria," Hunter said. Commanded. She blinked at him, distantly surprised that he called her by her name.

Faria focused on reigning it in, even as her vision dimmed, even as her heart stuttered. Moments passed, but she couldn't tell how long. The pain wracked her entire body. She felt as though her bones were bruising, tendons stretching, blood vessels bursting. She was losing her sense of self, of what it meant to live or die, to love or hate. Nothing had meaning, just the urge to continue until there was nothing left.

Finally, the emerald fire smothered the black flames until they were no more. She washed her water over the flames, the power flowing through her doused with the action. She was utterly spent, shivering with oncoming fever, barely able to keep consciousness.

Hushed whispers echoed around her, but she understood nothing. Faria felt her mother lean down and reach for her but Hunter was quicker. Without a word, he lifted her under her knees and neck, cradling Faria to his chest. His body heat did what it could to stop her violent tremors.

The queen's voice sliced through the fog, the only clear sound in a field of gasps and murmurs. Dread and resignation coated her words. "It has begun."

Then, darkness.

SEVEN

NELLIE

H oly Heck on Wheels. What. Just. Happened.

Faria was bent over the muddy ground, an aura of faint blue light emanating from her. A hush descended upon the crowd as water rose up and trickled away from her towards the flames, trying to douse whatever foul magic laid waste to the forest.

The light flickered as Faria raised her other hand to the queen but when nothing happened, Hunter stepped in and slashed her palm with a black dagger. Queen Amira stared at Hunter as Faria slammed her hand to the ground and this time the vibrating stopped, only to be replaced with a violent windstorm that nearly toppled Nellie face first into the mud.

The blue light pouring from Faria faded to a faint purple as honest-to-goodness flames flared to life on top of the rivulet of water she created.

They changed in color from blue to red then violet. The same type of flames that flared to life in the library a few days ago. So that answered that question. The power came from Faria.

The queen stared transfixed at what happened before her, but Nellie's eyes were on Hunter, who laid his hand on Faria's shoulder. The sound of her gasp was lost in the rush of whispers around them. No male could touch the queen or the princess without permission, except for those they chose as their partners. Nellie thought that must be what the whispers were about but as she looked around, all eyes were on the Forest.

Violet flames changed to a brilliant green as they leapt around the black fire and Faria let out a pained scream.

She's gonna kill herself.

Shouts and exclamations resounded around her as Faria's flames devoured the other. The fire died down, bit by bit, until nothing was left but Faria's magic. Soon the water sputtered that out, too.

Faria fell to the ground, gasping for air, and to the shock of all gathered, Hunter reached over and picked her up. He stared at each person in turn, challenging them to do something about it. All avoided his gaze as if he were an Alpha, exuding his power to demand their respect and obedience.

I wonder if Hunter is a shifter, Nellie thought. *Only the dominants in my clan commanded that type of power.*

Queen Amira and Hunter shared a long look, her face solemn as a silent message passed between them. He nodded at her as he walked away toward *Mentage*, Faria in his arms.

The crowd quickly parted to let him through. Exclamations rippled in their wake.

"She is the Chosen!"

"She is the Fated!"

"She is the Destined!"

"She brings the reckoning!"

Over and over again, words surrounded her, and those still left standing fell to their knees in reverence.

This was just a hint of power in the battle to come. Faria nearly killed herself trying to douse a fire, and yet the Prophecy said that Faria would need to...combine with this evil? It was a warning, right? Suspicious timing for it to happen on the same day as the fire outside of Athinia.

Whoever was the source of that evil magic would be there soon. Nellie felt it in her bones.

She wound her way through what remained of the stunned onlookers, her boots squelching in the mud. Warlocks and elves called to the wind to carry away the burning scent of dying things, while the farmers went back to harvesting what crops they could before nightfall.

She had so many more questions than answers, and as she made her way inside *Mentage*, she knew the best person to answer would be Hunter. There was a reason why Faria's magic flared in his presence and she wanted to know why.

Making sure she was in all of her tiny human glory, Nellie turned the swagger up to a ten and began the search Hunter. No one could deny her when she was on full blast, and that was what she intended to be.

She only hoped he responded to her.

HUNTER WAS NOWHERE TO BE found the rest of the day or that night. He wasn't in Faria's wing when Nellie got there, but Faria was tucked into bed and unconscious. Nellie felt her friend's forehead, expecting her to be burning up, but she was cool and clammy to the touch. Faria stirred in her sleep and burrowed deeper into the down comforter. Nellie made sure she had water on the table next to her bed and added another log to the fireplace before heading back out.

She went to the healers' wing, an area in *Mentage* that allowed all practicing and credentialed healers to make their tonics and brews for the whole of Athinia. Healers switched between there and the hospital in the city, though they often preferred to be in Athinia where most of the action took place. Though she conducted a thorough search, the healers said Hunter had not come around.

Rather than risk anyone's suspicions by roaming the grounds, Nellie opted to stand guard outside Faria's room instead. Some kitchen staff left food that never got eaten, and Faline came to see what Nellie was up to. Nellie promptly told her all she witnessed and said she planned to remain outside Faria's room until Hunter arrived. Not even the king visited, though Nellie figured he was still sorting out the ordeal outside of Athinia.

Queen Amira arrived at midnight. She raised her eyebrows at Nellie before entering Faria's room, and left only moments later. Her face was pale and sweaty, and there was a slight tremor in her walk. Nellie desperately wanted to know what was going on, but no one asked the queen something like that, and her ambition from earlier had deflated.

The next morning Nellie found a small bowl of oatmeal and fruit next to her makeshift bed on the stone floor. She felt grateful to whoever thought to leave her food as well, realizing how ravenous she was.

It wasn't until nearly noon when Nellie finally tracked down Hunter. She found him studying the ground at the edge of the fields where it met the Forest, the same place where the fire battle had occurred. Nellie almost made it to him but then he slipped into the trees, gentle as a passing shadow.

He often hunted for food for the carnivores at *Mentage* and Athinia, so it wasn't strange that he went into the Forest. What *was* weird was that he was weaponless. No bow, no arrows, no axe. That, and he stuck to the shadows, trying to keep out of sight. If that didn't spell suspicious then Nellie didn't know what did.

She considered changing into a bird but thought better of it. A meter into the Forest she stilled. There was no sound. No birds. No wind. No water. It was as if a shield blocked all her senses. As if the evil residue killed even sound.

A voice broke the silence. "What are you doing?"

"Jeez Louise, Hunter!" Nellie gasped as she turned around, hand on her racing heart. "You nearly killed me alive!"

"That makes no sense, Nellie." Hunter cocked his head at her. "What are you doing here? It isn't safe."

"Well, I was following you, of course," Nellie replied. There was no sense in denying it. She batted her eyelashes and glanced up at him. He towered over her—in this body, she was at least two feet shorter than him.

"It's just that sometimes a girl needs a nice older gentleman to look after her in these scary times, is all."

He gave her a blank look. "I know what you are."

His words took a moment to register. Nellie's mouth turned to sandpaper and she lost the ability to speak. After a few tries, she said, "Um... what?"

"Change." The command echoed in the air.

Nellie meant to protest but she felt the unbearable need to listen to everything he said. The pressure squeezed her body but more than that, she found herself *wanting* to listen to him. Anything he asked for she would have gladly abided. If he told her to slit her throat, she would have done it. Nellie hadn't felt that type of compulsion since her clan leader forced her into banishment by making her walk through the Gate of All Realms, and even then, he'd had to wait for the blood moon.

What was Hunter, to be able to do such a thing?

"What are you doing to me?" Nellie said through gritted teeth, the pain squeezing the air from her lungs. "Stop it."

The pressure lessened, but only enough to let her know it was still there.

Nellie considered running her mouth with a few choice words, but then realized that Hunter had some sort of magic that far surpassed her own. The realization that there was a lot she didn't know about him struck her. In fact, she didn't know anything at all. What if *he* was the source of evil?

Slowly, Nellie backed away, her bones protesting with the movement as they longed to fulfill his command.

"You needn't fear me." Hunter had the decency to look embarrassed and any compulsion left over was immediately lifted. "It has been a while since I used that voice and I forgot how strong it could be."

Yeah, okay, Nellie thought. *That sounds sane.*

"Nellie, I know this is not your true form. You are a shapeshifter and you are suspicious of me. Let's talk. Change, please."

Well, Nellie certainly couldn't deny the truth. She was a better fighter in her natural body, so she changed bit by bit until she looked like herself. Apprehension gripped her, but she thought his compulsion helped coax the change along because it wasn't nearly as painful and it didn't take as long as usual.

"What the hell are you, Hunter, if that's even your *real* name." Nellie's deeper voice almost surprised her as did the anger that came out of it. She didn't have to bend her head so far back to look at him and she poked his chest with her finger, making sure he felt every bit of irritation that she felt toward him for daring to use magic on her.

"It is a name I have chosen, yes. You can still call me that. As for what I am, it is forbidden for me to say. I'm not someone you need to fear."

"Oh, that's convenient." Nellie tapped her foot on the ground, jazzed up from being caught and by the thought of actually getting some answers. "Forbidden by whom?"

"I cannot say that either."

"Great. Well, what can you say?" Nellie noted his stoic face, his clenched fists. He seemed as though he were wrestling with an invisible barrier, like something blocked his mouth from saying too many words.

"Though I can't say what I am, I can tell you I'm not your enemy. I am here to protect Faria. At all costs. Whatever it takes. And so are you."

The way he repeated almost verbatim what the queen had said mere days ago sharpened her interest. "What do you mean so am I? I was banished here."

"When you walked through the Gate of All Realms, you could have ended up anywhere. With dragons, trolls, on a fire land, underwater with mermaids. The Fae, wherever they are now, heavens forbid. That is why it is a punishment to your people, no?"

"What's your point?"

"You ended up *here*, Nellie. This is where you were meant to be. Why the Fates sent you here. For this." He gestured to the dead earth around them. "For Faria."

"What is 'this'?"

"It's the start of the apocalypse."

Cripes. If she needed confirmation, that was it. "That's awfully dramatic."

Hunter stared at her, his expression blank. The silence went on for an uncomfortable moment.

"So, um—" Nellie fumbled with what she wanted to ask him. "What are your abilities, what do you know of the Prophecy, and what magic do you have that can help us?"

He let out a long-suffering sigh. "I don't have full use of my powers. I don't know why. Because the Fates deem it so," he said, shrugging. "You should not even know this much, but I see you for what you are. You should not hide yourself, especially not now." He paused for a moment. "There may come a time soon when you won't need to anymore. The queen is starting to get reckless."

"What does that mean? Does she know what you are and why you are here?"

"Not what I am. She likely now suspects that I am some sort of protection."

His answers were starting to tick her off. If he made a big show of exerting some power on her then why not explain more about his purpose?

"I need you to do something, Nellie."

She cocked her head to the side, taking in his strong features. The freckles that threatened to dance over his nose, his sharp jawline, his russet hair curling just around the ends. Nellie felt a pang inside, one of deep longing that she hadn't felt in a while. Suddenly she wished it was Endo in front of her, seeing her for who she truly was instead of Hunter.

"Why do I get the feeling I won't like what you're about to say?" Nellie finally said.

"You must follow the queen. She needs our help and she is likely to reach out to you soon."

"She already gave me a cryptic call to arms, Hunter. No need for you to add to the pressure."

"The time will come when she will ask things of you. And you must do it, no matter how impossible it may seem."

As if saving Faria wasn't enough?

"There is something I must do," Hunter said, turning away from her.

"Wait—" Nellie yelled, but there was no point. Hunter disappeared, blinking out of existence. She found herself alone, the silence stretching on. The lack of life in the deadened forest unnerved her. She changed back into her younger form and ran out into the sunshine, away from the forbidding cover of the blackened leaves.

She took in her surroundings. The green rolling hills, *Mentage* sprawling behind lush gardens, birds flying overhead, workers getting ready to rotate their shifts for the afternoon. Everything was vibrant but a sense of foreboding still rushed over her, feeling as though someone watched her through the void in the Forest. Her eyes travelled along the perimeter of the trees and beyond, noting those bursting with golden life next to the offending area in front of her.

The overwhelming need to cry sprang forth with the thought of her home, her family. Though it was irrational, Nellie couldn't help but feel that she had brought this upon everyone. That it was her fault the apocalypse was on their doorstep.

She shook the feeling off. There would be plenty of time to cry. For now, it was time to plan.

EIGHT

THE QUEEN

Queen Amira's steps echoed against the heavy beating of her heart. Her silk gown flew in the breeze left in her wake, and she tried to keep her slippered feet from running to her daughter. What she was about to do was forbidden beyond measure. If They found out, the punishment would be unimaginable.

She reached her daughter's wing and felt Nellie before she saw her. The buzzing energy of the girl lit up an already loudly decorated hallway. Amira gave her the barest of glances. She knew Nellie had questions but wouldn't dare ask her—and to be honest, Amira wasn't sure she wanted to speak to the girl. It was too complicated to explain how she knew what she really was, that she knew she would be pivotal to Faria's success or downfall.

When Amira entered Faria's suite, the scent of jasmine and earth assaulted her senses, along with something else. She stood for a moment in the quiet, her nostrils working to scent what else was there.

Male. Familiar, of the forest and ocean, but not.

Hunter.

She stamped down on her anger before it had a chance to rise. Of course Hunter had been in her room, exactly as she had instructed. She should be grateful that he had helped her when he did; it didn't matter whether he was human or not. The moment he had touched her—forbidden as it was—Amira knew he was something else. What exactly that was, she wasn't sure. She was not given information about a male protector, only Nellie.

She squared her shoulders, steeling herself for what she was about to do. The line she would cross as soon as she entered the bedroom.

Amira could barely hear Faria's steady breathing over the crackling fire, yet it was all she could listen to. Her daughter, her precious child, was still alive. She was not yet harmed. There was still time to try to protect her, in whatever way she could.

She approached Faria's bedside, wishing her hand would steady before placing it on her daughter's cold forehead. Even after sleeping for several hours, Faria's powers still had not returned. It was too much too soon.

Amira steadied her breath before allowing part of her consciousness to brush against Faria's. It was easy to do, to get into her mind while she dreamed. She had barely entered into the darkened dreamscape when she was slammed backward and nearly lost her footing.

Amira raised her hands in front of her and was surprised to find an invisible wall, sturdy as if it were made of stone. Her gifts flared to life at the touch. This barrier was not Faria's doing. Someone placed it there. Someone much stronger than Amira.

She knew she should feel relief that someone thought to protect Faria in this way, but instead unsettled her. Who could have known that someone would try to enter Faria's mind? Was it Them, knowing she would try to tell Faria the truth, or was it an ally, protecting Faria from what was to come?

Amira pushed with all her might, her mind against this wall, trying to break it down. It wasn't until she poured a bit of her essence into it that it started to give. Without much more than a thought, the barrier disappeared as if it were never there to begin with.

Shaken, the queen stepped forward, bracing herself for another unknown attack, but none came. She sat down in the empty space, waiting for the images of Faria's dream to manifest.

The Forest of the Dawn erupted around her, filled with more life than Queen Amira had seen in years. Birds chirped, deer frolicked, and even the fish in the stream bubbled up every now and then. Bright hues of blue, green, and orange filled Amira's vision. The trees felt alive, the breeze heavy with the scent of orange, jasmine and vanilla. Exotic scents normally found only in the Spring Garden.

Her heart ached from how alive Faria was, from how vibrantly she viewed the world.

From how little she had allowed herself to know her daughter.

Faria appeared then, dressed in the normal gray tunic she insisted on wearing, a bow in hand. Hunter stood behind her, correcting her positioning. Amira's eyes narrowed at the image. She knew Faria had this infatuation with him—it was obvious by how viciously she practiced weaponry with him and how excited she got over their verbal sparring—but she hadn't realized how deep the infatuation ran. She could feel Faria's longing from here.

Amira cleared her throat.

The image of Hunter faded and Faria whipped around at the sound. Shock and embarrassment crossed her face. "Mother!"

"We don't have much time, child. Please, follow me."

Amira strode into the Forest, where silence and wind replaced the lively sounds. She didn't have to look to see if Faria followed; she could hear the grumbling from her daughter as she tried to keep up.

"This is a new one, even for you." Faria's anger echoed in the silence. "This is a serious invasion of privacy."

Amira stopped in the clearing closest to the Gate of All Realms, where magic was strongest. Though this was only the dreamscape, the vitality of the magic vibrated her blood as if she were standing next to it fully conscious.

The portal was hidden from all in Anestra. The exact location of the Fae and Human Realms, among others, just a blink away. Even in the dreamscape, the force of its magic was undeniable. Only a select few knew how to find it; the consequences would be dire if everyone knew what lay so close to them.

"Where are we?" Faria rubbed her hands down her arms. "I've never seen this place before."

"Never mind all that. There is something you must know."

"I feel like my skin is jumping off of me," Faria said as she gazed in the direction of the portal. "I feel the need to run over there. It's taking everything in me just to stand in place."

Hmm, interesting. Her gifts must be strong enough to feel it, even here. Good. She needs to remember this place.

"There are rumors," Amira said. "Of you being the Chosen. The Prophecy, evil meeting good. It's true. It's all true."

"Prophecy? What?" Faria gazed around. "This is one weird dream."

"This is no dream!" Amira hissed. "Listen, please! My blood strengthens our realm, but protection is fading just as I am."

"Fading? Impossible, Mother. You are centuries away from that."

"There is no time." Amira waved Faria off. "When I was challenged as queen, as you will one day be, I was told things, shown things that were both past and future. You need to know that everything I have done, it was all for you."

"This isn't making sense. I'm not to know of the trials! Why are you telling me this?"

"I cannot say more on that, not now. Evil comes. Faria, listen. You will be challenged, tested. Hurt. You will break." Amira's voice wavered as she tried to keep her strength. She couldn't be emotional and hold herself to the dreamscape at the same time. "You must rebuild. You must come back from it. You will feel all hope is lost, but it isn't. My daughter, I love you with everything, all that I have. My protection on you will come to an end soon and then you will learn the truth about everything. Please, Faria. You must endure. You must survive."

"You never told me you loved me before." Faria's wide eyes stared at her. "You're scaring me. I don't understand what's happening."

Feeling herself starting to fade, Amira willed her voice to linger in the growing darkness. "Survive, Faria. Endure, then survive. Choose life. Everything depends on it."

The queen tumbled through the air as she was tossed from the dreamscape and into another place. Here, and not here. Disembodied voices hissed in the darkness around her, sinking their anger into her bones.

"You speak too much, Queen." The words echoed inside her head, the pain of it erupting from behind her eyes.

"I did not tell her the circumstances," Amira said, pleading. "I did not break the rules."

"She will not remember."

"No! She must!" Sobs raked through her body. "Please."

"She will forget all when she awakes. You cannot change the Fates. Not yours, not hers. Do not anger Us further."

Queen Amira slammed back down to reality and all remnants of the dreamscape and the other place disappeared. Seconds passed—or maybe minutes—as she fought to regain her composure, as she fought to keep the sweeping wave of nausea at bay. Her hands shook as she wiped the sweat from her brow. She should not have come, but she needed to try.

It was all she had left.

NINE

FARIA

Blistering, searing pain. Emptiness. Heartbreak.

Something is missing. What am I looking for?

Hate. Revenge. Desperation.

A light.

Sweat-drenched sheets tangled around Faria's feet and her body hung halfway off her bed. It took a minute for her to realize she was in her room, tucked under the covers. She wasn't being tortured. She wasn't lost. Those feelings slowly receded to the back of her mind.

Why am I still dressed? She felt like she'd spent the night drinking too much elderberry wine. A dull ache throbbed behind her eyes.

Slowly, memories came back. Fire. Flame. Water. Whispering. Then him, putting her to bed. Tucking her in. Telling her he would make it right. What did that mean?

Then there was that dream. Most of it was blank but those *feelings*. Even dimmed as they were, Faria couldn't shake it. Every moment of consciousness had her grasping onto their fluidity like water. The queen had been there, but she couldn't remember why. It felt important though, and nagged at her like a gnat. Did she tell Faria something?

Goddesses above, this light is so bright.

Nellie burst into Faria's bedroom in a cloud of energy, taking away any hope for more sleep.

"Fifi! You're awake!"

"How can I not be with you bursting through the doors like that?" Faria grumbled, lifting the sheets over her head.

"I've been waiting for you." Nellie pulled the sheets back down and gave her a reproachful look. "I can't believe you didn't tell me."

"Didn't tell you what?"

"About how powerful you are! About your—" she looked off to the side conspiratorially before whispering, "magic. Everyone keeps talking about you. It's all over Anestra by now!"

Perfect. "What? What are you saying, Nells?"

"How you're Chosen! The 'One Who Was Prophesized!' The Redeemer! The Most Glorious Gal of All!"

Faria laughed at her absurdity. "They certainly are not saying that."

"Well, most of that anyway." Her foot shuffled along the rug. "I thought we were besties." Her wide, innocent eyes shone with a hint of tears.

"Besties?" Faria smiled at her, teasing her choice of words.

Nellie scrunched her nose in disgust. "You really need to pay better attention to the things I teach you. Buds for life! You know, BFFL!"

"Earth is weird," Faria said, rubbing the remaining sleep off her face. Nellie's words began to sink in. "Wait, what? Chosen? Prophecy?" That nagging feeling itched in the back of her mind again.

"Yes! How could you not tell me? I thought you told me everything."

Faria watched Nellie for an uncomfortable moment before responding. "Nellie, we are different ages, different species, and I am future queen. Yes, we are besties, as you say, but I can't just tell you everything. Some burdens are for me, not for you."

The young girl shot her a dazzling smile. "Aw, it's okay. I get it. We all have our secrets." She winked. "At least I can tell everyone that I'm besties with *The One*."

"If you call me the Chosen One again, I swear on the three goddesses I am going to scream." She rubbed her temples, a headache looming. "And what does that even mean? There are millions of prophecies or something, isn't there? Where is the proof?"

"Um, hello, do you remember what you did? You made freaking *fire*. Purple fire. After making *water*. And then your fire ate the evil fire. Like full on swallowed it whole! And then your water put out your fire like it was no biggie."

Faria's head pounded.

So now I'm going to doom our race because I won't choose a partner and have a child before the age of eighteen, but also, I'm going to save us because I am supposedly the Almighty One? Faria never believed in prophecies. There were so many, most of which never came to pass, and there would be many more to come. Most of it was silly ramblings of Ancients, probably their idea of a joke…but to be the one to bring on Armageddon?

This was more than Faria's heart could deal with.

Speaking of her confusing heart…"Hunter."

"Oh, yeah. People are definitely talking about that one, too." She gave a devil's grin.

"Gods. Now I really have to avoid him. What did they say?"

"Ha. Avoid him? I wouldn't bet on it." Nellie chuckled to herself. "Anyways, they're saying how *lucky* he was to be right there when you almost ate mud. How *fortunate* you were to have a big, strong, male to carry you to bed." She raised her eyebrows at Faria as she made a show of taking in her surroundings. "I see nothing exciting happened, though."

"Nellie!" Faria's cheeks flared. Everyone was so caught up in wanting her to have a child they seemed to have lost their filter.

Faria wondered what her parents made of it. She snorted to herself. They were probably encouraging the rumors, even if it was about a human. "Of course nothing happened, I passed out. And, excuse me, a big, strong male? I mean he is good looking, but I didn't *need* him. I could have done just fine on my own."

"Oh, I would need him any day of the week," Nellie said.

"Oh, my gods! You are a child! And anyways, people must know that nothing is going to happen between us. That it can't." She didn't miss the raised brows or secret smile Nellie gave her. She played with her bedspread, pulling a thread loose and twirling it around her fingers. "Plus, we fight constantly. He is cocky beyond reason; his skill is as impressive as it is irritating. And then he carried me! How embarrassing. He wants to get far away from me and all this drama, I'm sure."

Nellie stuck her hip out and tapped her toe. She looked frazzled, dressed in the same simple shift as yesterday, dirt slung across her nose and her braids undone. "You're delusional. Also, Hunter is out in the hall waiting for you."

"What!?"

"Oh yeah, he joined me in my vigil outside your rooms a few hours ago. I told him I would announce his arrival." She bent at the waist with a dramatic flourish.

Faria leaped out of bed and ran her fingers through her hair. She opened her wardrobe and went through silks and fine velvets before deciding on a pair of brown riding leathers and a light green tunic. *Chosen One* or not, she wasn't about to start dressing in frills and bows. She strapped on her leather boots then tossed back a few berries from the tray Nellie had brought in, willing the sugar to stave off her impending migraine.

"Nice choice," Nellie said, looking Faria up and down with approval. "Can I come with you?"

"Come with me where?" Faria was nearly breathless at the thought of facing Hunter again so soon. What would she even say?

Stupid girl. You don't like him. You don't want his company, and you aren't curious at all about what he wants. "What does he want?"

"You're going into the Forest, of course!"

She would keep her curiosity at bay. She refused to ask Nellie what she meant. "What do you mean? Why would we go in there?"

Nellie smirked. "Rumor has it he knows a thing or two that he wants to teach you."

"I don't know what that means," Faria said, shooing Nellie out of her bedroom.

"You'll see."

Faria crossed the entryway, the smell of fresh cut jasmine tickling her nose before she opened the door. Hunter stood rigidly in similar leathers to hers, his tunic red and a simple brown vest covering it. He wore sheaths on his forearms and ankles and was armed to the teeth in various knives and daggers. A pair of bows and two quivers of arrows were slung across his back. He looked dangerous. Hunky, Faria begrudgingly admitted to herself. A chill passed through her.

They stared at each other, unspoken words palpable between them. She shifted her feet, suddenly self-conscious. *Pathetic.* She refused to break first.

"Nellie said you were here." She cleared her throat. "What can I do for you?"

He looked up and down her body, taking his time as he measured every inch of her. He handed Faria a bow. "You're coming with me."

TEN

FARIA

Faria and Hunter strolled across the fields toward the Forest of the Dawn. After two nights of overnight frost, the morning's sun seared her and sweat prickled her scalp. Although, if she were honest with herself, it might have had to do with her proximity to Hunter. He strode ahead of her, shoulders tight, knuckles straining against the bow he held.

"So." Faria strode quicker to keep pace with him. "I wanted to thank you, for what you did."

"It is my pleasure to serve you, lady."

His formality grated on her nerves. "Do we really need to be so formal after…everything?"

"Yes."

Okay, then.

Faria didn't quite understand what she did to make him so distant. She figured him walking away from her two days in a row had been because of his bruised ego. Now, she wasn't so sure. Perhaps he was intimidated by how powerful she seemed to be.

She snorted. His arrogance seemed to be rubbing off on her. She'd have to make conscious efforts to change that, immediately.

They passed a few workers in the fields, several of which yelled out to her, calling her their Chosen. Others just stared or bowed low to the ground. They had never revered Faria in such a way. She rarely saw such deference even for the queen. It wasn't their way; the Agostonna Royal Family strove for a more casual existence. She had gotten bows of the head and tiny curtsies. Never anyone on bended knees.

Faria acknowledged them but with small bows and waves, but kept her distance. They acted as if she were a goddess come to life. It seemed as though she was going to have an even harder time finding a life partner. No one would get within twenty feet of her.

She looked toward that vile spot that marred their once pristine land. Now that the excitement was over, she saw how bad the destruction really was.

And it was even worse than Faria imagined.

The trees were bent in a silent, black scream. No leaves remained— only charred wood petrified in position, as if hoarfrost had frozen them in place. The ground surrounding the trees was burnt, with black veins reaching out toward the field of crops. Even at this distance, she could see how far the damage went.

Faria could almost hear that terrible energy calling to her, forcing her to get closer against her will. She had to know what it was. Maybe if she learned more about it, she could decipher the source. Maybe if she answered the call, she could find out who would do such a thing and learn their next step. Magic sang in her blood. Just a taste of its power...

The darkness stretched before her feet. She was bent down, her hands hovering over the inky blackness, right where she had stood nearly two days ago. Faria didn't remember walking over there.

She shuddered at the malice that leaked over the ground. She felt it stroke against the pure essence of her gifts. She thought she wanted to learn it, but instead it reached out as if it were learning her. As if it were a sentient being. Yet, Faria could not step away, the feeling reverberating throughout her body. Even the pebbles seemed to vibrate, as though they were trying to dispel the evil that corrupted them.

Faria watched her own hand reaching out. Something seemed to sing her name. If she could just touch it, she would know how to control it, and then nothing like the other day would ever happen again—

"Ouch!" Faria's hand stung and turned crimson from the sharp whack of Hunter's bow, breaking her from her reverie. "What in Aurelia's Garden is your problem?"

Hunter's fist clenched at his side. "Don't touch it." His lips were drawn with barely suppressed anger.

"I can feel it. I don't think I stopped whatever it was at all." Faria looked back to the ground. "I think I changed it."

"Yes."

"Yes? That's all you have to say?" Faria stood from shaky knees and spread her arms wide. "Thank you so much for explaining any of this. You are really, very helpful."

"First of all," he said, nostrils flaring, "I do not need to explain anything to you."

Faria bristled with indignation. "Excuse me?" She wasn't used to anyone being so rude to her, not even him.

"Secondly, what happened here was dangerous, ancient, and evil. And now the *Chosen One* wants to touch it?" He said it as if she were simple minded and it stung more than she wanted to admit. "Do you have any idea what could happen?"

Faria's annoyance crept ever closer to anger and if she had canines like the Fae, she knew they would have started to lengthen. As it were, she bared her teeth at him anyway. "I already touched it, remember? I doused that fire. What difference does it make?"

"You were closed off to it before and now you're practically trembling with how eager you are to accept it."

"If I learn it, I can control it. I don't think it will harm me. I can feel that my essence will accept it, somehow." The thought was only mildly unsettling. "I don't know how to explain it."

They were less than a foot away from each other, standing toe to toe, each wearing a reflection of the other's incredulity.

"Accept an unholy, ancient evil?" Hunter leaned closer, his voice dropping even lower, caressing a part of her that Faria didn't want responding to him. "That is a very dangerous statement, Lady Faria." His voice was like melted chocolate, settling into her, wrapping her in its embrace. The gold flecks in his eyes glowed, and she could taste a hint of violence in the air. She craved it.

"Not more dangerous than what is going to happen if I can't control it," Faria hissed back at him. A warm breeze shimmered over them, their hair dancing in the wind.

She drew closer to him until they were a breath away from each other, unable to turn away from his stare. His anger urged her forward, as if she had something to prove to him. She would always accept whatever challenge he presented.

"If I know what it is, what it wants, then I can get stronger. I can protect my people, our land, from whatever it is that is coming. This was just the beginning. I must learn more so I can do more. Can't you see that?"

He didn't respond and Faria became painfully aware of how close he was when his every exhale brushed her cheek, tickling the skin beneath her ear. Her fingers twitched at her side as she suppressed the ridiculous urge to run them through his hair.

Faria could see from her peripheral vision a scattering of workers inching their way closer to them. Gossips, all of them. They wanted to see Faria do something magnificent, no doubt. She was starting to feel like a carnival act.

One glance at the gawkers and Faria realized what caught their attention. The wind whipping around her and Hunter was not natural. Everything—everyone—was as still as the trees. It seemed that only she and Hunter could feel that preternatural wind, could feel the hair whipping across their faces. She had no way to explain it.

Hunter leaned in, his lips brushing the outer shell of her ear, whispering words only she could hear. "You cannot control Fate. Do not try." He abruptly turned and strode back toward the Forest, leaving Faria freezing in his sudden absence. The wind died as he walked away.

"Come," he commanded over his shoulder.

Not wishing to cause a bigger scene, Faria followed, thinking of all the ways she was going to annoy him once they got to their destination.

She took one last glance at that darkened patch of earth and felt a longing for what she left behind. A desire, like she was walking away from her destiny. Yet she could not help but wonder, as Hunter turned and waited for her, if instead she was walking toward her future.

THEY WALKED FOR SEVERAL MILES in silence. The farther away they were from the darkness, the more the Forest came back to life. The warm gold of the leaves interspersed with green from the evergreens seemed far brighter. The birds chirped louder and water from a nearby stream babbled happily away. The air felt clean, crisp, and smelled of chestnuts and the last of autumn.

It had been a while since Faria explored this far into the Forest. She breathed in deeply, centering herself, mentally preparing for whatever Hunter had planned for them. Each cleansing breath helped her to regain control, helped her feel more like herself. She knew she lost all common sense when she was around Hunter but being this far into nature was freeing, in a way.

It felt so different here. The trees were older and the air moved differently in her lungs. The scent of spice and dirt were heavy, exotic, different from the usual moss and loam. There was a sense of peace, of calm here. Everything felt as though it belonged and worked with each other and she could not help but wonder how she never discovered this part of the Forest before.

"What is this place?" Faria asked in the quiet stillness.

He was silent for so long she thought he would ignore her. "The Forest has many secrets."

Even his evasive shortness with her couldn't affect her mood. Faria closed her eyes for a moment, relishing this new feeling. All of her came alive. She could feel the core of her gifts waking up, stretching as though from a long nap. It sang through her, flowing through her blood.

They stopped in a field filled with wildflowers. Faria glanced at Hunter. Rays of sunlight and shadows flitted around him. He looked so different here. Less human, more like her kind.

Like something Other.

"I know this place," Faria realized. That itching feeling in her mind nagged at her again. The field, the trees, and that incessant humming in her blood.

"You don't," Hunter said. The space between them felt distorted. Sensations were heightened, the distance between them feeling so impossibly far, yet she heard him as if he were standing a breath away. Faria wondered again what type of magic ruled here.

"No, really," Faria said, making her way over to him. "I think I dreamed of this place."

He cocked his head to the side. The green of his eyes shone in an ethereal way, catching her off guard. They were beautiful, almost iridescent, like sunlight reflecting off a forgotten sea.

"What are you?" Faria blurted out, repeating the words that had made him walk away from her just a few days ago.

A hint of a smile crossed his face this time. Faria glided closer to him, enough to reach out and touch him if she wanted to. And she did want to, she realized.

"Right now, I'm the one who will take your training to the next level," Hunter replied.

He tossed his bow to her and dropped the quiver of arrows at his feet. He removed his leather belt and stepped out of the gauntlets around his ankles. After gently laying down his weapons one by one, he turned to face her. "You know the basics already, but we will review them first."

"The *basics?*" Faria replied, crossing her arms. "Please. I can spin circles around you."

"Today will be target practice," he continued, ignoring her. "Both with the bow and some throwing daggers."

"Does my mother know you've kidnapped me?" She almost chuckled at imagining the color her face would turn. To be out in the middle of the Forest with him. It would drive her crazy.

"The queen is very aware of what we are doing."

Smiling tightly, Faria asked, "Why must you suck the fun out of everything?"

"You cannot expect me to not tell the queen where I am taking her daughter, especially now when there is a clear threat to the Queendom."

He had a point, there. Faria stared at him, wondering if she should tell him she knew he wasn't human.

"For the sake of transparency," Faria said, "I know you are no more a human than I am." She leaned into him as she spoke, their bows the only thing keeping them apart. "I don't know what it is about you, but I can sense it."

His eyes roamed her face. He drew an arrow, nocked it, and whipped around, firing at a target too far in the trees for Faria to see.

"Your turn." He stepped aside, deliberately increasing the space between them.

The control he had over both his weapons and emotions unnerved her in more ways than one. The more she tried to rattle him, the more undone she became. She felt drunk from the air, from the power she felt flowing in her veins, and was almost giddy from his presence and wanted to impress him.

The bow was the only reprieve she had from his gaze. Honey colored limbs sanded smooth rested under her fingers. The weapon was powder soft, yet firm and supple. The grip was slightly ridged, the clefts of which held her hand perfectly no matter how she tried to move it. Faria nocked an arrow and drew the string back as tight as she could, testing its strength. It didn't matter the power she gave; it did not whine or break. This was an exceptional weapon.

"I don't recognize this bow," she said. "Is it from Anestra?"

"No," he said. "Find your target."

"Where did you say your people came from?"

Hunter smirked and pointed deep into the forest, outside the safety of their glen and into the darkness beyond. "Your target."

"I can't see anything. How deep is it?"

He raised one perfectly sculpted brow. "Use your instincts, Princess."

With magic already thrumming through her body, it was hard to resist the gooseflesh that erupted over her exposed skin.

Shaking it off, she closed her eyes, picturing the target she used to practice on when she was a child. Somehow imagining the rudimentary piece made it easier, like she couldn't miss if she tried. She could see the rough straw, the bullseye made from stained elderberries. She could almost hear the laughter of children running through the fields, smell the fresh-turned earth from planting season.

Inhale, exhale.

The arrow released with a snap. Faria opened her eyes, wanting to see if it had hit. She glanced at him for approval but narrowed eyes were his only response.

"Again." The command echoed in the air around them as he pointed to a spot farther to the right of where she stood. Faria shifted position, nocked a new arrow, and fired.

Again.

Again.

Minutes passed but Hunter said nothing, only pointed to new areas of the field, new places in the darkness beyond the glen for her to aim toward.

Sweat dripped down Faria's face by the time she had gone through both quivers of arrows. Shadows deepened across the field and a slight breeze drifted through the wildflowers, bringing with it a welcome reprieve from the unseasonable heat.

"Let's eat." Hunter said from beside her.

"Aren't we going to collect the arrows?"

"Soon," he said as he sat on the ground. "First you need something to eat."

Faria realized he was right. She had left that morning without a full meal and had slept for hours before that.

Hunter reached behind him for his belongings, opening the small pack nearest to him. Inside was fresh fruit, nuts and flattened bread.

"Can I ask you something?" Faria ventured.

He broke off a piece for himself before handing her the loaf.

She took his silence as permission to continue. "Do you know what caused that fire?"

"Something ancient and evil."

"But *what* exactly?"

"I believe we will all find out soon."

She rolled her eyes at his cryptic response. "Do you think it's related to the warlocks? The unrest that is happening outside Athinia?"

He chewed slowly and Faria admired the lines of his jaw, watched his throat as he swallowed. "You know the history behind the Great War, right?"

She was surprised at the question. The Great War had occurred a thousand or more years ago. "Of course. Thousands perished. The Warlock King wanted to steal our lands. He studied dark magic for years, created unholy creatures to aid him in his mission. No race was left unscathed, but we survived."

Hunter's face turned stony. "Not all survived."

Indeed, not. The Val had sacrificed themselves to protect the Royal Bloodline. Her bloodline. "The Val made the greatest sacrifice, releasing their magic as a last-minute attempt to protect my ancestors. Without their magic, they could no longer protect themselves and were little stronger than human. What they did brought upon a mass extinction to their race for the sake of mine surviving."

He nodded. "The warlocks realized they would not succeed. The magic of the Val was too great. Their creatures died, along with much of their own magic source. The king set a curse upon the Royal Bloodline, thinking to damage it enough to end it. That is why your family no longer can bear male children. Why you are lucky to have one child at all."

Suspicion struck her. She was well aware of her history, and his response seemed less than innocent when he laid it all out like that. "Did you bring me all the way out here to remind me of my duty to my people?"

"No, lady." He brushed the crumbs off his hands. "I mean to say that perhaps the warlocks are tired of their power being so diminished. Perhaps they feel resentment towards the Agostonnas."

"But, why? We provide everything for them. They are our citizens. They are no different than any other elf or human."

"Perhaps they don't like that."

Faria thought about it. The warlocks living and working at *Mentage* were all so pleasant, so amenable. She would never think there would be something amiss with them.

And yet....

"So, you think it's connected?" she asked again.

He shrugged. They sat in silence while they finished eating. The sounds of the Forest echoed in the glen. It was beautiful, listening to nature's song, but soon Faria started to squirm. She never spent so much time with Hunter before, not alone. She had never had a civil conversation with him, either. It was strange, sitting there with him.

She studied the planes of his face, the calluses on his hands, the same ones that held her not long ago. She didn't particularly like the direction her thoughts were heading in and she wondered why the queen believed it necessary for them to be alone.

"She knows I can help you," Hunter said.

Faria's eyes shot to him.

"It was written all over your face. You should really work on that." He ate slowly, staring off into the distance.

"Wow, you sure know how to charm a lady."

He turned to face her, his stupid, perfect lips forming a cocked smile. "You have no idea the ways I can charm another, lady or not."

She was not going to respond to that. "Are you going to tell me where you're from?" she asked instead.

"No." His face remained passive as he chewed his bread.

"Does my mother know what you are?" Faria tried scenting him again, but he smelled the same as always. Equal parts of the earth and not. He raised his eyes toward the sky as he ate, his back straight, his legs crossed in front of him. Faria wondered why he felt the need to be so rigid when everything about the Forest loosened her up.

"I suspect that now she has an idea."

"Now…?" Faria prompted with a mouth full of berries. "Why now?"

Silence.

"Okay, why does she think you can help me?"

"Because of who I am."

"You are incredibly infuriating," Faria said. She hated when he did that—gave her non-answers. She hated the way it made her feel. Like he had all the power because he had all the answers. She was starting to realize how young and naïve she felt in his presence.

Hunter stood up and brushed his hands along his pants before taking a drink from his waterskin and handing it to Faria.

"What are we working on now?" Water drooled down her face as she drank.

He glanced at the sun and shadows. "Target practice. Daggers, this time."

He stooped down to collect a handful of small weapons as Faria said, "A man after my own heart."

Hunter stiffened.

"I mean—it's just an expression," Faria stammered. "Nellie teaches me things. I didn't mean that *you* were after my heart." *Shut up, shut up, shut up!*

Instead of responding, Hunter shoved a knife into her hand. Its hilt was warm after being tightly held in his grip.

"I am after no one's heart," he finally said. He stepped aside and pointed in the same direction as the first target. Faria thought that was the end of the conversation until he said, "It isn't allowed."

She tucked that piece of information aside for later and aimed toward the first target. Again, and again, he pointed in the same areas as before, only slightly higher this time. Faria worked quickly, watching the daggers flip end over hilt as they sailed in the air, wondering if she was actually aiming at anything at all.

The sun had nearly set by the time she finished. They walked in silence, the chirping of birds and crunching of their boots the only noise accompanying them. Faria kept her eyes to the ground, searching for the glint of her arrows or daggers. There were only leaves, twigs, and the occasional small critter. No weapons in sight.

They soon came upon a much larger clearing than the glen they had practiced in. This one was surrounded by tall trees, the canopies extending high into the sky. Their crowns created a ceiling of golden leaves blocking out any remaining light. A rough X was carved into seemingly random trunks.

Faria's mouth gaped when she saw all forty arrows and fifteen daggers interspersed among the trees.

Every single shot had hit its mark. Every. Single. One.

"How did I do this?" Faria said, looking at each target with equal parts surprise and unease. "I thought you were making me aim at nothing, looking at my form or maybe messing with me."

"I wanted to see something," he said as he gathered his weapons.

"And?" Faria swallowed. Somehow, those arrows and daggers had known exactly where to go.

"And I was correct."

Faria worked her jaw and stamped down on her annoyance, recognizing another feeling she had. Fear.

How could I do this?

"I heard once when I was very young that the Chosen would be a proficient markswoman," he said. "That she would be able to just think of it and she'd hit her mark."

"I never heard anything like that before," Faria said. She never paid much attention to anything having to do with the prophecies, though. She thought they were just another elven legend created centuries ago. "Where did you say you heard this, again?"

"I didn't," he said, raising his brows at her. "Nice try."

Faria grumbled. "Okay, and so you experimented on me why? To see if I was actually who they say I am?" She was almost offended, even though she wanted nothing to do with being the Chosen One or the supposed Prophecy. "Did you doubt it?"

"No, I always knew who you were," he said. "But I wanted to see how much of what I knew was the truth."

"But the other day, when you had me throw daggers at you, I kept missing."

"That's because I'm faster than you." He continued pulling arrows from the tree trunks, their shafts wavering slightly from the force of his strength.

"So, what does it all mean?"

He said nothing as he placed his weapons back in their holsters.

Faria should have helped him, she knew, but she was too fired up to concentrate. Leaves kicked up in her wake as she paced the forest floor. It was almost full dark now, but the light of the moon was bright enough to aid her lowlight vision. She could still see every glint of metal Hunter tucked away on his body.

He was silent as they walked back to the glen. Faria had never been this deep in the forest at night. She might have been terrified of the stillness of it if she hadn't had so much on her mind. The wind whispered its secrets to the canopy above and flowers below, the scent of cinnamon and jasmine overpowering her when he finally responded.

"It means," he said from behind her, "that I have to be careful."

Maybe it was the heady scent of spices or the incessant humming Faria felt in that part of the forest, but her emotions were hard to control. His lack of answers infuriated her. She whipped around and nearly collided with him as he stepped closer to her.

Faria's heart raced, breathing in his scent. "What do you mean you have to be careful?" She didn't know why she whispered it, but there was something about the way his eyes shone in the night, nearly feral in appearance. A light breeze tickled her neck as if reminding her the wind carried secrets and if she said anything too loudly, the world would irrevocably change. "What do you have to be careful about?"

His expression was unreadable and he looked down at her, barely a breath away, and leaned in.

Faria's heart pounded and she was absolutely certain he could hear it, but there was nothing she could do to stop it. For a moment she thought he might kiss her, but she chastised herself at the thought. Absolutely, in no way, would that happen. Ever.

Still, she stared at the lush contours of his lips as he crept closer, wondering what they would feel like. He inhaled when he got as close as he dared, his nose impossibly close to the sensitive spot on her neck as he whispered in her ear.

"Everything, Faria. I must be careful with everything."

He lingered a moment before turning away, finding the trail that led back to *Mentage*.

Trouble, she breathed to herself. *I am in serious trouble.*

ELEVEN

NELLIE

Torches along the stone walls sputtered, casting long, dancing shadows across the scrolls scattered on the oak table. A low babble of voices could be heard in the Athenaeum, dulled to a low murmur thanks to the heavy wooden door.

It had been almost three weeks since Nellie had first tried to enter this room. Now she and Faline pored over endless documents, looking for anything that might give them a clue on what to expect from the Final Battle. Anything to give them an advantage over an unnamed enemy.

It was absolutely, excruciatingly dull.

Nellie stretched and leaned back in her heavy wooden chair. A pleasant fire crackled behind her and she was thankful for its warmth. Faline perused their latest haul of papers, scrolls, and books. They had ordered tea long ago but it sat next to the fire, forgotten in their quest to find more information.

The only thing they had learned was that there were three separate forces at hand. At some point, the three forces—including good and evil—would converge. They weren't sure what the third force was supposed to be, so really, they were back to almost nothing. Even Faline's longstanding friendship with the Secret Circle proved fruitless, though she thought about visiting with them personally to try to glean their secrets.

Nellie wished she could have gone into the Forest to watch Faria's lessons rather than sit in a dusty room in the center of town. She was sure that whatever happened there was much steamier than what she was doing. She smiled to herself, remembering the previous day when she had watched them return from their session. Hunter looked extremely agitated, and Nellie had it on good authority that he often spent his evenings drinking in Athinia, turning down any female company for the night.

Faria, on the other hand, couldn't stop saying how infuriating and rude he was, but she always said it with a smile which made Nellie think that *something* else must have happened, though Faria never spoke of it.

"I think we should continue tomorrow," Faline said. She stood and yawned, stretching the kinks from hovering over scrolls all day. "I have a feeling we will need our rest tonight."

Nellie nodded, grateful Faline had suggested it before she did. It was nearly midnight and she was exhausted. Though it would be a quick walk back to *Mentage*, she still felt weird about being out so late at night. Athinia was safe, but everyone knew nothing good happened in the dark.

They left their books laid out, trusting that no one would be able to get through the spelled door, and walked through darkened bookshelves in amicable silence. She was grateful beyond measure for Faline's company. With Faria busy day and night, she found that she was lonely without her friend.

The crisp night air whispered across their faces as they walked the road leading back to the main hub of Athinia. Unsurprisingly, Nellie could hear the revelry and merriment that spilled out of the taverns ahead onto the square. When they turned the corner, bright lights twinkled and people danced in the street. A fiddler sat in the corner with his case open, willing to accept any donation for the cheerful tunes he played. Despite her exhaustion, Nellie stopped and enjoyed the moment.

This was one thing that wouldn't have happened where she came from. Her clan used to have parties, but they were quieter, more subdued. Here, laid out in front of her, was pure joy. Whatever they felt—elf, human, and warlock alike—they expressed through their bodies. There was a certain type of freedom to it. As someone who was often trapped in a body that wasn't really hers, Nellie relished the moment, living vicariously through them.

"Is that Endo?" Faline asked, peering through the dancers.

Nellie's eyes shot up, looking for the warlock. Her stomach gave an uncomfortable twist when she saw him, arms locked around a beautiful elven woman. They hopped together in time to the beat. She watched as his dark hair blew across his forehead, sticking to a thin layer of sweat. Strong hands shifted between the female's waist and back. When the song ended, he bowed to her and kissed her hand before she walked away. His raised eyes landed on Nellie.

"Let's go," Nellie whispered to Faline, pushing her along. She didn't want to have to talk to Endo, not tonight. Not when she was too tired to act like he didn't look so much like her human mate. Too tired to control her emotions.

"Too late," Faline mumbled as Endo made his way over.

He stood tall, much taller than her four-and-a-half-foot frame in her current form. He smiled down at her as she tried and miserably failed to keep the flush from creeping up her cheeks.

"Hi, Nells! Faline. Have you ladies come to dance?"

"Goodness, no," Faline said, a smile playing on her lips. "We were just doing a bit of late research for Her Majesty. We were headed back home, now."

"Mind if I join you?" Endo asked. "I've had enough for one evening."

Nellie let out a small choking noise, but Faline elbowed her quickly. "Of course, you may."

They walked along in mostly companionable silence, each taking in the busy nightlife. Restaurants were still packed, patrons eating either on rooftop patios or decks overlooking the river. Street vendors sold hot chocolate and desserts, the scent of caramel and cocoa warring with each other. The stars twinkled overhead, adding to the winking storefront lights. Nellie sighed. If she were able to speak to Endo as the woman she was rather than the girl she pretended to be, it would be the perfect evening.

"What's on your mind?" Endo asked, picking up on her thoughts.

"I was just thinking what a lovely evening it is," Nellie said. "It was nothing like this...when I was younger."

His eyebrows knitted together. "Would you like to talk about it? The human realm?"

Nellie froze for a moment, unsure of how to answer. She would give anything to talk about the food, the amusement parks, and the internet. It would be nearly impossible to do so without giving away why such things were so important to her, why she could never enjoy them as a member of her clan. He couldn't know about a clan at all.

"There is so much to say," she started, "and not much at all. It is a cruel place. Filled with violence, unrest, such hatred. It can be scary, especially for a woman or someone considered different. It is very archaic, compared to here. Some people are persecuted for who they love, for the color of their skin, for being their true selves. It can be dangerous."

"That sounds awful," he said. "Why would anyone be persecuted for who they love or what they look like?"

"It's complicated," she replied, not wanting to get into the specifics of it. "But it is also a place filled with magic. Not this kind of magic." She indicated the city, the edge of the Forest of the Dawn. "Human magic called technology. We are able to speak to anyone in the world, no matter where they are, with a small device we can carry in our pockets. There are huge parks filled with different rides. The concerts are insane. The food is incredible, especially pizza. That is one thing Anestra just doesn't have."

"That is surprising," Faline said from beside her, "considering the number of humans we have here."

Nellie nodded. "True, but most humans end up here by accidently going through a Gate. They come with nothing of value, have no idea what sort of beings exist in other realms. Humans aren't taught about other beings at all. The ingredients grown here do not taste the same as there. And perhaps it is just too hard to try to replicate something so perfect, knowing that it'll never be the same..."

She trailed off as a sadness settled into her. She didn't have much left on Earth besides her mate. She had no family and didn't care for her clan, but there were certain comforts that she wished she could have again.

Endo sighed from next to her. "I do understand, to a point," he said quietly. Nellie felt Faline slow her pace, suddenly interested in a picture frame on one of the store fronts. "I have not seen my homeland in many years, and it will likely be many more until I do again."

Nellie considered that. Endo was a warlock from Wendorre. She wondered if he was familiar with the dissent among his kind. "Wendorre is a few weeks' ride...why haven't you gone back?"

For a moment he didn't answer, and she worried that perhaps she had pried too much. He looked around them, making sure there were no eavesdroppers. "I cannot. It is a difficult journey, and to be honest, there isn't much to go back to. Our land is dying...there are hardly any children left. The people are sick. Less crops are yielded each season. There is no leadership." He shook his head. "It would not be the way I want to remember it, and I worry if I go back then I will never return here."

Nellie reached out to touch his arm. "I am sorry for that," she said, meaning every word. "It must be hard, living in a land so prosperous, when the one you come from is having difficulties."

He considered her words. "I love Anestra and am forever grateful to the queen for taking in so many warlocks, for letting us live where we wish in her land, for letting us use our dwindling kernels of power so we don't forget how to. But there are others—"

"Endo!" A sharp voice cut through the night. Nellie jumped at its briskness. "We gotta talk to you."

Endo blanched, giving Nellie an apologetic look. "Must be something about the work for tomorrow," he said. "Have a good night, Nells."

Nellie squinted her eyes down the dark alleyway where the voice had come from. It sounded familiar, but she couldn't see anything apart from shadows. She felt Faline brush up against her.

"Unusual," she murmured. "Endo works for Hunter and that is not Hunter that called for him."

Nellie looked sidelong at Faline. "I suppose I could…find out," she said.

A severe look crossed Faline's face and their eyes held for a moment. She nodded her head. "Be careful," she said. "I'll meet you back in our rooms."

Nellie gave her a small smile, then casually walked over to the shadow of a building, checking to make sure the coast was clear.

Being a rare shapeshifter that could change into anything had its advantages. As far as she knew, she was the only one in existence to be able to shift. She only had a few complete changing cycles, but the fear in her clan's eyes was evident. Being exiled from them was inevitable, the way they held onto their superstitions and prejudices. It was an old, deep, hatred they had. All of them, except her mate. The only one to defend her when she was banished for a crime she didn't commit.

Nellie had only moments to shift before risking exposure. She felt the sharp pains of her bones shrinking in size. Her nose hardened as a beak replaced it and her back burned where wings sprouted.

Soaring into the sky, she relished the feeling of air through her wings, for the freedom she felt to be such a little thing with no one to answer to.

Except she did have a task to perform, and quickly. She was exhausted from research all day and each shift drained her a bit more. She flew in slow circles, searching the alley Endo had disappeared down. At first, she saw nothing but darkness. Then, behind the shadow of the buildings that lined the forest, she saw three dark orbs of eerie green light. The type of light that only warlocks could conjure.

She banked on a breeze, careful to remain unseen and unheard as she swooped down into the tall grass. With hardly a thought, she changed into a mouse and scuttled along, careful not to bend any grass blades and arouse suspicion.

It was risky, but she had to make sure Endo wasn't involved in whatever was happening with the warlocks. Needed him to not be involved.

The greenish orbs softly glowed as she approached three large bodies. She recognized the back of the one closest to her as Endo. The other faces were too deep in flickering light for her to make them out properly.

"As I was saying, I don't know when he's arriving, but my sources say it is soon." The gravelly voice came from the scarred face of Smyth Wylock. He had worked on the fields and in the stables at *Mentage* since long before Nellie's arrival.

"Obviously," answered a voice dripping with ego. "Anyone with eyes can see that. Even the scum we live with knows." His face was covered but Nellie cringed at that voice every time she heard it. It belonged to that jackass Crispin. He dressed like he ruled the place, and his stalking gait was abhorred by all he tried to court, male and female alike. Nellie suspected he was a traitor from the moment she witnessed him threatening Callum.

"Shh," Endo said. "Don't talk like that. You never know who might be listening." His feet were restless against the grass and he shifted around to make sure no eavesdroppers lurked in the dark.

"No one is here," Smyth said. "I would have sensed it." Nellie didn't doubt it. He sometimes worked on the night watch because of his uncanny ability to sense anyone who approached. It was a wonder he didn't sense her now, though she likely had her current body to thank for that.

"Even so," Endo said. "I'd rather not get caught by anyone, least of all have word get back to the queen at this hour."

"Oh, please," Crispin drawled. "As if she could do anything, now that we are so close to being rewarded. Imagine the gifts he will bestow upon us once he is here." Nellie could practically see the gluttonous glow of his dark eyes, his sneer shining off the orb he held.

"We don't even know who *he* is," Endo said. "What if he's been here all along, waiting for us to mess up? Or testing us?"

Smyth snorted. "'Course he's testing us. You think he wanted us to rally the impressionable younglings for fun? Convincing humans to start fires across the border of the land as well as Athinia just to keep the king and the Guard busy? He wants to see how far we are willing to go."

"We were only able to convince a few to our side," Endo said. "They are too loyal to the Agostonnas. It won't be enough."

"Speak for yourself," Crispin said, puffing his chest out. "Just tonight I convinced at least ten more to join the cause."

"Oh, for crying out loud." Smyth smacked Crispin on the back of the head, his scarred hand flickering in the orb light. Nellie wondered what could have caused such an injury, especially one that wasn't healed either by the warlock's natural healing ability or through *Mentage's* own personal healers. "We need more if we are to take back our power from the queen."

Take back their power?

Nothing moved in the silence that followed, save for the flowing light that hovered above their hands.

Endo's soft voice broke the silence first. "I don't like betraying our queen, but—"

"She betrayed us first! Centuries ago!" Crispin's scathing reply curdled Nellie's bones. "Did anyone know who she was? No. She masqueraded as a human, begging for sanctuary in our lands. Our ancestors knew a trap would be set and she did it!"

"There is still no proof." Endo forced the words from his mouth. "We have never met who we now serve. We're going on blind faith. The queen has never done anything wrong to us. She is a kind ruler, giving us whatever we asked of her within reason. It doesn't feel right."

"Except take our land, our people, and our power with her." Smyth chewed his lip. "No one knows how old she really is. They *say* it's just a century, but it wouldn't explain why her image is all over old warlock tapestries. Or how this land started to prosper exactly when our power dwindled." He paused to take a breath. Crispin flicked lint off his coat as if he were bored with the conversation.

Smyth continued. "Look, I'm not saying that what we're doing isn't wrong, but helping our people is right. If he can restore the power to our kind…think of it, Endo. Our women will no longer suffer. We can have children again. Children! When was the last time you saw a warlock child survive into adulthood?"

"I was the last one, as far as I know." Nellie couldn't tell if she felt sorry for Endo or angry at him for being involved in this mess.

She was reminded of something her mother used to tell her growing up, when she felt sad about moving from place to place, sad about not having a father.

"Memory will have a funny way of creeping out of the deepest recesses of your mind. It will play with your emotions and make you feel an echo of pain, of love, or betrayal, whispering it back to you on repeat. It is heartbreaking and shocking each time, but remain firm in the present, girl. The now is what your attention needs."

Her mother was right. The present did need her attention. She had three defectors standing right in front of her who had admitted to inciting the angry protests. She wished she had real magic to capture and deliver them straight to the queen. In all honesty, she was surprised the Contract they had signed didn't include inciting anger. It was smart of them to use humans who had no magic tied to the land.

Endo turned in Nellie's direction, his tanned face and bright blue eyes illuminated by the green from his orb. "Someone is here."

"Impossible," Crispin's oily voice said. "I'm much better attuned to our magic than you and I can say with certainty no one is here but us."

"I agree," Smyth said, though he looked around as well. "I sensed nothing approach us."

"Then you two are fools," Endo said. "I feel its emotions. Sorrow and anger." He glanced right over Nellie's head. She stilled, not daring to breathe. "We need to get out of here."

Smyth put his hand out to Endo before he could move away. "Wait."

Clenching a fist in the air in front of him, Smyth muttered something under his breath and suddenly Nellie's neck felt as though it were in a vise. Small squeaks came from her as she tried to choke down air, anything before she passed out.

"What are you doing?" Endo asked, alarmed at the concentration on Smyth's face.

"Killing whoever it is." His gruff voice held no hint of remorse.

Endo ripped Smith's arm away, swatting it down to the side. "Are you crazy? We can't just kill at will. We don't know who it is! This isn't what we are."

"Haven't you been paying attention?" Crispin asked as he turned back toward the direction he had come from. "This *is* what we are now. This is war."

"Whatever it is, is dead," Smyth said. The orb hovering in front of him went out as he veered toward the road that led out of Athinia, carrying a sack against his back. "No human can survive what I just did."

Endo stayed behind as his companions retreated back to whatever hole they had crawled out of. Air filled Nellie's lungs again and the bright spots in front of her eyes ebbed. She nearly lost control of her disguise, but her life depended on hanging on for a little longer. There was no doubt in her mind that if she were human, she would be dead. She didn't want to imagine what her old clan would say if they knew she survived this long only to be killed as a field mouse. Pathetic.

"I can feel you there," Endo whispered as he bent down toward her hiding spot. Though she knew he couldn't see her or know what she was,

Nellie panicked at the possibility of being discovered. "I don't know who you are, but Crispin will find you. He may have acted like no one was there, but I can guarantee he put out a tracking spell just in case. It is dangerous here, and if I knew where you were, I would probably have to kill you myself now that you know of our betrayal."

Nellie held her breath, willing him to leave. To say more.

"He is coming, you know. They're right. War is upon us, but it doesn't have to be this way. We just want what she stole from us. If we could just have our power back, then we would leave. There doesn't have to be any bloodshed. He promised that."

Endo sighed. "If you are against us then I am sorry for what might happen to you if the queen denies us what is ours. You've been warned."

He walked away into the night but Nellie still kept her breaths shallow. She didn't know how long she stayed there, her mind reeling with information.

The queen stole power from the warlocks? Why would they think that? Who could possibly know something like that, if it were true?

Three dissenters worked right at *Mentage*. They had probably started the fires on the edge of the villages to spread fear and distrust among the warlocks. It was no wonder some had been getting restless. Just the other day, Faline had said that a handful never showed up to work, out of the blue.

And Endo. Sweet, caring Endo. He used to play with Nellie during her first years in Anestra and had always snuck her special treats. She had a crush on him the moment she saw him, but of course, masquerading as a child prevented her from acting on her desires. He looked to her as a sister, as everyone did. He was young, too. Maybe twenty, at most, if she had to guess. Still a child, especially for a warlock who could live decades past humans.

Nellie wanted to warn Faria, but with the princess's eighteenth birthday coming up and her never-ending training, Nellie didn't know when she would have the chance. That, and it would be nearly impossible to tell her without revealing what she was. Though Hunter insisted she could be herself, Nellie wasn't quite ready to reveal her betrayal. She hated keeping this secret from her friend.

Making her way back to the shadowed alley, Nellie shifted into her thirteen-year-old body and hurried to the main road. It was late—nearly one o'clock in the morning if the groups of revelers leaving the town were any indication.

In the distance, leaning against a fence post, Nellie saw Crispin and Smyth. They whispered to each other, casually nodding at passersby. Though their bodies were at ease, Nellie saw the way Crispin pitched his head as if listening to something in the distance. She willed her heart to slow, to blend in with the group in front of her. By the looks of it, they had all drunk their fill that evening.

The group ahead of her laughed so she laughed with them as they passed by the two warlocks. Nellie told herself to keep looking straight, to avoid all eye contact, but her curiosity was stronger. She had to know.

She breathed a sigh of relief when no one called out to her. It wasn't until she got to the trees leading the way to *Mentage* that she risked looking back. His eyes met hers and he cocked a half smile. She felt like a mouse caught in a cat's trap, especially when he gave her a tiny nod, as if telling her she was marked.

She needed to get to Faline, to Hunter, Queen Amira—anyone who would listen—to warn them of all she had heard. To ask if any of it was true. To see what could be done to rectify the situation.

Most of all, to make sure the death mark placed upon her could be removed.

TWELVE

FARIA

The nightmares continued with renewed vigor almost every night. Faria would awake hours before dawn in sweat-drenched sheets gripping her like a vise. Now she lay in bed, her heart pounding, her fight or flight response kicking into overdrive. This time she didn't want to fight.

The darkness was coming for her. She could feel it.

Faria untangled herself from the bedding and shuffled to the washbasin next to the window. The chill seeped through the glass and even though she wore thick leggings and a nightshirt, her nightmares left her frozen. She splashed cold water on her face and glanced outside. The Spring Garden took on a glowing hue this time of night. She started to look away but caught movement out of the corner of her eye, nothing but a dark shape among the lemon trees. She stilled, rallying her power to attack whatever lurked outside of her bedroom.

A faint orb of white light appeared, hovering in the hands of a lone figure. Faria would recognize those sharp cheekbones and the tightness around that mouth anywhere. She let out a frustrated sigh, though she had to admit she was relieved to see that it was only her mother.

What was she doing, lurking in the gardens at such an hour?

Faria put on a dressing robe and thick wool slippers, then snuck out the sliding glass door onto the patio. Scents of peony, jasmine, heather and lemon nuzzled her. Though it was the start of winter, the magic that kept the garden blooming was still hard at work ensuring the plants and flowers in stayed their prime.

She walked along the blue stone path, under archways green with ivy and between trees blooming with lush red and purple leaves that glowed in the night. She pulled her robe closer as a breeze tickled her exposed skin.

She felt her mother before she saw her, felt the anger emanating into the night. Faria wondered if returning to her nightmares would have been less daunting.

"Mother," Faria said, approaching the queen who sat upon a wicker bench, thick vines creeping up its legs. She bowed her head and as she looked up, she saw her mother's dark eyes tighten at the gesture. She wasn't sure if her mother's anger was directed toward her, but she had the sudden image of a viper. She swallowed but held her head high. "Is something the matter?"

The queen scanned her from head to toe and her muscles relaxed slightly. "I couldn't sleep," her mother said.

Faria stepped from foot to foot, unsure of how to act. It wasn't common for them to spend any amount of time alone together—not for many years, and certainly not at this hour. "Neither could I."

"Tell me of your dreams," her mother said, piercing her with a fierce stare. Somehow the queen knew what plagued her daughter. "What woke you this night?"

Faria felt strange speaking of it in the open, as if whatever evil lurked would beckon at her words. She heard the order in her mother's voice, however, and knew it was something the queen would not let go of.

"I have been having nightmares for weeks. Months." She hugged her arms around herself. "They used to just be flickering images, a feeling of terror, nothing concrete."

Queen Amira sat still, light hovering above her hands.

"They started getting clearer the past few days. Bone chilling screams. The howling of strange animals." She paused, not sure how much she should divulge. She wanted to forget her nightmares altogether and worried what her mother might think if she shared the details. She lowered her voice to a whisper and continued. "This time, it was a clear picture. An entire, horrible scene."

"Tell me, Faria," the queen said. "Give me as many details as possible."

"Did something happen, Mother?" Faria asked, wondering if perhaps her mother was here for some other reason than to listen about her dreams. "Is there a reason why you're asking?"

Her mother's lips moved to a tight frown, but she did not answer.

Faria shivered again, despite the warm air permeating the garden, but this time she felt an inkling of her power stir. A hidden ember of flame in her core that ignited, as if it felt sorry she was freezing cold. Instantly her skin warmed.

The queen raised a brow. "Seems like we have a lot to discuss if you are able to have such control over your abilities now."

"Hunter has helped me these past weeks," Faria said. She shifted her weight. She didn't want to talk about Hunter with her mother. "I thought he gave you daily updates."

The queen hummed and lifted her hand. "Continue, daughter. Tell me of the nightmares."

Faria took a trembling breath.

"I was in a cottage on the outskirts of Anestra. A short way away from the Barren Plain. There lived a family of warlocks. They looked so familiar to me."

The queen scanned her face but said nothing.

"The world shook with violence while clouds gathered outside. Thunder rumbled menacingly over the shack. I was angry, so angry. My hands reached for a bone knife hanging from my belt. I cut my hand and allowed blood to flow onto the table. Black blood. It reached a woman across from me and lifted into the air, hovering inches from her face before lazily entering her mouth as a snake to its den. Within seconds she changed from pale to purple, her eyes pleading for mercy. But I didn't have any mercy in me."

She glanced at her mother whose pale face shone with not just worry, but a touch of fear. "Are you sure this was you, child, or did it feel as if you were possessed in someone else's body?"

Faria didn't want to think about the way it felt, the loathing she felt toward the woman. "I don't know. The hands didn't look like mine, but I felt every inch of hatred running through my veins."

Her mother nodded. "Continue."

"Her body…it e-exploded, pieces raining around me, around the remaining two, squelching along the floor, walls and ceiling. The smell was putrid, but I could feel myself smiling, drinking in the terror of the man and child who were still alive…. Next thing I knew, I was standing outside, and I sent a simple fire spell toward the cottage. I set the roof to flames. Then I woke up."

"A fire spell?" The queen's gaze sharpened. "Are you certain it was a spell, not something innately of you, your gifts?"

Faria thought back to how it felt, realizing the lack of ember she felt in her veins. "It came from me but it was not of me."

Her mother pursed her lips, contemplative. "How real did it feel?"

"As if I were just there," Faria replied. She swallowed down the fear still threatening to choke her. "Mother, I have never been so far as the Barren Plain. How could I know the location this dream occurred?"

"I do not have all the answers," her mother said. Her face remained distant, lost in thought. "I will tell your father to check in with the Outpost, see if they have any news."

Faria nodded. "This felt different than…" her voice trailed off.

Her mother caught on. "Than the visions you have been trying to keep from me?" She gave Faria a pointed look then shook her head. "I think, because you are what you are, you are in tune with the vile being that plagues our lands."

"So, he is here, then?"

Queen Amira changed the subject. "I received news not long ago. We know three of the warlocks who seem to be leading the most recent unrest."

Faria felt a surge of anger, of protectiveness over her lands. She hardly recognized the coldness of her voice as she said, "Who?"

Her mother looked her straight in the eye. "Crispin." Faria sneered at the name. He was a jackass intent on bedding anything that moved. "Smyth." She raised a brow, surprised. Smyth always felt like a grandfather to her. Kind, helpful. Polite. She looked at her mother, waiting to hear the third but she saw the hesitation. She waited, unwilling to prompt her further.

"Endo."

A gush of air whooshed out of Faria. "Impossible." No, she refused to believe that the sweet warlock she grew up with, the one who trained their people in all manner of weaponry, had anything to do with this. He was so gentle. Powerful, quiet, but sweet. "Are you certain?"

"I trust my sources implicitly."

"What are we to do?" She couldn't imagine what her mother might do to them. There had been peace in their lands for as long as she had been alive. Her mother was cold and distant to her, but never cruel, especially not to their people. The Contract the warlocks signed upon entering Anestra would have activated, voiding their powers if they broke the terms to their agreement, but that hadn't happened.

"Continue your lessons with Hunter. Work harder on your control."

Faria felt anger surge again. "I have perfect control."

The queen raised a brow. "Is that why the flowers around you are burnt to a crisp?"

Faria looked around her and saw that indeed the plants were no more than ash. That she could do such a thing without being aware was unsettling. Maybe her mother was right. She reined in her feelings, working to keep the mess of her emotions contained. Once she felt calm, she sent a rush of soothing magic toward the plants and watched as they came back to life.

She expected her mother to praise her abilities, but instead the queen rose from her perch. "Sleep, Faria. You have a long week ahead of you."

"What do you mean?"

"We will have guests by the end of the week. You will need to train as much as you can and then help entertain them."

She had almost forgotten that her mother wanted to arrange her life partnership. Almost forgot that whatever she felt toward Hunter would amount to nothing.

A stone. She felt as if she were a stone sinking to the bottom of a lake, pressure from the water rushing over her, with no one to save her from drowning.

She turned her back on the queen and walked away.

"YOU AREN'T CONCENTRATING."

Faria huffed an exasperated breath before focusing her eyes back on a stick in front of her, attempting to light it on fire.

Hunter leaned on a tree across the way, dressed in a fleece-lined tunic and thick pants, his breath visible in the air. His arms were crossed and he watched her in annoyance.

They spent the morning running through the Forest over rough terrain. Despite her lack of sleep, Faria managed to keep up. Mostly.

She pushed large stones and did pull ups off tree branches—anything he deemed necessary to build up her physical strength and endurance. They took time to go over a new set of daggers. Tiny black blades with pieces of leather-bound metal as the hilt, barely large enough for her to grab onto. He said they were best for stabbing between bones.

Lunch that day was quiet. She had grown used to his cocky smiles, and had expected them. She played into it and flirted shamelessly with him. She made it clear to him that she was open to having fun in a different way, a more *mature* way, but he always brushed her off.

It was easier now, this almost-friendship they had bordering on something else. In the middle of the Forest, where all energy seemed to converge, it was a relief to not hold back her feelings, even if she did embarrass herself at times. Though he dared to get too close, to find reasons to place his hands on different parts of her, he never gave any indication that he wanted to take it further. No matter how many times she propositioned him.

It was unusual, then, that they ate in silence. Her exhaustion hit her and she really wasn't in the mood to strike up conversation. Judging by the dark circles under his eyes, neither was he.

Now, she sat cross legged and staring at that stupid stick, envisioning Crispin's face. What she wouldn't give to actually set him on fire. She felt the need rush through her, stronger than her need to breathe, felt the flames lick her bones, felt it her next exhale.

The trees surrounding them caught in flame. She swore, tired of failing at this one simple task. Of having no control. Of not knowing what her future looked like.

"That's not very lady-like, Princess."

She gave him a gesture that *really* wasn't lady-like.

The corners of his mouth turned up as he watched her return the trees to normal. She found she enjoyed this new ability of hers. As much as she could damage the land, she had the ability to restore it, and that gave her a sense of hope she hadn't felt in a while.

He prowled closer to her, flipping one of the tiny daggers between his fingers. "What's bothering you today?"

"You mean besides you?" She didn't really know why she said that. He wasn't bothering her at all. Or maybe that was the problem.

"Has something happened?" he asked, scanning her face, taking note of her rigid posture, the steel in her eyes.

"Nothing you need to worry about."

"Is this about the warlocks?" She forgot that he would know about Endo. "About their deception?"

"What will happen to Endo?" She didn't care as much for the others but for him...there had to be a mistake.

"I don't know. They haven't been found, yet."

She jumped up, ready for action. "Then let's look for them."

"Easy there, Princess." He placed his hand on her shoulder, the warmth settling into her bones. It soothed her icy temper, the way she wished to harm all who wronged them. She felt her muscles relax, her body turning to jelly.

"What are you doing to me?" She made eye contact with him, saw the tightening of his mouth.

"Nothing." He stepped away from her, leaving her cold again. "But we aren't finished here, and you can't go traipsing off into the unknown."

Her attention snagged on the dagger again. "I have never seen a blade like that before." She reached out as if to touch it, her hand hovering inches above his. She felt an energy coming from it, or him. It hummed through her, calling to her.

"It's an old weapon." He stopped moving but didn't hand it to her, as if waiting to see what she would do.

"It looks brand new." She raised her eyes to his, hand still outstretched, waiting for the dagger.

"That's because of the *Drogosterra* blood."

"*Drogosterra*? You mean the fabled dragon beasts."

He nodded. "They were last seen in the Great War. Disappeared the same time the Fae did. No one knows where they went."

"So, this weapon is thousands of years old."

"It was a favorite of some Val soldiers, or so the story goes. The blood of the *Drogosterra* hardens the blade, makes it unbreakable."

Surprise rippled through her. He had a great many assortment of weapons, but he had never mentioned having something that once belonged to the Val. "Why aren't they in a museum with the others?"

His face was carefully blank as he handed it to her. It felt different than other weapons she had handled before. They usually felt cold and unrelenting in her hand. This dagger, however, seemed to almost settle into her fingers, as if it were an extension of herself.

"I have my ways." He gave her a full smile, one that showed off his dimple and she felt her stomach tighten. Felt more than that, actually. Holding this weapon made her feel powerful. She had to be one of few in recent memory to handle a blade such as this.

A warm breeze rippled through the meadow, causing the tall grass to sway in its wake. It brought with it the scent of the ocean, though they were so many miles away from it, and something a bit spicier. Like cinnamon, but not. She inhaled deeply, the scent calling to her almost as much as the weapon. She lost all sense, all reason. All control.

Hunter took a step back when she smiled at him, aware of the sultry way it spread across her face. "What is that?"

His nostrils flared. "Not sure what you mean."

"You don't feel that? You don't *smell* that?"

His stillness should have unnerved her, but it didn't. He shook his head once.

She bit her lip, closing the gap between them. "Am I doing this, whatever it is I feel?" She still held the dagger but reached out her other hand, boldly placing it on his chest. She felt it heaving, as if he couldn't get enough air, though he looked as though he were unaffected.

"If what you are 'feeling' means you touching me, then yes. You are doing that." He grabbed her wrist as if to push her away, but he didn't move. The gold halo in his eyes were molten, as if he were on fire on the inside. She understood that. She had felt flame flow through her every day since she had ignited her power.

"What is this—ouch!" She cursed, looking down at her other hand, which was now dripping in blood. The breeze disappeared, the hypnotizing scent along with it. She watched the blood pour down her hand.

"Shit," Hunter said, backing up. She wanted to laugh at him, never having heard the human curse on his lips before, but the sharp stinging was too distracting. "If I knew I had to retrain you on how to handle a weapon, I would have never handed that over."

She winked at him, *winked*, of all things, as the blood poured out of her. "I know how to handle a weapon."

His mouth quirked to the side. "You're beginning to sound like me."

"Ugh, you're right," she said, as she finally inspected the cut. She had squeezed the dagger too hard and saw two separate lines slice down her palm from where the blade had penetrated.

"It looks deep. We should head back to the healer. I don't want you to lose too much blood before your body starts to mend itself."

She ignored him, investigating the grooves from where her blood poured. She concentrated and watched as it slowed to a trickle. Dropping the dagger, Faria held her other hand over her exposed palm, imagining what the healers did for injuries like hers. She pictured her skin stitching back together, felt the itchy sting as her flesh did her bidding. A light blue glow emanated from her hand, soothing the irritation.

"No need," she said to Hunter as she turned to face him. "All better."

A muscle in his jaw clicked. "That's...new."

She pursed her lips. "Indeed." Suddenly, complete exhaustion overcame her as she wobbled from side to side. "I'm uh... not feeling too great," she said, breathless.

The last thing she saw before darkness claimed her was the flaring of Hunters eyes and firm hands reaching for her.

COLD GRASS SCRATCHED AT HER exposed arms and the backs of her hands. The sun was lower in the sky and hovering inches over her face were a pair of deep green eyes.

Faria flushed at his closeness, unprepared for the way her mouth salivated as her gaze lowered across his cheekbones to his full mouth. Brown hair hung over his forehead, and a rope necklace with a single coin dangling over the collar of his tunic. She became all too aware that his hands were placed on either side of her head, the upper part of his body nearly covering hers. Too aware that they breathed in time with each other.

"Um...hello," she said weakly. Stupidly.

"What the hell was that?" His voice was tight, his eyes hard chips of emerald ice.

It took her a moment to realize where she was and for the vision to come flooding back to her. The burnt house from her dream. Ashes floating in the breeze. The stirring of the charred wood and then from it, a bird of fire, its wings blazing with flame and heat. It crowed loud and deep, then veered north, disappearing on the horizon.

"How long was I out?" she asked, trying to get up. He placed a hand on her collarbone, keeping her down.

"Long enough," he growled. "What. Was. That."

"Get off me," she said, baring her teeth. How dare he speak to her like that. "I don't have to answer to you."

She gripped his wrist, leaned forward, then swung her leg around his waist, flipping him so he was pinned to the ground. His hand still gripped where her neck met her shoulder, and though she was in the position of control, she found it hard to breathe.

She leaned in, painfully aware of every part of her body touching his. She could have licked the sweat off his neck if she wanted to.

"Don't," she whispered, "growl at me."

Something sparked in his eye, something predatory. It went beyond his usual cocky manner. Went beyond him trying to rile her. His smile was slow and lazy, his teeth sharp against the fullness of his lips. Faria tried not to move, tried to control her breathing. She felt a breeze through her hair, smelled the salty ocean water and driftwood as the fire in her veins clashed with the ire in his eyes. He licked his lip, her eyes zeroing in on the action. She hated herself, hated the way she couldn't breathe, couldn't think. She wondered if he could hear the pounding of her heart, the rush of her blood flowing quickly to other places in her body.

"Careful, Princess," he said, his voice just as low as hers. The world was a rush of color as she was slammed onto her back. "You're letting your emotions show." His eyes slid from hers to her neck, then out to the meadow surrounding them.

She glanced to where his attention now lay, gasping at the rays of sparkling sunlight as they dazzled over a ring of beautiful flowers. Their veined leaves were on fire and their petals shimmered as if they were made of liquid silver.

"What is that?" she breathed.

"I don't know," he said. "Manifestation of what you're feeling. What is it that you are feeling, Princess?"

She whipped her head back to his, spotted his predator's smile. He knew what she felt. She didn't have to say it. She swallowed her desire and annoyance.

"We need to get out of here," she said, the fire in her veins sputtering out. "I have to see my mother."

Hunter pulled off her and tried to help her up, but she swatted his hand away. A dark chuckle escaped him. "You going to tell me what all that was about?"

She thought about not answering, but she somehow thought he would find out anyway. "I saw something I need to tell her."

"You had a vision?" All laughter fell from his face. "What did you see?"

She shook her head. "Does everyone know about all my abilities?" She bit down her irritation. "I can't make sense of it. A burning house. A bird shooting from the ashes. It was made of fire. If I didn't know better, I would say it was a—"

"Phoenix," he said, cutting her off. "You saw a phoenix? Where did it go?"

"North. It shot up into the sky and veered north."

His eyebrows furrowed.

"Does it mean something to you?" she asked.

He shook his head and gave a noncommittal reply, busying himself with the rest of the weapons. She bit back a frustrated retort and surveyed the meadow. It had changed since they first arrived. She had no idea what type of plant she had summoned, or what could be made with liquid silver and flame. She pictured how the meadow normally looked, trying to put it back to how it was. She felt a shimmer of power release from her, blanketing over the land and when she opened her eyes, she saw it was done.

She felt Hunter staring at her but she wasn't ready to meet his gaze. She had a whole mess of feelings to work through, not only her new ability to heal wounds, but also the pull she felt toward him. Most of all, she needed to decipher this new vision and how it seemed to be a continuation of her nightmare. She needed to speak to her mother.

Most of all, she wanted silence. She wanted to clear her head, to not think about Hunter. Her future partner was due at *Mentage* in just a few days. What Faria needed was a distraction, to wash away all thought of who currently occupied too much of her time. She knew exactly what she needed to do.

She led the way out of the Forest, feeling the weight of his presence the whole time.

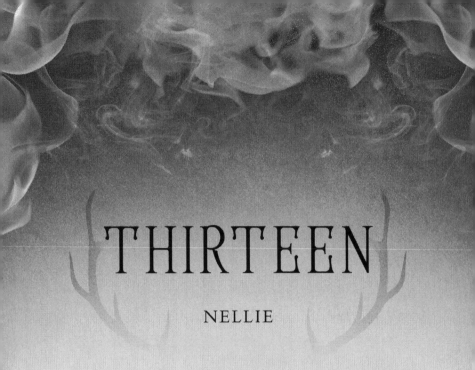

THIRTEEN

NELLIE

"I don't like this."

Nellie slid her feet into a pair of green velvet slippers that matched her tight-fitted black pants and loose green shirt. "It's perfectly safe. Even the queen said so."

Faline leaned against the wall, worrying her lip. "I know what she said."

Grabbing a pair of pearl earrings, Nellie turned and glimpsed herself in the floor length mirror. Freckles covered her tan skin though the winter solstice was right around the corner. Her hazel eyes were bright, and her loose brown curls flowed over her shoulders. She fixed a band of pearls along the crown of her head, a traditional style of elves. She smiled, pleased with her appearance.

"Faline, this is the first time in five years that I am in my own skin!"

Nellie twirled, delighted laughter bubbling up from her. "With permission, that is. I admit that I'm nervous. The threat of others discovering what I am is terrifying, but knowing the queen is on my side certainly helps."

"You are not to reveal who you are. Or what you are," Faline said as she fixed a thick cloak along Nellie's shoulders. "You are only to find him, get what information you can, and get out."

Nellie rolled her eyes. "Faline, this is the first time I can be a woman." She looked at herself in the mirror again. "Or girl? Why do I still look seventeen? I would be nearly twenty-two on Earth."

"I suspect your magic is recognized by the magic of the land and it has slowed your aging, as would happen if there were a whole clan of you here. Much like how warlocks and elves age slower. If they were in your realm their aging would likely speed up."

That's exactly what she thought. "Well in any case, I plan on enjoying myself. I know the queen is using this as some kind of secret mission, but I am looking at this as my first night of true freedom. I plan on eating, drinking, and," she pressed on over Faline's grunt of disapproval, "perhaps even finding a male my age to kiss."

Faline pursed her lips but a smile soon sprouted. "You are right, my child. You are perfectly capable of handling yourself."

"I am. Plus, I still need time to find him."

"You will likely see Wil and Reed out in Athinia. Queen Amira has ordered them to trail Crispin if they can find him, and then we will know for sure if the tracking spell is still in place. They don't know who you are or what you're doing, so you needn't fear discovery by them."

"Won't it be obvious that two of the Queen's Royal Guard are roaming the city?"

"They'll be undercover on a date. They won't be in uniform, just a couple enjoying what the city has to offer this evening."

Nellie was glad for that. She loved Wil and Reed and didn't think they spent enough time together as just lovers outside of their Queen's Guard duties. She glanced outside. The coming night gave her a rush of butterflies.

Faline smiled at her. "You will do fine, Nellie. Enjoy yourself."

She beamed. "My name is Maggie tonight." Her smile dwindled. "I wish I could tell Faria—that it could be the two of us roaming the town together. Getting into mischief." She shook her head. "I don't know that she will ever accept the real me, that the betrayal will be something she can overlook."

"It will take time." Faline rubbed her shoulders, soothing her. "But she will come to love you just the same. And Faria has requested to be alone this night, anyway."

Nellie nodded. "Okay, well. I'm off!" She grabbed a coin purse and slid it into an inner pocket of her brassiere. She noticed Faline's raised eyebrow. "What?" she asked innocently. "It's the safest spot for it." She winked and left for Athinia.

It was said that the honey cheesecake served at The Phoenix Fire had been voted best in the land.

She planned to see if that were true.

THE PHOENIX FIRE WAS MANY things to Athinia. It was the true heartbeat, the central hub for locals and out-of-towners alike. It was where the ale could always be counted on to be fresh, where local musicians were guaranteed a spot to play, and where—for a price—one could find a tasteful partner for the evening.

Nellie sipped her glass of elderberry wine and sighed, rubbing her belly. She had to admit, the cheesecake was a fine dessert. She looked around at the revelers now spilling out onto the street, dancing to a rendition of a sea shanty sung by what looked to be an old elven sailor. He sat on a stool in the corner, slapping his hands in time to the beat, crooning about mermaids and sea men tossing themselves overboard to get a closer look.

She tapped her toe to the tune, wondering, now that she was good and toasty, where she would begin her search for Endo. She debated whether or not to pay the bill, but opted for one more round. The fire roared in the large hearth that took up nearly one whole wall, and though the floor was sticky with stale ale, she felt much too comfortable to leave just yet. She flung her arm out to catch the barkeep's attention and instead felt it unexpectedly slam against something hard and covered in fur.

"Oof," the cloaked figure said. "Excuse me—"

"I am so sorry!" Nellie yelled over the music. "I wasn't paying attention."

She saw the curve of his smile under the hood of the furry cloak.

"Well, well, well. I suppose it serves me right." He removed the covering, and Nellie realized she was staring into the face of none other than Endo Ceridian. "Seeing as how it was me who bumped into you last time. Hello, Maggie."

Nellie swallowed, suddenly grateful she hadn't consumed another glass of wine; she already found it difficult to speak. She gaped at him.

"Mind if I join you?" He indicated the open seat across from her. "Unless you'd like to be alone..."

"No. I mean yes! I mean, no I don't mind if you sit with me," she stammered.

Endo chuckled, removing his cloak to reveal his usual dark leather pants and golden belt. His navy sweater turned his eyes into a stormy ocean that she wanted nothing more than to get lost in.

"Would you like another drink?" he asked as he got a server's attention. "Looks like you had an elderberry wine? Gotta be careful with that stuff. Des has a warlock buddy of his add an aging potion to it. Makes it taste like it was aged for decades rather than years. Really packs a punch."

"That it does," Nellie said, noting the fuzzy feeling in her fingers. She should really say no, but she didn't know when she would next have the freedom to be in her own skin, to have this time with Endo. "I think I would like one more."

Endo put in the order then fixed his gaze on her. "I've been hoping to run into you," he said. "How have your first few months in Anestra been?"

"Busy, actually. There has been so much to see and do. Acclimating has been a bit overwhelming. So many things are similar to Earth and yet, so different."

He nodded, taking a sip of his whiskey. "I imagine it has to be a bit of a shock to realize this place exists, and then to try to live according to the rules of the land. I imagine it's even more intimidating for non-magic users to suddenly be around so much power."

"That was actually not too hard to get used to. I read a lot of fantasy novels and had always wondered what a life filled with Fae males would be like."

Endo's booming laughter drowned out the fiddler's music. Nellie stared in wonder at him. She didn't think she'd ever heard him laugh so openly before. "Well, I'm sorry to disappoint that your company for the evening isn't one of the Fae but instead a mere warlock."

She suppressed a smile as she bit her lip. "I think you'll do just fine."

They stared at each other and Nellie could feel the fuzzy feeling shift from her fingers to more inappropriate areas. She took a sip of wine, making sure to drink slowly so she wouldn't lose sight of her mission. "Where have you been, anyway? I've looked for you a few times at *Mentage* but it seems I always miss you."

He shrugged. "Here and there. I actually just got back into town the other night."

"Oh? Where did you go? I always wondered what the rest of Anestra looked like outside of here."

His smile faltered. "Why are you so curious?"

She didn't skip a beat. "Are you kidding me? I'm in a mythical land filled with mythical creatures! If you only knew about the types of worlds I used to read about. It's exciting to think about what else is out there."

"Well." He shifted closer. "It's a beautiful continent, but everywhere else is much like here. There aren't as big of cities, except for maybe Mercy Bay, but there is lots of open land, mountains, more magical forests than just this one. I traveled to the mountains, just north of us."

"The peaks you can see in the distance on a clear night?"

"Yep, Caranek Peaks. I heard there was a city of gods if one was able to get through it."

"Did you?"

He looked down into the swirling amber liquid. "No, I couldn't find a way."

Nellie took another sip of her wine and wondered if she would be able to remain sober long enough to glean more information without sounding suspicious. "I wonder what a city of the gods would look like. We don't have anything like that on Earth."

"Legend has it that if you make it to the city, you can awaken those who sleep there. The goddess Farrah was said to have created her own temple before she was laid to rest."

"I don't know much about the gods and goddesses of this realm, but I can say with absolute certainty that I would never want to awaken any god of Earth. To do so would be as good as starting the apocalypse."

Endo smiled at her. "It's so strange," he said. "You remind me so much of this human girl, Nellie. Do you know her? She's very spunky, always speaks her mind. She lives at *Mentage* as well."

Nellie took a gulp of wine, impending drunkenness be damned, and swallowed loudly. "Nope, can't say that I do." The fiddler was playing a jig so lively that people crowded into any available space to dance around the tables. "Would you like to dance?"

"Come on," he said, leaving coin on the table. "Let's go outside. We'll get trampled in here." He curled his long fingers around hers and a new type of nervousness took hold. It had been so long since someone showed interest in her. So long since she could act on her feelings. She only wished it wasn't with a traitor to the queen.

They jostled their way through dancing couples and large groups throwing dice. The music was just as loud out on the square. He led her around the side of a building, into its shadow. Nellie had a fleeting fear that he was taking her somewhere to harm her, or at least to corner and question her.

A beautiful stone patio lay beside the river with twinkling lights hovering around its perimeter. One edge of the patio held two-person wicker tables, and stairs descended toward the riverbank. One other couple danced on the side closest to the water, swaying to music only they seemed able to hear. Here, the noise of the tavern barely reached their ears.

"Okay, how did I not know this was here?" Nellie wondered, tightening her cloak against the wintry evening breeze. She surveyed the empty lawn before the riverbank.

"I'm certain people know it exists, by why would they want to leave the heart of the party if they didn't have to?"

"That's a good point," said Nellie.

Endo led them to the edge of the water, taking in the beauty of the night. Nellie's mind strayed to the upcoming celebrations. The winter solstice was the following week, along with Faria's birthday. She wondered how many people were going to attend the extravaganza. "The princess turns eighteen next week. I hear there is going to be quite the party."

Endo nodded. "I hear that as well. A night carnival, right?"

"I can't wait. I haven't been to anything like that in... years. It'll be interesting to see how magic changes it. Will I see you there?"

He extended his hand to her. "I thought you wanted to dance."

She allowed him to lead her back to the patio, the twinkling floating lights acting as their personal spotlights. "There's no music," she said as he placed his other hand on her lower back, inching her closer to him.

"Shh, listen," he whispered. Nellie strained to hear anything besides the distant hoots and laughter from the taverns. Before long, a soft humming noise murmured around them, building up to a one-note tune. More voices hummed, creating a harmony. It flickered on and off and Nellie had a sudden vision of fireflies.

"What is that?" she asked, careful to keep her voice soft so as not to startle the sound.

Endo nudged her into a simple dance, swaying her back and forth. "No one really knows," he said just as softly. "These voices started eighteen years ago, along with the rumors of fabled beasts roaming the Forest. Some say they are sprites, declaring to everyone they have returned. Others say it's simply a noise a certain plant makes when the moon beam hits them. No one has been able to locate the source so far."

"That's a beautiful thought," she said. Plants that sang in the moonlight? That was true magic.

She allowed Endo to move her to the melody, enjoying the comfortable silence between them. She studied his face, wondering how someone so sweet could be caught up in any trouble with Crispin, of all people, and how he could be a traitor to the queen. It didn't make sense. The wine had loosened her lips enough that she knew if it remained quiet between them, she was likely to blurt out her questions.

"Maggie," he said, "can I ask you something?"

"Of course," she replied, thankful he broke the silence first. "I'm an open book."

"Is anyone courting you?"

She burst out in a chuckle and for a moment the humming ceased. She waited until it started again before she spoke. "No, not at all."

"Did you leave someone at home? In your realm, I mean."

Nellie stilled. "Why do you ask?"

"It's just that you've avoided looking in my eyes this entire evening together. I can't help but wonder if it's because someone else is on your mind or perhaps you feel guilty about being with me this evening."

She couldn't possibly tell him that if she stared into his eyes, she would surrender whatever modesty she had and tear off his clothes, regardless of who was there to see. Instead, she went with the safer answer. "There was someone back home, but that doesn't matter now."

"Was it serious?"

She didn't want to talk about it, but she still found herself saying, "We were mates. The bond broke when I came here. I no longer feel him and it's as if a piece of me is missing, and nothing but ghosts and shadows have taken its place."

"I'm sorry you have to feel that pain. I didn't realize humans have mates."

Oops. "Soulmates. It isn't something every human believes in, but I knew after just one night."

"It's okay if you want to talk about it. I really don't mind."

"You want to talk about the former love interest of the woman you're holding in your arms?"

"Maybe if you get it out then you'll find some closure. You'll be able to look at me, perhaps, and want to get to know me. You'll learn to trust me."

Nellie desperately wanted to believe that was true. It had nothing to do with anyone left on Earth and everything to do with the dangers of his association with Crispin, but she couldn't tell him that. She blew a stray hair out of her face. "I suppose if you want to know about it..."

"I do."

She felt comforted by the warmth of his hand in hers and decided it would be okay to talk about it. "I had known him for years. My mother and I—we didn't have a set home. We traveled around the country, living here and there. She got a job where she could. I changed schools every year, sometimes multiple times a year until she decided to homeschool me. She never really explained why she could never settle down, but she had a need to see as much of life as she could. She said staying in one place too long was dangerous for the body and the mind.

"It was hard for me. Hard to make friends, hard to date. Once a year we always went back to this state. This territory," she amended at his confused look. "I saw him in a crowd and our eyes zeroed in on each other. It wasn't the first time I had seen him. I'd known who he was since I was around eight or so. But this particular week we were there and I just... knew.

"One night we drove around and parked in this parking lot and looked up at the full moon. It was so bright, it blocked out the stars. We talked about everything—shows we watched, books we read, but also what we wanted out of life. If there was something greater than us. A higher power."

Nellie's stomach clenched at the memory. "We spoke for hours and he held my hand and nothing had ever felt so perfect. Knowing I would leave in a few days didn't matter because we connected, then. Afterward, we went to an ice cream shop and ate our cones and he said he missed me already, and asked if I could stay.

"I told my mom I thought I met the one and she said I was just a teenager, experiencing attraction for the first time. That it would pass and there would be others. But there never were any others. After my mom passed away, I went back to that state, that territory, and found a way to survive on my own until I came upon others like me who took me in. He was part of that group and we were inseparable for months. Until I ended up here."

Endo stayed quiet, though Nellie was sure he had many questions. "That sounds really special. It isn't often that one can find someone they connect with on a level that extends beyond the physical."

"I'm certain you have no problem with that," Nellie said. "There is so much more to you than just your good looks."

"Do you think I'm handsome, Maggie?" his smile turned sultry, his voice a bit lower. He tightened his grip on her waist, bringing her closer to him.

"Don't let it go to your head," she said. "Anyway, you know it's true. It's not like you're caught up in whatever unrest there are among the warlocks."

He stiffened. The smile slid off his face, replaced with something stony and distant. "What do you know about it?"

"N-nothing," Nellie said. She couldn't believe what an idiot she was. "I stay at *Mentage*. I saw that black fire that consumed the Forest. I know there is something happening."

"You would do well to stay out of it," Endo warned. "That's terrible power. Humans needn't get caught up in it."

"You aren't involved, are you?" she asked, dropping his hands. "Is it you I should be staying away from?"

"You needn't fear me, Maggie. Goddesses above, I know I don't have the right to ask you, but can you trust me? It will all work out."

He twirled her then, and she was lost to the sensation of being in his arms. She knew that perhaps he was dangerous, or at least associated with dangerous people, and she didn't want to trust him. But the beautiful humming from the forest and the soft twinkling of the lights added to the heady feeling her wine gave her. She allowed herself to enjoy the moment, uncertain whether another like this would come.

"Maggie?" his low voice rumbled near her ear. "Didn't you say you came here with your family?"

"Mhmm," she hummed, eyes closed, enjoying the vibration of his voice running through her.

"But you just said your mother passed away before you came here."

Her eyes flew open, her mind blank. She found words difficult. "Yes. That is true. But family is what you make of it, isn't it? Those I came with I consider my family."

He didn't say anything but she could tell by the way his eyes glazed over that he was trying to use his natural ability to pick up on her feelings. She tried to control her heartbeat and it wasn't until she felt the tension leave his shoulders that she loosed a breath.

"Yes," he said after a time. "Family is what you make of it. I've seen it first-hand. That young girl I mentioned earlier, Nellie? She was found wandering the Forest one day and one of the queen's most trusted friends adopted her without question. She must have been frightened, to have been alone. Don't you think?"

Nellie swallowed. "I imagine that would be terrifying for a little girl to come here alone. So fortunate someone quickly claimed her."

"I always thought the Forest did something to her," Endo confided. "Her signature didn't read like the other humans. It was there, but hiding just underneath. I always swore there was something magical to her."

Nellie felt sweat start to prickle at her as she fought to keep her face unreadable. "Really? How interesting. Did you ever ask her if she really was only human?"

"No," Endo said. "I wanted to allow her privacy. But it's curious…"

They were no longer dancing, but they still held on to each other, the humming a faint background noise. She didn't want to ask, but she still found herself saying, "What's curious?"

"You feel to me the way she does," he whispered. "And now I'm kicking myself for not asking her what makes her special."

"How interesting." She didn't want to talk about how close he was to figuring out her secret, how he was only moments away from putting it all together. She did the only thing she could think to do.

She kissed him.

He tensed, hesitating only a moment before he gripped her waist, pulled her tighter to him, and thoroughly kissed her back. His tongue brushed against her lips, a silent request for more, and she opened up to him. They were a clash of tongue and lips and she poured all of her confusion, her guilt, her attraction, and her worry into him. He took every inch of what she offered.

He placed his hands on her cheeks and he broke away, staring into her eyes. She breathed heavily, waiting for him to say whatever was on his mind. "I know you," he whispered. "I know I know you."

The hair on the back of her neck stood on end as the feeling of being watched swept over her. She took a step back from him, peering behind him in the darkness.

"What is it?" he asked, but a moment later he tensed, subtly shifting her behind him. She blanched when she recognized the drawling voice that dripped from the shadows beyond the twinkling lights.

"Who, or perhaps, what, are you hiding behind you?" Crispin's voice filled the empty space, dousing the heat between them.

"What are you doing here, Crispin?" Endo crossed his arms, positioning his body better to keep her out of sight. "You're supposed to be back at camp."

"Well, I was, but then I decided to enjoy the…delights Athinia has to offer. I was just leaving when I picked up a trail I felt compelled to follow," Crispin said. "So, I will ask you once again, who are you hiding from me?"

Endo looked over his shoulder at her, his face inscrutable. Was he putting it together? Did he realize it was her who overheard them as they plotted to overthrow the queen?

He looked back at Crispin and stepped aside, grabbing her hand as he did so. "This is my friend Maggie. She's new here."

Crispin stepped into the light, a sneer plastered on his face. He took his time looking her up and down and it left an oily feeling over her body. She suppressed a shudder and glared at him, refusing to let him see how much he disturbed her.

Endo growled low and pulled her closer to him. "What you seek isn't here, obviously." He said it as if he knew the object of his search. Nellie's mouth went dry. She could barely keep up with all the lies and secrets between them all.

"Maggie," Crispin said, walking closer to her. "You wouldn't have happened to see a little blonde thirteen-year-old, would you?"

She looked around her, noticing for the first time how very alone they were. "I don't see anyone else here, do you?"

He leaned in and inhaled deeply, as if he were taking in her very essence. A cruel smile played on his bloodless lips. "I don't, but my... compulsions are never wrong. If you see anything, let your *friend* Endo here know."

He took one last look at her then scanned the riverbank beyond them before bowing and walking away.

"Tell me he's not a friend of yours," Nellie said, her voice shaking.

Endo cupped her face and placed his forehead against hers. "I don't know how to explain what's going on. With him—or with you." Nellie opened her mouth to protest but he silenced her with a swift kiss. Just that brief connection left her knees weak. "Don't deny it. I have my suspicions, but I dare not speak them to the air. We don't know who is listening."

She swallowed and waited for him to continue. The ethereal humming had stopped and now the only noise was the rushing of river water and the occasional laughter from the main square.

"If I'm right I..." his whispered words trailed off. Nellie was starting to feel lightheaded. Her palms were sweaty and her mouth was dry. The haze of the wine had completely worn off from the rush of adrenaline upon Crispin's arrival. Her secret had almost been revealed, smothering the joy of the kiss she had been waiting five years for. She vaguely wondered where Wil and Reed were and if they knew Crispin was in town. Faline was going to lose her mind once she told her everything.

Endo licked his lips then continued. "Is the person standing in front of me the real you? Is this… true?"

She hesitated a moment before nodding. It was as close to an admission she could give him.

A look of relief washed over him. Nellie imagined things would have gotten real uncomfortable if he thought he just made out with a thirteen-year-old.

"I need you not to find me," Endo said. "I'll look for you when it's safe. When I know you won't be on anyone's mind."

"What do you mean, when it's safe?" Nellie finally asked. She needed to hear him say that he had willingly chosen the side of evil. She needed to hear him say he'd made a mistake.

"You are an impossibility," his voice he whispered in her ear, holding her close. "An impossibility that I will protect. I will see to it that you are safe."

He raised her hand to his mouth and kissed her knuckles, his blue eyes boring into hers. He turned and walked away, leaving her feeling affronted at the audacity he had in claiming her, yet she couldn't help but feel a sense of relief. She knew, more than anything, that he would not land on the wrong side of this impending battle.

She tightened her cloak around her and made her way back to the square, allowing herself to be swallowed up in the carefree laughter and joviality of Athinia at night.

Her mind reeled. For all that had occurred, she realized that she'd found out little more information. In fact, Endo's revelation of who or what she possibly was would not go over well with either the queen or Faline. She had almost nothing to report except that they had tried to pass through Caranek Peaks for some reason. And he had confirmed that whatever was coming was definitely evil, and Crispin's tracking spell was most certainly still in place.

Nellie hoped she didn't lose the queen's favor, that she could still be of use to her while they figured out ways to protect Faria.

She had the sinking suspicion that no matter what they did, it wouldn't be enough.

FOURTEEN

FARIA

The blessed numbing sensation that followed the burn of alcohol was what Faria liked best when she came to lounges like these. She settled into soft pillows, prepared to watch the dancers in the center of the carpeted floor. Gauzy fabrics in reds, purples, and black hung from the ceiling and doorways, giving a sultry, boudoir feel. Each alcove was spelled to hide the viewer within, allowing for total anonymity. Only the walls held muted light. *Inhibitions* was the perfect place for indiscretion.

The jewel she gave the bouncer helped.

Soft strings rippled through the air, and though Faria couldn't see the other patrons, she felt a collective alertness as dancers shimmied their way onto the floor. These humans were breathtaking. The men were shirtless.

The gold dust that covered their skin shimmered from sporadic lighting along the floor. Their faces were shrouded in shadow, though with her low-light vision, Faria could see designs painted along their foreheads and brows. The women were dressed in gold bodices and long flowy skirts with slits up the sides. Gold chains wrapped around their waists tinkled as they swayed. Symbols drawn in fluorescent paints glowed along their bare skin.

The dancers twirled around each other as if they were one entity with one breath, its only goal in life to tell its story through movement. Faria was enraptured by the beauty of it, by the freedom of their movement. She felt a pang of jealousy. They seemed so alive, able to share such passion with those who hid in their own private alcoves. Faria wondered if everyone else hiding their faces needed a moment of freedom, too.

She swirled the milky substance in her cup and knocked back the rest of it. As if summoned, a server came with a replacement. Faria placed her hand on his wrist and smiled up at him. She couldn't tell if he recognized her, though he wouldn't have said if he did. All workers signed a magical binding contract that ensured the utmost secrecy.

"Will you keep me company?" she asked, patting the soft cushions beside her. "For a little while?"

His warm eyes turned molten and his returning smile made her ache. Yes, she would enjoy his company. "I will return shortly." His voice drawled like melted honey. She wanted to get lost in its sticky sweetness.

Faria took a sip of her new drink and leaned her head back, closing her eyes. She allowed the music to thrum beneath her skin, allowed the drink to take its course and light a fire within. This wasn't the first time she had snuck out of *Mentage*, nor was it the first time she sought the company of another, but this time held more importance for her. The suitor her mother intended for her was expected the following day, so her freedom was at an end. She wanted one last night to do what she desired, rather than what was expected of her. That, and she really needed to get the feel of Hunter off her skin. He occupied her every thought and knowing she couldn't act on it was unbearable.

She knew *Inhibitions* was the perfect place—the only place—in Athinia where someone like her could seek the company of another and not have it return to the queen. Faria inhaled, the scent of spice mixed with something familiar permeated the air. It didn't matter what it was. The scent called to her as the music did.

The cushions shifted next to her and a smile played on her lips as he tucked a strand of loose hair behind her ear. His breath tickled her neck as he leaned in and said, "There you are, Princess."

She froze. Faria's stomach bottomed as her eyes slowly opened and glanced next to her. Her breath quickened as she took in a loose black shirt, golden skin of his chest exposed. She noticed the square jaw, the curve of sinful lips and finally met blazing emerald eyes, a halo of yellow fire glinting in the low light. She swallowed hard.

"I know my good looks leave others speechless," he said, "but you usually have something scathing to say to me." Though his tone was playful, Faria noticed the murderous intent in his stare and chose to say nothing. She wasn't sure she could form the words. His presence was always distracting, but she had never seen him dressed so casually, never seen him in such sinful lighting, never had been so painfully aware of every place his body heat penetrated her. She licked her lips.

"What are you doing here?" he demanded. "What were your intentions with *him*?"

That shook the shock from her. "Excuse me?" she said. "What I am doing here seems painfully obvious." She kicked back the last of her drink for good measure, both to annoy him but also to steady her nerves. "As for my intentions with him…" She trailed off, allowing the soft moaning sounds around them to speak for themselves. His eyes widened with understanding. She raised a brow, challenging him to say something. He only stared, a muscle in his jaw working as he undoubtedly swallowed all the words he wished he could say. She was slightly disappointed by it.

"I paid extremely well for my secrecy tonight," she said. Her skin prickled with awareness as the energy pulsing from him blanketed her. The music, the dancing, the low lighting. It was all too much to be here with him. "How did you find me?"

"Why did you come here?" he asked instead.

"I know I've consumed plenty of this lovely drink tonight, but I'm fairly certain I just answered you. More than that, I don't owe you an explanation. I'm your future queen. You don't get to question what I do."

"I do when it puts you in danger." His eyes flickered to her lips. She licked them again, slower this time, and the pulse in his neck quickened.

"The only thing I'm in danger of," she said each word slowly, letting them sink in one by one, "is being touched by a male who wants me. Not the Chosen One. Not the princess. Just Faria."

"With a stranger?" he asked. He inched closer, and she felt the danger rolling off him. It ignited a flame inside her and it was all she could do to keep her powers under control. The last thing she needed was to incinerate the club because she couldn't control her emotions. "With someone who doesn't know what makes you burn?" His mouth was against the shell of her ear. "With someone who doesn't properly know how to worship the female behind the power she harnesses?"

"What are you doing here, Hunter?" She tried desperately not to have his words affect her, but she failed to keep her voice from shaking. A sudden invading thought cooled her down. "Did you come here for female company?"

He cocked a smile and for a moment she thought he wouldn't answer. She didn't know what she would do if he didn't deny it. Finally, he said, "I came for you."

She shook her head, not wanting to believe it. She was surprised when tears sprang into her eyes. She quickly closed them and willed the ache in her throat to go away. Once she was certain her voice wouldn't tremble, she said, "I came here to get the feel of you off my skin. You invade every thought. Every feeling. I cannot—will not—spend my last night, free of any obligation and expectation, pining after a male I can't have."

"May I—" his voice broke off and she opened her eyes, searching his face. He swallowed. He seemed to decide against whatever he was about to say and shifted away from her.

She was determined to restrain herself from him, but it appeared her body had different plans. "Yes," she said, grabbing his hand and placing it against her cheek. "You have my permission."

He slid hand into her hair, gripping it enough that her head pulled back. His other hand stroked her cheek, then her neck, until he slid it behind her back, pulling her flush against his body. He had all the power but this time, she wanted the control.

She laid a hand against his chest and pushed him back into the cushions. She straddled him, allowing all the soft pieces with her to meld with the harder bits of him. His hands gripped her hips and he let out a soft hiss as she adjusted herself until she was flush against the only part that mattered.

She stared down at him, a coy smile on her face. Slowly, he leaned forward, his lips a breath away. This was what she wanted, what she needed. The quiet anticipation nearly set her on fire. A thought struck her. It had been a while since she lay with a male and she wasn't sure that she could keep her flames under control. Perhaps this wasn't the best idea.

He veered away from her mouth and instead nibbled on her neck and she knew, as her blood ignited, that there was no possible way she could keep her powers from manifesting. As if he had the same thought, he whispered, "As much as I would love to see all the wicked plans you have for me, I would rather go someplace more private. Where I can worship you and watch you fall apart as you scream my name when that flame ignites."

Yes, she wanted that. Needed that. "Your arrogance knows no bounds," she said. He nipped her neck, his tongue following to sooth the tiny hurts.

"It's not arrogance, it's confidence," his voice rumbled in her ear. "I—"

Whatever he was about to say was cut off by a scream in a nearby alcove, followed by a crash. Hunter shot up, nearly tossing Faria to the ground as he pulled a dagger out from a hidden holder up his sleeve. Faria raised her skirt, revealing a similar holster and removed her dagger as well. She thought how silly it was for her to brandish a weapon when her magic was a weapon, but future queen or not, it was best not to use magic against another unless absolutely necessary.

Hunter glanced at her, at the weapon she held, a look of incredulity on his face. "Is that one of mine?"

She smiled sweetly at him. "Could be," she said, knowing damn well it was one she stole from one of their last practices.

He shook his head and together they left the private comfort of their nook and approached the one they heard screams from. The music had stopped, and the dimmed lights were raised. A few patrons looked out from behind their curtains but none approached, recognizing Hunter and trusting him to take care of the problem.

"Get off of me!" a female screamed. Hunter ran forward and threw back the curtain, Faria on his heels. He threw a male off of the woman as if he weighed little more than a bag of sticks.

"Are you alright?" Faria asked, rushing to the woman. Tears streaked down her face and the front of her tunic was torn, but she had a fierce glint in her eye.

"That thing doesn't know how to take no for an answer," she said.

Faria whipped her head around to the offending male. Though he wore a hooded cloak, she thought she recognized his scent. "Crispin," she whispered.

He took off, sprinting for the exit. Hunter shot after him but stopped from the doorway and looked back at Faria. That one look said it all. She knew their night together would not happen. She nodded once at him, a signal to let him know that she understood. The safety of the Queendom came before her satisfying any urges she had, regardless of her freedoms.

Shocked murmurs from witnesses interrupted her thoughts, and though she valued her privacy, Faria removed her own hood and revealed herself. The patrons quieted, surprised to see the princess, their Chosen, in such a place.

She cleared her throat. "I apologize for the interruption," she said, her voice strong and clear despite having a sinking feeling that her mother would soon find out where she was. "We do not tolerate such behavior and will ensure that the offender in question will be punished. Please, allow me to refill your drinks so you may enjoy the rest of your evening." She signaled to the servers for another round.

The lights dimmed and the music restarted. The dancers walked back out onto the floor and Faria heard echoes of, "Thank you, Princess." She passed bowed heads as she made her way to the owner of the lounge.

"Princess Faria," Shane said. "I am so sorry you had to reveal yourself. I will do everything in my power to ensure no one speaks of your presence here."

"It's alright, Shane. I believe that will be impossible." Faria sighed and took out a bag of coins. "This should be enough for everyone's drinks. If there is any leftover, send a bit of food as well. Some hummus and bread. That drink of yours really packs a punch."

He bowed to her as she left. Regret filled her as she walked home. The drink made her bold, she knew, and she would never get another chance with Hunter. It should have been harmless fun. The way he spoke to her, what he promised to do to her. Her toes practically curled in her slippers.

Faria bumped into a passerby, lost in her thoughts. "Pardon me," she said.

"Lady Faria!" the passerby exclaimed. Her heart sank. "We were not told you would be in the city tonight."

"Wil," Faria said. "Reed. How lovely to see you. Well, don't interrupt your evening on my account." She winked at them and walked away before they could say anything else. She almost thought they would follow her back home, but both seemed to be distracted by something. Good. Perhaps they'd learn what happened and would aid Hunter in his chase to find Crispin.

Back in her rooms, basking in a hot bath, Faria allowed her thoughts to stray to whoever awaited her the next day. She wondered if he were kind, if he would be intimidated by her power. She hoped her mother would have chosen someone equal to her.

She hoped, for the sake of their Queendom, that it worked out.

FIFTEEN

FARIA

An air of change was upon them, and Faria knew it was more than just the coming solstice she felt in the hours before dawn. She slept little, worrying if Crispin was caught and the memory of the way Hunter had felt between her thighs.

He wanted her then, no matter the consequences. She wondered what it would have been like, if they had followed through on what they felt. She wished she could blame her boldness on the alcohol but they both knew that would be a lie.

The sun was not due to rise for another hour, but she could wait no longer. She dressed in thick leggings and a long sweater, strapping on a dagger. She grabbed a warm winter cloak and a pair of mittens, then ambled into the Forest. It was quiet except for the occasional chittering of a critter, and every now and then she came across flowers and fallen leaves that glowed phosphorescent in the moonlight.

She did not fear the Forest, but she was on edge. There was a sense of awareness that prickled her skin, as if the Forest were waiting for the change to arrive as well.

Faria conjured a large flaming ball that hovered above her hands, using it to warm herself from the chill of the wintery morning. She paced around the glen, trying—and failing—to keep her nerves under control. Streaks of lightning shot through the sky, though the threat of a storm was not there. She knew she conjured the electricity, knew that it reflected her electric anticipation of seeing Hunter again.

She sat on the tufted grass, the fireball hovering in front of her. She sought some quiet place in her mind to meditate. She inhaled the scent of lilac and jasmine tickling her nose, even now at the start of winter. With every exhale she imagined pushing out the fear and worry that had built up over the past few hours. With every inhale she took in more of the life from the Forest, more of the magic deep within its roots, more of that incessant hum she only heard when she was in the glen.

She felt him before she saw him. Her magic pulsed, the fireball flaring brighter before dissipating altogether. The scent of ocean and spiced bark hit her, calling to her. Every molecule waited in quiet eagerness for his arrival.

He sat next to her, keeping a polite distance away, and wrapped his arms around his knees. He had dark circles under his eyes and his hair was disheveled as if he had been up all night.

"Did you get him?" she asked, referring to Crispin. They needed to glean information in whatever way they could. Her heart dropped when he shook his head.

"I don't know how he got away from me." He raked his hands through his hair. "Nothing gets away from me."

"How very arrogant of you," she said, keeping her tone playful though every nerve of her body was taut, as if she were an arrow and he was the target.

He smiled faintly. "Confidence, Princess."

"That's right...I believe you were going to prove all that confidence to me."

"Faria—"

"Don't," she interrupted. She didn't need to hear his rejection to feel it. "You don't have to say anything. It was a moment and it passed. It's not a big deal."

His nostrils flared but he remained silent. They sat almost as if they were strangers. She didn't want it to be weird between them, but she also felt as if it was her last chance to be honest with him. Who knew how quickly she would be expected to do the bonding ceremony once that male arrived? Butterflies pounded in her stomach and she felt light-headed, but she had to get what she wanted to say off her chest.

"I want you to know that I find you irritating, arrogant, and infuriating to the highest degree." He raised a brow but she continued, avoiding his stare. "Half the time I'm with you I consider setting you on fire. But the other half...it's *you* setting *me* on fire. Every look you give me, every touch. I drown in it. I know it's probably just physical attraction and I don't blame you because, look at me," she stole a quick look at him, smiling. "But you need to know something, before I won't get the chance to say it again.

Before this part of me is trapped in the arms of another."

He growled low in his chest, his eyes glowing an eerie iridescent green in the approaching dawn. He waited for her to continue and she steeled herself, preparing for rejection.

"I want you to know that in all the months I've had to find a life partner, I've refused to settle for so many reasons. I don't deserve anyone who is less than my equal. I need someone to challenge me. Someone who makes me laugh but also makes me want to pluck my eyelashes out one by one. Someone who doesn't back down from a fight. Someone who puts up with my mood swings. Someone who can handle my power and all that it brings with it. Someone who looks at me and sees *me* instead of some Fates-cursed female sent to fulfill some nondescript prophecy." She swallowed the bitterness down and looked at him. "If given the choice, I would have chosen the one I wanted to fall in love with. The one I wanted to give my body, blend my soul with. If the option were there, I would choose you."

The humming thrummed her blood, her heart pounding against the admission. He was quiet as he searched her face. Too soon, he looked off into the distance, his jaw clenching. She scented him and while she did detect annoyance and anger, she also felt the spicy tang of lust and a sweeter taste underneath.

"You don't have to say anything," she said. "I'm sure you don't feel the same and that's okay." It would eventually be okay. After she drowned in her humiliation.

His silence echoed louder than any other sound the Forest could have produced. She stood quickly, brushing grass and dried leaves off of her.

"Let's just forget I said anything," she said. "What are we going to work on today?"

Hunter glanced up at her with a look of regret and somehow that hurt more than his silence. Did he regret the words she said? Did he regret touching her the way he did or the things he said? She could handle his rejection, but not his regret. As if everything about her were a mistake.

He stood to his fullest height, his body towering over her. His energy made him feel larger, taking up more space, invading hers. She welcomed it.

His hand reached as though to touch her face, but he stopped short, his fingers barely grazing her cheek. She looked at him warily. She needed him to say nothing. She needed him to say something. Her heart echoed in the empty space between them.

He moved, his body a blur as he picked her up and pressed her against a tree. She barely registered the bark biting into her, instead focusing on her legs wrapped around his waist as her fingers gripped his hair. His lips were on her and there was nothing gentle about it but she didn't care. They didn't have time to be gentle.

The humming in the background grew louder and she was vaguely aware of flames surrounding them. She knew they wouldn't harm her, knew they were a manifestation of everything she felt inside. His hips rolled into hers, his tongue exploring her mouth, her neck, her collarbone. It felt like freedom, like release, like a piece of her was missing and she didn't realize the depth of that loss until he filled it. She pressed him closer, demanding he give more because it wasn't enough.

His mouth tore away from hers. His heavy breathing mirrored hers, as if they were gasping for something other than what the other gave. He was her oxygen. His eyes blazed with a holy green light fit for the gods, the flames around them reflecting off the golden halo. She felt he could see straight through her.

He lowered her legs to the ground, his harsh breathing ragged in her ear. His breath was warm on her neck. "I will never be an option."

He walked away, the flames dying in his wake.

"I WILL NEVER GET TIRED of looking at that butt," Nellie sighed next to her. The young girl had been waiting for her when she'd left the Forest, and they both took a moment to watch Hunter's retreating back. Faria tried to tamp down the sting of his rejection, though she knew he was right.

"Nellie! Why am I not surprised?" Faria looked at her, noting the dreamy expression on her face. "You always know when I need you. How have you been? Staying out of trouble?"

Nellie sashayed her hips back and forth ahead of her as she glanced over her shoulder. "I always stay out of trouble, baby."

Faria couldn't help but chuckle. "Come on," she said as she playfully bumped her, pushing all thoughts of Hunter from her mind. "Our guest should be arriving soon."

"Wait, Faria." She hesitated at Nellie's use of her full name. She hadn't called Faria that since her first month at *Mentage*.

"What's wrong, Nells?"

Nellie stared at the ground then over Faria's shoulder. Faria had an overwhelming sense that Nellie was older than thirteen, and that she just wanted to protect her from any harm. A child so young should not look or feel so old.

"I've been wanting to talk to you for days. It's about—"

"Darroc." Faria finished for her.

"Yes, exactly! How did you know?" Nellie's gaze followed Faria's, her face mirroring the princess's shock.

A brilliant, shining white stallion trotted up the path leading to the gates of *Mentage*, its muscles protruding from under its incredible coat. It was the largest creature Faria had ever seen. Mounted on that breathtaking animal was an astonishingly good-looking male. His skin was a rich brown, a beautiful contrast to the stallion he rode. His dark hair was parted just off to the side and he wore the most brilliant shade of azure silk, the silver buttons on his coat reflecting off the sun. Even from here, Faria could see he was well-built as if he'd spent his life doing manual labor.

The stallion stopped in front of the girls and waited as all six-foot-three-inches of warlock male stood before them. He smiled at them. A dimple on one side appeared as he bowed low.

But it wasn't the beautiful animal, the clothes, or his good looks that took Faria's breath away. It was the pair of deep, violet eyes that finally held her gaze.

The eyes of true warlock royalty.

It was said the true royals no longer existed and that was why their diminished power never returned after the Great War. The queen took in so many warlocks that had defected to give them renewed sense of purpose. To feel as though they belonged. The Agostonnas took care of them and shared their land, treated them as equals. The warlocks helped make the land more fertile with the little power they had left and in return they wanted for nothing. It was why it didn't make sense they were starting a rebellion. As far as everyone knew, they were happy in their replacement home.

But here was proof that someone existed all along, and he came at the queen's invitation. Faria had a feeling it wasn't mere coincidence. What this her plan for stopping the rebellion, for saving both their people? The queen had only told Faria that his name was Darroc, nothing else.

It was clever, though why wouldn't she tell Faria from the beginning? She would do anything to keep their people safe. If she said she knew of a true Royal or her plans of stopping the rebellion, maybe Faria wouldn't have fought so hard on this arrangement. Maybe.

Darroc stepped closer and reached for Faria's hand, pressing his soft lips to her skin. Instantly her blood vibrated, like it knew something she didn't. Like it recognized him. She couldn't tell if that was a good thing or not.

"Lady Faria." His baritone voice commanded respect without forcing it, rumbling like a storm going out to sea. "I have longed to meet you for quite some time."

"Darroc," Faria replied with as much confidence as she could muster. Real warlock royalty! They felt as fabled as the Val. "I hope your journey was well. We expected you here sooner."

"Yes, my travels were delayed about a week ago," he hedged. "There was…no news?"

"None, as far as I know," Faria said. He breathed easier at her reply. "I'm sure you will want to rest, but first I will personally escort you to Queen Amira and King Dennison. All who enter *Mentage* see them first.

I'm sure you understand."

"Of course. Your queen was more than generous to offer me a place to stay. I'm very much looking forward to thanking her."

Faria started to lead him away but a small hand on her shoulder drew her back.

"Faria, I must speak with you," Nellie said.

"Not now, Nells." Faria shook her off. She felt guilty—she hadn't seen the girl in weeks and what she had to say seemed important. "Perhaps Faline will need help with setting up for tomorrow. I'll catch up with you later." Faria smiled at her before turning away.

It wasn't like Nellie to be so serious with her, nor was it like her to not swoon over handsome males, child or not.

Faria looked back at Nellie before rounding the corner and saw her still standing there, jaw clenched shut, arms crossed in front of her.

Something was very wrong, indeed.

SIXTEEN

NELLIE

S
he stood in the ancient hallway, observing the Throne Room through the magical stone wall. It was a cavernous room with large windows situated high up on the walls, allowing the sunlight to reflect off the shiny surfaces of the marble floors. Banners of the Agostonna royal crest hung from cathedral ceilings. A black velvet carpet ran through the center of the marble floor and stopped before a dais, where Queen Amira and King Dennison sat upon their thrones.

Each throne was carved from black marble. The queen's had a high back and spanned out in the shape of wings. Black flames gave it the impression of being on fire. The king's throne depicted a *Drogosterra*, rather than a firebird, its scales winding down the chair's spine, its mouth open in a mighty roar.

Queen Amira's dress was as regal as Nellie had ever seen. Long sleeves billowed down her arms, covering her tightly clasped hands. The skirts of her dress were violet, shimmering with silver as if they were made of ethereal rays of moonlight shining through a starry night. The bodice was plain, with silks tightly bound around her tiny frame. The neckline was limned in what looked to be diamonds. Her long, dark hair was pulled back in the traditional elven warrior way, braided on one side and pulled tightly to the crown of her head, upon which an antler crown rested. While the queen often dressed well, it was rare that she presented herself in such a way; equal parts ruler and warrior. The sharp lines of her dark face made her look more fierce than usual, and though she plastered a smile, tension was evident straight through her back.

King Dennison sat to the left of the queen, wearing the same dark tunic as the workers at *Mentage* normally did, though the vest he wore was made of fine leather embroidered with gold and silver leaves. His dark hair was left down and brushed just past his shoulders. A severe look was set upon his usually cheerful face. He wore a band of gold around his forehead. His skin was fair to the queen's dark, contrasting in perfect harmony. His deep amber eyes shone with anger. The Queen's Royal Guard stood in front of the dais as sentries, though Nellie could see that all were armed with swords and daggers along their belts.

The doors creaked open and Nellie watched as Faria and Darroc walked down the carpeted aisle, stopping just before the dais.

"Mother, Father, allow me to introduce Prince Darroc L'Azare, the last remaining Royal of Wendorre. Prince Darroc, Queen Amira and King Dennison Agostonna."

Darroc bowed deeply to the queen and king. "Thank you for your hospitality, Queen Amira," he said as he stood from his deference. "It is a pleasure and an honor to receive this special invitation to *Mentage*. You have no idea how long I have wished to visit."

"Yes, it was nice to finally receive an acceptance from you, though it did take me offering you a chance at my daughter's hand to convince you." Though she remained smiling, her next words were ice. "It seems as though the prospect of war was not as concerning to you."

"Ah," the prince said. "Though it may not seem it, your offering a place by Faria's side was a fortunate coincidence in timing. I was gathering information from what remains of the royal council to figure out how to best handle these *rebellions*, as you say." He straightened his jacket before continuing. "As you know, my kingdom has not fared well for quite some time."

The king clenched his jaw. "*Princess* Faria," he corrected Darroc. "Yes, how strange it is to see that warlock royalty still exists. Certainly, one would expect your power to have been restored."

Darroc shifted his violet eyes from the king to the queen. "Indeed. The rightful power will be restored, soon."

The scent of threat was a violent current in the air. Nellie knew he referred to the Queen stealing their power, which she had learned from when she eavesdropped on Endo, Crispin, and Smyth. She didn't think Darroc would be so bold as to bring it up. The Royal Guard placed their hands on their swords, ready for action at the queen's word.

No one in the Throne Room said anything. The king and queen looked deadly while Faria glanced between the three of them, confused.

It was clear she didn't understand what was going on, which meant the queen never told her the theory about the warlocks' power being stolen. Nellie had the sudden clarity that Darroc had not just something, but *everything* to do with what had been happening in Anestra.

Anger speared through her. How could the queen invite him to *Mentage*? How could she think to choose him as a life partner for Faria? Nellie had to be wrong. The queen would never put her daughter in such danger.

Faria interrupted her thoughts. "With your permission, I'll show Darroc to the gardens…" she said, her voice trailing off in the tense silence.

"My lady." Darroc lightly touched her on the arm. Nellie froze at the gesture, as did everyone else in the room though, the prince seemed oblivious. No one touched the future queen. Except Hunter. "If I may, I would like to know where your mother received such a beautiful bracelet. It reminds me of one my own mother used to have."

Faria politely shifted away from his touch, narrowing her eyes at her mother. While the queen dressed well, she never wore jewelry except during celebrations. This was no celebration.

Nellie glanced at the Queen Amira's wrist. She had raised her hand to Wil to open the doors and her sleeve had slid down, revealing the adornment. Nellie probably wouldn't have noticed it if Darroc hadn't said anything. The bracelet itself was a thin cuff made of some type of metal. By the way it shone, most likely silver. Within the cuff looked to be some sort of substance that moved, like clouds or water, and it swirled delicately back and forth. It was a strange piece, certainly not elven-made.

"It is a family heirloom, passed down for generations." The queen's voice sounded evasive to Nellie and she wondered what the queen might be hiding.

"How interesting. My mother's has been lost for quite some time. It was a unique design, made by one of our most trusted jewelers. I was under the impression it was the only one of its kind."

The unsaid accusation hung tangible in the air. The Royal Guard clenched the handles of their swords as one. Still, the queen said nothing as she waved her hand away, dismissing Darroc and Faria from the room.

Nellie watched the king and queen for several moments longer, but they simply shared a long, worried glance before they, too, left the Throne Room.

Were the rebel warlocks right? Had the queen actually stolen their power somehow? What was the connection with the bracelet?

Nellie needed answers, quickly. She pulled aside the tapestry of the Val, listening for anyone walking by before stepping into the hallway.

"Nellie."

She halted the screech leaving her throat, jumping at the sound of her name.

"Hunter, I swear to goodness one of these days I'm going to do serious harm if you keep sneaking up on me like that. How did you know where I was?"

He half smiled but most of his attention was back on the tapestry as if he'd never seen it before.

"I am leaving." He said the words without taking his eyes away from the scene in front of him, his brows furrowed in concentration. "Did Faria choose this tapestry?"

"Yes, she did. Wait, excuse me?"

He turned to look at Nellie, his face serious as it ever was. "I am being summoned. Even now, it is hard for me to stay here when I am being compelled elsewhere."

"Who is calling you? What does that mean? Does Faria know?"

His green eyes hardened but he showed no other emotion. "She cannot know. It does not matter. I cannot interfere."

"I'm so tired of how cryptic you are!" Nellie whisper-shouted at him, running her hands through her hair. "You can't leave now. She needs protection!" She quickly explained about the awkward encounter she had just witnessed. She paid particular attention to his face when she told him about the bracelet and accusations that Darroc made. Still, he remained passive.

"On second thought, I must speak to the queen."

"I'm coming with you!" She ran down the hall, trying to keep up with him. Whatever he was, he had the speed of an elf. Nellie thought that the edges around his body started to blur.

Hunter stopped in front of the Council Room. Only Enis stood guard at the door. "I must speak to the queen," he said.

Enis looked him up and down. "I don't think so," she said. "She has a lot on her plate."

The door sprang open and the queen herself ushered Hunter in. She looked over her shoulder. "You too," she said. Nellie barely had enough time to register the shock of the queen actually speaking to her. Normally anything she wanted went through Faline. She hurried inside before the queen changed her mind.

"I'm not sure that Nellie should be here for this conversation," Hunter said. His fists were clenched and Nellie noticed the veins on his arms popping through the muscle on his forearms. Whoever or whatever was calling for him must be getting impatient for him. His body shuddered with how hard he worked to remain in place.

"She will not repeat what she hears," Queen Amira said. "Say what you need to."

"You cannot give Faria to him."

Nellie's eyebrow raised. That was bold.

"You cannot give me orders."

"Do you understand who he is?" Hunter asked through clenched teeth. "Who he *really* is?"

The queen swallowed, her face carefully blank. "Yes."

"How could you?" The words rumbled through the Council Room as a sense of displeasure increased. Nellie shifted from foot to foot, wishing once again that she had minded her business.

Whisps of breath became visible in the suddenly frigid air. "Need I remind you who you are speaking to? You do not get to question me. You do not give me orders. You do not tell me what I am to do with my daughter. Everything I do, *everything* I have done, has been to protect her. You know as well as I that we cannot change what the Fates deign to pass."

"She is not prepared for this type of danger," Hunter said. "She cannot do the bonding ceremony with him. It will not save Anestra."

Nellie shivered, wondering if she would make it to the fire in the hearth without being noticed. The queen stared Hunter down. "I suggest that if you do not wish to see harm befall Faria, you stay away from her."

Her mouth tightened and her eyes took on a blue luminescence. "And if you do not want to risk him discovering what you are, I suggest you stay away from him as well."

"I am to protect her with my life. Even you cannot remove me from my duty."

"And I am trying to protect yours. Do not make things worse."

Hunter vibrated violently, then simply popped out of existence. The slight widening of her eyes was the only indication of the queen's shock.

The room warmed up again and Queen Amira sat at the table in the middle of the room, hands folded in front of her. The silence stretched on, and Nellie wondered if she should try to pop out of existence, too. She cleared her throat but said nothing, waiting for the queen to tell her something—anything—about why she needed to hear all that.

"I suppose you have questions," she said.

"Yes," Nellie breathed, relieved at the opening. "Do you know what Hunter is? What did he mean that it's his duty to protect her? Who is Darroc really? What does your bracelet have to do with anything?"

Queen Amira raised a brow and Nellie realized she had just admitted to spying on them. The queen let out a long sigh and rubbed her temple.

"I do not know exactly what Hunter is, but I have strong suspicions. No, I will not tell you what those suspicions are. It is his business to tell you if and when he is ready."

Nellie frowned. She was really hoping to get the dirt on him.

"As for who Darroc really is. It is obvious he is royalty, though he is not the prince he claims to be. The bracelet is not your concern." She gave Nellie a pointed look. "I allowed you to listen for several reasons. First, I know you would have tried to eavesdrop anyway. Second, I could not tell anyone what the danger to our land was. I am still forbidden to explicitly speak the words. You heard what Hunter said. Take what you will of it. Third, I need to remind you that you must protect her at all costs."

Nellie wanted to protest. She wanted to question the queen more, to demand answers. She expected Nellie to sacrifice everything for Faria and she would, but she deserved to know why. Instead, she bowed her head. "I will protect her with my life. But I still don't know what you expect of me. My kind is not welcome here."

"If you were not welcome here then you would not be here," Queen Amira said. "Soon, I will have need of you. I will request from you what you might not be willing to give. There will come a time when it will seem the weight of the realm will rest on your shoulders—as it does on us all. I cannot and will not apologize for it, because it will be as essential as anything else in this dangerous game we are to play. Do you understand?"

"Is this dangerous game tricking Darroc somehow? Do you know a way to prevent the Prophecy from coming true?"

The queen said nothing, but Nellie had the suspicion she was on the right track. Whatever powers were at work were far stronger than the queen, and for all she was asking of Nellie, she truly believed Queen Amira would have given more detail if she could.

She nodded her head anyway. "I will do what you require of me." Nellie gave a slight bow as the queen waved her hand to dismiss her.

"And Nellie, you and I cannot meet again while he is here. It is too dangerous. I will send word when I require you."

Nellie left the Council Room feeling more confused than ever. The queen had an idea of what Hunter was, but would not say. She had all but said that Prince Darroc was the evil taking over the land, though he may not actually be a prince. She was going to be asked to complete impossible tasks, but she must do so anyway. And above all, the queen expected her to protect Faria.

She needed to find Faline, fast. She needed to see if her adoptive mother had answers and if not, then guidance on how she was to proceed with Darroc there. She was in more danger than ever since she didn't know if he could detect her kind. It seemed Endo and possibly Crispin had picked up a different signature from her. She could only imagine what their leader knew of her.

"Why are you so important?" Enis asked as Nellie passed through the door. Nellie had almost forgotten she was there.

"I wish I knew," Nellie replied before walking away.

SEVENTEEN

FARIA

The contrast between the frigid winter air and the warm breeze blowing through the Spring Garden disoriented Faria. Beautiful scents of fresh daisies and grass tickled her nose. It felt crude, almost, to look past the garden to a gray landscape. Though it was her favorite place in *Mentage*, she felt strange sharing it with a stranger. With a Prince of Wendorre. With all the guests they had hosted over the years, Faria had never entertained a prince before, and certainly not one she was all but betrothed to.

Wilhelm and Reed followed close behind as Faria led Darroc along the stone path, stopping occasionally to point out her favorite plants. She never had guards follow her before, though since this prince was a complete stranger and she was the future queen, it made sense to have someone close by. Normally she would be indignant, but after what she witnessed in the Council Room—the thick tension between the queen and Prince L'Azare, and then how angry her father was…it was enough to have her on guard as well.

He was alluring, there was no doubt about that. But something was off. Faria scented him but it was just a symphony of warlock. He smelled of magic and earth. There was nothing to suggest anything otherwise, no glamour for her to see through. And yet, when he grazed her arm, it almost felt like her blood reached for him, as though it recognized who he was.

Or perhaps warning her of *what* he was.

Either way, it was compelling and terrifying, but she didn't altogether hate it. After her earlier rejection from Hunter and the inevitability of a bonding ceremony between the two of them, Faria knew she should put forth the effort to at least get to know Darroc. Perhaps she would learn to develop feelings for him, and if not, then the arrangement could certainly ease the tension between their races. A diplomatic union would be the best for all parties involved, no matter how much turning away from the one she wanted hurt. *See? I can be a team player.*

They walked in silence until they reached the jade fountain in the center with the Stag, Lion, Bear, and Phoenix all pointing north, south, east, and west.

"So, care to explain why you were rude to my mother?" Maybe she should have tried harder in her lessons with Faline on how to entertain foreign guests.

Prince Darroc took a moment before answering. "Apologies, Lady Faria. I was merely shocked to see another bracelet of its kind. It was extremely rare and after it went missing…well in any case, I apologize."

"It isn't me you need to be apologizing to, it's my mother. She was kind enough to invite you to stay with us at *Mentage* and more than that, she has been taking care of your people for decades, and her mother before that. Why haven't you been taking care of them, anyway? Why do so many flee to Anestra to the protection of the queen?"

Darroc's nostrils flared. She had struck a nerve. Good—she wanted answers. "May I tell you a tale, Lady Faria? An old warlock legend?"

Her interest was piqued. She knew almost nothing about warlock legends. Many warlocks who moved to Anestra weren't interested in holding onto their dying culture. She thought it sad, but understood the need to start over; their desire to remake themselves was something she often dreamed of as well. She motioned for him to continue.

"Long ago, there was a benevolent king who loved his people more than anything in the world. Anything, other than his beautiful wife. The king and queen had been together for centuries, but the queen's health was quickly declining. Desperate for help, the king sought out their most gifted jeweler, who was said to have the ability to create life's essence in the shape of a jewel. It would allow the wearer to remain alive, keeping their life force close so it would not slip away to join the gods. The cost for such a gift was high, but the jeweler said he would do it for free to help his queen.

"Days passed and soon the queen could no longer move on her own. She was pale and losing weight quickly. She had no appetite and her beautiful face once filled with laughter had turned sullen and aloof. The king demanded the jeweler to hurry, for his queen was dying and had only days or maybe hours left. The jeweler assured the king that he was nearly finished, but in order to capture her life's essence, he would need something that only she could provide.

"The king did not understand. What was it that his queen could provide but no other? He soon realized it was her magic."

Darroc stopped in front of the phoenix, gazing intently at its open scream. "Would you like to hear the rest of it?" he asked.

"Yes, please." Faria said, shifting closer to him. He was a magnificent storyteller. His voice enchanted her. He could probably speak of soil and rocks and she would listen.

He leaned in, speaking softly the rest of the legend, never removing his eyes from the phoenix.

"A warlock queen's magic is unique because it only reaches its full potential once she is mated or has a child. It is part of the reason why we revered our females so. Why it would be a horrible crime if something were to happen to them. A queen's magic is what gives life to the king's magic. Though we are a patriarchal society, one is never at the height of their power without their partner there to guide them."

Faria trembled at his words and the implication behind them. A warlock queen. That was what he sought from her, from their arrangement. A way to help restore their power.

"To give the queen's magic away, well, that was not for the king to decide. He brought the jeweler to see his queen, to ask her blessing to finish the jewel that should keep her alive. She reached her hand out to the jeweler and asked for him to lean closer. She whispered words no one else heard, and then the jewel was complete.

"The king snatched the jewel out of the jeweler's grasp, gazing closely at it. It seemed to have been made of diamond, but liquid. Swirls of clouds stormed inside of it. Its shape was that of a crescent moon, a sign of change to come. He slid the jewel onto his beloved's wrist and waited for something to change.

"But nothing did. The queen's eyes closed and though her breathing was even, she slipped into a dream state. Wracked with fury, the king lashed out at the jeweler, demanding to know what his mate said. The jeweler said he could not repeat it even if he wanted to, as the magic was her own. He did not understand the language she used, though it completed the jewel. He claimed it should work but the king grew tired of waiting. He decided to take matters into his own hands."

Darroc was quiet for a few moments, and though Faria was eager to hear the rest of the story, he seemed as if he needed time to collect his thoughts. The passion with which he wove his tale was inspiring, as was the way he held on to his peoples' legend as if it were his own story. She felt ashamed for not learning more about her own histories. Faria had spent so much time fighting everything her mother wanted from her just to spite her. Maybe it wasn't too late to learn. Perhaps there was a legend she could share with Darroc as well.

"The king was desperate, and he did the only thing a desperate warlock could do in the name of love. He relinquished almost all of his magic, save one drop, in an effort to preserve his queen. It was a dangerous game he played. The king's magic was what allowed his people and land to thrive. Without it, they would fall into ruin. He knew he was gambling the future of his race away, but it was his only chance at saving his mate. He had to believe it would work. That hope was all he had to hold onto.

"But it wasn't enough. The king poured his magic into his queen, willing it to revive her. To make her whole again. But instead, she burnt to ash. The king stared in disbelief, shock shutting down his every thought. He was meant to save her, not kill her. Still, he did not leave her side, nor did he allow anyone to take away her ashes.

"The Kingdom of Wendorre mourned, not just for the loss of their queen, but the loss of their magic as well. Warlock—male, female, and child alike—suffered. Sickness and disease as they had never known ripped throughout the kingdom. Plants withered, the fertile ground dried and turned desolate, and soon the warlocks' long life spans came to a close. The king sacrificed his people for nothing.

"He took vigil for weeks, never leaving their bedchamber. He, too, stopped eating. His only son could not help, either. He had to watch to the warlocks' rapidly deteriorating health. He saw his land die along with the people he had learned to love.

"But then, the ashes began to stir. The king could not believe it. He was delirious with lack of sleep and thirst, but it happened again. The ashes rippled until soon, a giant phoenix erupted where his beloved once lay."

"A phoenix?" Faria interrupted. Darroc jumped as though startled, looking down at her with annoyance. "Phoenixes aren't real, are they? I thought they were one of the fabled creatures from Earth. No one has ever seen one before."

"No one currently *alive* has ever seen one before," Darroc said. "And anyway, this is warlock legend. Not all legends are accurate, are they?"

"Yes," Faria replied. "All legends have a kernel of truth. Perhaps the truth of this one is that the king created a phoenix, something that is everlasting, because he hoped to forever preserve his queen. The magic he gave up worked, but it worked in its own way."

Darroc gave her a half smile. "Indeed, you seem to be ending my story for me. Yes. The king's magic did work, but as magic has a mind of its own, it created its own version of the truth as well. A phoenix cannot die and is always reborn.

"As it were, according to legend, when this phoenix rose from the ashes, there was a cry among the warlocks. Water—blessed, much prayed for water—fell from the sky, soaking up the dusty, arid lands. People were starting to regain their magic. Within hours, crops were fully grown as if they never went anywhere to begin with. It was a miracle!

"The phoenix remained in the kingdom for several months. Word got out that the king turned his queen into an animal to save her. No one knew the truth of it, that the king transferred all of their power onto an animal, except for the king's son. That is, until the phoenix disappeared.

"No one knew where she went, but once she left, the warlocks realized what the king had done. He did not save them. He betrayed them. He gave away their essence, which was now tied to a creature they knew nothing about.

"The king knew the phoenix would return, though, so he waited. While his people grew old, while they succumbed to disease, while they tried to plant crops and yield fish, he waited.

"There was an uprising, and though the king regretted seeing it happen, he did nothing to stop it. His desire to live had diminished. He had given everything to his queen but still, she left, taking with her everything she had.

"But while the king held on to hope, his son could not. The prince could no longer stand watching his people suffer. The king still had a drop of magic left, which would pass from father to son upon death. Though the prince fought with himself, he soon became convinced that he must kill the king, so that the power would move onto him. The prince did not have a mate and therefore no one that he felt a weakness for. He knew he would be able to grow and harvest that power and restore the warlocks to their glory.

"The prince approached the king when he was alone. The king, tears in his eyes, knew that the prince came to him with murderous intent and did not stop him from slashing his throat. And the prince, filled with grief, held the king's body until it turned cold.

"Word spread at what the prince had done but rather than be cheered as a savior, he was cast out. Worse than that, there was no transfer of magic. There was nothing left except for the little kernel of power each warlock had. With no prince and no king to lead them, they soon left Wendorre. Those that remained behind did so with one hope in mind that the phoenix would finally return home."

Faria watched Darroc as flickers of emotion passed through him. Anger and sadness at war with each other. It was in the droop of his shoulders. In this way his fists clenched by his sides. The way his pulse quickened in his throat.

He stood near her and though they did not touch, it felt as though he held her close. Faria was enthralled by him. He was a magnificent storyteller, his every word enchanting her. It took a moment for her to get her bearings again. She found her hand reaching out to Darroc. Her knuckles barely grazed his arm before the movement broke him from his reverie.

"It seems I owe you another apology, Lady Faria."

"Why is that?" she asked.

"Because that was a heavy story to burden you with when we only just met." He shrugged. "I always felt close to those stories, ever since I was a boy. They haunt me every so often and after seeing your mother and that jewel and now this statue of the phoenix…I am reminded again of what my people lost. But it is not your burden. Not yet, anyway." He cocked a smile and winked at her.

"I am sorry you feel so strongly, but I envy you." Faria walked away from the fountain. A rustle in the bushes behind them let her know that Wil and Reed were not far behind.

She wondered what they thought of the prince's story. "I never cared to learn all the legends of my people or where our gifts came from. Not really. I know they come from the three goddesses, that their magic when they laid to rest is what nourishes this land with magic. I never cared to learn beyond that. Never tried to figure out how much was truth or fiction created to make us appreciate or fear our gods. I almost feel as though I have no connection to that aspect of myself. I love my people, I love my land, and I love what we represent. But I'm afraid I'm still too selfish to lead. I don't know that I could ever make the sacrifice that the prince in your story made. If I would murder to save my people."

The weight of her declaration pressed on her. Faria wasn't sure where the words came from but she knew the truth of them as she said it. She never confessed something so emotional to anyone before, not even to Hunter, with the exception of that morning. This warlock prince made her feel so at ease, like she could reveal anything to him.

Darroc considered her words then pulled Faria to a stop. Again, he dared to touch her and though she should have, she didn't hate it. The way her blood sang electrified her. She could feel the pulse of energy emanating from him. If that was the power she felt now, she wondered how much it would grow once they did the bonding ceremony. Once she became his warlock queen.

"You say that now but when it comes time, you would do what needs to be done."

"How do you know?" she asked in earnest.

He shrugged. "It is Fate."

Faria rolled her eyes at him. "Fate can shove it. I don't believe in fate."

"In time, Lady Faria, I think you will." He dazzled her with another smile and she felt another part of her shield melt away. He seemed so sure of himself. So sure of her, though he'd never met her.

"How much of that story was just a legend?"

"My people are not much for storytelling. I am sure some parts are exaggerated, but most of it is based on fact. The prince did actually kill the king who did actually relinquish his magic to save his mate."

Faria considered his words carefully as they strolled through the garden. She stopped at an overgrown rosebush, marveling at the way its petals shimmered in the sun. A thought struck her.

"How are you here, then?"

"What?" The prince stilled at the question.

"If the king and queen both died and they had one son who never had a mate, then how are you here? It is clear you are true warlock royalty. Your eyes cannot change that."

Darroc stared off into the distance.

"Unless," Faria continued, "You are not who you say you are. You do not come from Wendorre. Or your legend is just that. A legend."

"I assure you; I am of Wendorre."

"So, what's your story then? How are you here?"

"Perhaps that is best told another time," he said. He walked to one of the doors leading into the Atrium. "I am tired, Lady Faria. I am sure your guard would not mind showing me to my chambers."

Reed looked to Faria with his eyebrows raised, waiting for approval. She almost snorted at that. Neither him nor Wilhelm waited for her approval for anything. She did appreciate it, though. They wanted to show that she had the power here, not him. Smart.

Faria nodded her head and waved goodbye to Darroc. He was mysterious and he did tell lovely stories, but still, Faria couldn't shake the feeling that something was off. She understood his behavior toward her mother, though she did not approve. That whole exchange was odd. Her father was never angry and yet he had looked ready to pummel him. Faria felt that it went beyond Darroc's disrespect toward her mother. Like she was missing vital information about their guest.

The mid-afternoon sun beat down on Faria despite the cold and the smell of roasted nuts and vegetables permeated the air. Her birthday celebration was in a few days, and even from the garden, she could hear the bustle of workers setting up. It was expected to be a huge celebration, with both solstice and her eighteenth birthday within a day of each other.

The theme Faria wanted was a night carnival, so there would be fire dancers, jugglers, illusionists, and much more. People from all over Anestra were expected to flood to Athinia with a select few staying at *Mentage* as the queen's personal guests. Though Faria hated being the center of attention, she found that she was looking forward to the festivities.

She shuffled her way inside but drew up short. The queen stood in the window, watching Faria, her lips pursed.

Once again, Faria wondered why her mother insisted on a bonding ceremony with Darroc, especially when she clearly disapproved. Faria had to assume it was because of who he was, that their union would staunch the problem with the warlocks and reunite their two countries. She had a feeling, though, that there was an ulterior motive. The queen had her secrets, that much was evident.

The question was whether those secrets would help them or destroy them.

FARIA AWOKE FROM A DREAMLESS night and was grateful for the reprieve from her nightmares. Rays of the morning sun reminded her that this would be her first morning without Hunter in months. She felt an ache as she remembered the feel of his hands on her hips, his tongue skimming along her neck, the urgency with which he had kissed her. She groaned, pulling the covers off her. If only she didn't know what he tasted like, maybe she wouldn't miss him so badly.

She quickly changed into leggings, a plain brown tunic with a layered wool sweater over it, and slid on thick boots. She'd be escorting Darroc on a tour of the grounds after breakfast. She felt a flutter of nerves, though she wasn't sure how to feel about them. Darroc was charming and something about him oozed elegance, but she disapproved of the way he spoke to her mother and his arrogance bordered on the line of cruelty rather than confidence.

Faria opened her door, surprised to see Enis and Wil waiting for her. Enis gave Faria a slight bow before turning, leading the way to the Great Hall for breakfast.

Faria raised her brow at Wil. "Is there a reason for the welcome committee?"

Wil gave her an apologetic shrug. "Queen's orders, Lady Faria."

She sighed through her nose but didn't reply. She knew she'd have to get used to having guards around everywhere she went.

A hush descended outside the Great Hall as Darroc walked up the opposite hallway, Reed escorting him. He wore all black, from his pants to his dress shirt to his overcoat. The purple of his eyes contrasted brightly against the fabric and his tanned skin showed a lifetime of being exposed to sunshine. Groups of people crowded the hallway, whispering.

Gossips. All of them.

He gave her a slight bow. "Good morning, Princess." Annoyance prickled at his use of her title, though she knew it was irrational. He couldn't know what hearing it meant to her now, how much it ripped her heart that it came from the wrong person's mouth. He held his arm out to her. "May I escort you to breakfast?"

She swallowed down her feelings and gave him a tentative smile.

"You may."

He led them to one of the few two-person tables, ensuring no one would be able to sit with or interrupt them. She was slightly irked; she loved sitting and speaking with her people, but she supposed she could use the opportunity to get to know him a bit more. It would be an excellent opportunity to question him more.

He started to fix her a plate then stopped at her raised brow. "My apologies," he said. "In my country males always serve their females. Old habit."

She took the sparsely filled plate and loaded up with biscuits and fresh fruit. "Apology accepted, as long as you remember two things. First, I belong to no one. Second, I love to eat." She smiled at him and tore into a cinnamon bun.

A slow smile crept along his face. "I will try to remember that."

"So, tell me how you came to be. How is there a royal warlock? Do you have family? What is it like in Wendorre?"

"So eager, Princess," he chuckled. She held back her cringe. "I don't know exactly how I relate to the original Royal family. The power that did not pass on to the king's son moved on to the most powerful male, which was an ancestor of mine. It automatically made him a prince. He was never crowned a king, nor was any other male after him."

"Where are your parents now? Are they ruling Wendorre in your place? And why did we think you were just a liaison?"

"My parents have been resting with the gods for quite some time. I barely remember them. The people of Wendorre know who I am. We have tried not to let outsiders know of there being a prince because our power has not been restored, and I do not wish to give any warlock false hope. I don't want them to return to a home where they cannot prosper."

"That makes sense. Is it desolate, then?"

"No," he said, biting into a strawberry. The juice running down his chin reminded her of blood. "It still has life and vibrancy and culture...but it is muted. Or so I hear." He cleared his throat. "Enough about me. What do you do for fun?"

"I train." She paused, uncertain if she should have told him that. Coming from such a patriarchal country, he might not approve of females being able to defend themselves. It also dawned on her that he may not know about her being the Chosen, or all of her abilities that came with it.

He paused, his toast hovering just outside his mouth. "What do you mean, *train?*"

She felt eyes staring at her, at them, and she looked around the Great Hall to find that not one person was eating their food. The occasional murmur flitted to her but otherwise it was silent. She heard the rumors, knew that everyone had assumed she and Hunter would be paired off. She was certain her people wanted to know what exactly she was doing with a warlock prince. She looked back at him and cleared her throat. "Everyone here is trained in self-defense and combat starting from when we are children. It is an important skill and my favorite hobby, one that I spend much of my time enjoying."

He frowned. "Females, too?"

Faria reached for her glass, the liquid quickly turning to ice at her displeasure. She casually put it back on the table, hoping he hadn't seen. "I am not sure if you forgot, but this is a Queendom. All females, if they are physically and mentally capable, are encouraged to learn. All females know how to properly handle weapons and protect their bodies against thieves and predators. Some of our strongest females make up the majority of our armies. All females—elf, warlock, and human alike."

Faria felt a rush of emotion from those at the table around her. Without trying, she could scent their pride, their acceptance and their love from every angle. She smiled to herself. She knew they worshipped her as the source of this ridiculous Prophecy, but she wanted them to accept her as their leader. She felt a sense of gratitude for being given this opportunity to prove that she would always defend them—especially against arrogant males.

"I see." Darroc looked around the room at the hostile stares and proud smiles from every direction and wisely moved the conversation in a different direction. "And who do you train with?"

She kept her face free from emotion. She didn't know why, but she certainly didn't want Darroc knowing anything about Hunter. "Those who are my equals."

"Well, lucky for you, I am an excellent fighter. Come, I wish to see where you practice."

She couldn't think of a good excuse to not show him. She was supposed to give him a tour of the grounds anyway, so she placed her hand in his waiting one and prayed to the three goddesses that Hunter would not be there.

The practice arena was empty, except for several children who were working on target practice. Darroc paused for a moment to watch them. "Is that one warlock?" he asked, his face open in wonder.

"Yes, a warlock and human mix, I believe. He has been displaying natural warlock tendencies. He can heal small wounds."

"Healing?" Darroc asked, surprised. "Really? That is not something we have seen since…I can't recall. Healing was the queen's special gift, before she turned into a phoenix."

"Yes, it appears so. He spends time with our healers to help make elixirs and focus his powers."

"Hmm," Darroc replied. "This land suits my people well."

There was an awkward pause. Faria couldn't help but feel that Darroc wasn't entirely pleased at how his people thrived under her mother's care. "Let's leave them to it. Down here is where the weapons are kept."

"What is your specialty?" he asked, removing his overcoat. He perused the weapons on display, then pulled out a staff, testing its weight.

"All of these. I am partial to a bow and daggers, but I am well versed in everything here."

He tossed her the staff then chose another for himself. "Let's see what you got."

A slow smile crept on her face. She supposed she should have been worried. She didn't know his exact age but she was certain he was far older than her and he looked to be in excellent shape. However, she was trained by the best Anestra had to offer and she was confident in her abilities. Something about challenging him, proving to him that she was formidable called to her.

Cold wind whipped around them, but neither reacted to it. They circled each other, maintaining eye contact. Faria watched for any tells he displayed, anything to give away what he wanted to do. She decided not to wait for him to strike first so she veered left and struck toward his arm. He easily swatted her away as if she were a fly. He dove for the center which she blocked with ease. He struck out again for her legs, her shoulder, her back. Each time she jumped, flipped, or parried away. She did the same to him, going left before driving right, shoving the full weight of her body behind each attack. On it went. Neither showed signs of exhaustion.

Another breeze whipped past them. Faria inhaled the overwhelming scent of the ocean and spice and she knew with every molecule in her body that Hunter was nearby. She dared not look away, dared not give Darroc a reason to draw blood first. His eyes narrowed, his own nostrils flaring. Wanting to end this sooner rather than later, Faria jumped to the right then spun into his body, pressing against him, and shoved the staff up his chin. He blocked, but was too slow to prevent the staff from hitting his nose. Faria smelled the tang of blood and stepped away, smiling at her victory.

Inky blood oozed out of Darroc's nose. She watched as he snatched a cloth from his pocket to staunch the flow. The blood came away red. She thought she saw a look of disgust on his face but his features smoothed out. He bowed to her, maintaining eye contact.

"A worthy opponent, Princess," he said.

"Don't call me that," she replied automatically, then wished she'd bit her tongue. She looked around them, searching through the small crowd of people who had come to watch them spar. Her eyes drew to a spot in the shadows beneath the raised seating. She knew he was there. Knew he watched her. She looked back at Darroc who had a cat-like grin on his face.

"Apologies, Lady Faria. It appears that title triggers something in you."

He cocked his head, his eyes traveling toward Hunter's hiding spot. "Care to share the reason?"

"No," she said. She reached for his staff and returned them both to the rack. "Let's continue on."

He trailed behind her as she led him around the rest of the grounds, her mind always returning to the one she couldn't have. She tried to engage Darroc in conversation but she found that she just wasn't interested in what he had to say. She answered his questions on their armies, their trade routes, their economy without a second thought, though she was careful not to give too much information away. He avoided anything regarding the rumors about the warlock rebellion.

She tired of him by mid-afternoon and opted to take lunch alone in her rooms. He seemed displeased at that, but said nothing as Reed appeared to escort him to wherever he wished to go.

Faria had laid in bed the rest of the evening, trying desperately to think of topics of conversation or questions she could engage Darroc in. Though her birthday was the following day, she found she was no longer looking forward to the party and wanted nothing more than to hide in the Forest with the one person her body came alive for.

A dress arrived at her door courtesy of Faline. She listened only long enough to learn that Darroc had a matching set before she nodded and closed the door.

She lay back down and was thankful when sleep finally came to claim her.

EIGHTEEN

NELLIE

Nellie loved going to the circus as a kid. Watching the clowns with their silly makeup perform tricks delighted her as a child, as did eating as much cotton candy as her mother would allow. One of Nellie's last memories of her mother before she passed away was of them at the circus, sharing peanuts and reminiscing over their life on the road. They had no one to answer to—simply traveled, learned, and explored how they saw fit. The sight of the multitude of tents around the Forest of the Dawn struck a chord of longing in her.

Deep purple and silver lined apparitions glinted in the setting sun and huge bonfires struck up, flames of brilliant red and orange casting shadows on the guests' faces. Everyone was dressed to impress, wearing fine silk or velvet garments, thick cloaks wrapped around them in the frigid air.

Cinnamon and spice mingled with the scent of chocolate and roasted nuts, while music weaved hypnotically through the air. Faria's eighteenth birthday celebration was well underway and guests from the furthest reaches of Anestra were there to celebrate their future queen.

Nellie felt her hips sway to the rhythmic beating of drums, so similar to the Celtic music she had once loved. Before giving in to the full temptation of losing herself to the music, she wandered over to the nearest fire where a crowd gathered, certain she would find Faria.

Her mouth dropped, aghast at what her brain tried to process. Faria was linked arm in arm with Darroc, wearing matching outfits of deep green silk. Not only were they prancing around in what appeared to be a coming out gesture, but the symbolism of the pair meant they were a unit and should be seen as one. Nellie was horrified. Seeing them as a couple made everything much more real, and the danger more urgent than before. She had to find a way to get Faria alone. The only saving grace was that Faria looked as uncomfortable as Nellie felt.

Nellie caught Faria's eye and cocked her head toward the trees, indicating she wanted to speak to her, but Faria rolled her eyes and shrugged. She would never be able to get away from the crowd. Nellie understood. She wanted to be fair and give all a chance to speak to her. She would just have to follow Faria around wherever she went.

The crowds parted as Faria and Darroc made their way into the tent nearest them. They watched for a few minutes as illusionists manipulated the air around them, creating snow from nothing. A winter wonderland appeared for guests to explore, complete with an ice rink.

To Nellie's amusement, Faria seemed to pass on the fortune teller's tent. She probably had quite enough of people telling her what her future looked like. The couple paused next to another bonfire, one in the middle of the carnival, where people of all races were dancing a popular jig. Onlookers clapped and cheered on the dancers, the feeling of merriment affecting all who watched. Nellie kept her eye on Darroc and got a sense of satisfaction when Faria turned down a dance with him.

As she turned to leave, Nellie watched Darroc grab Faria and say something in her ear. Faria's smile dropped from her face. The bonfire next to them flared brilliantly in response before she plastered a smile on her face and walked away, Darroc trailing close behind her.

How dare he touch her like that? Nellie was furious. Just as she was about to follow, a hand clasped on her shoulder, keeping her in place. She turned and looked up into the eyes of Hunter, whose face reflected the same fury she felt. He shook his head and motioned to the shadow of one of the tents.

"What the hell, Hunter?" Nellie whispered at him. "I didn't think you'd be back so soon."

"Now is not the time to interfere," he said quietly, never taking his eyes off Faria and Darroc's retreating backs.

"Did you see the way he touched her? Now is definitely the time." Nellie tried to leave again but was pulled back. She gritted her teeth at him.

"Damn it, Nellie," Hunter swore. She was taken aback. He never lost his temper and she appreciated the fierceness, although she wished it wasn't directed at her. "Yes, I saw it. I am forbidden to follow, and I will not have him discover who or what you are. It isn't time, yet."

Nellie understood now why Faria was angry about all the rules surrounding her. "You are *forbidden?*" she said. "Are you not supposed to be her protector? He hurt her. She needs protecting. Now get a move on it."

"She can and will hold her own against him and as much as I hate it, he cannot discover me, either." Hunter quieted as someone walked over.

"Hey, Nells," Reed said. "What are you doing over here all alone?"

"I'm not alone," Nellie said, confused. She cut her eyes to Hunter who shook his head once. "I mean, I'm surrounded by all this magic! It's overwhelming for a young human such as myself and I just needed a moment."

"Well, if you want a dance later, let me know!" Reed said, walking toward a waiting Wilhelm. She watched as they linked arms and continued enjoying the celebration. Nellie felt a familiar pang in her stomach. She was happy to see other couples, but she wished she could be in her own body dancing with Endo again.

"They can't see me," Hunter said. "I am to remain hidden tonight."

Again, she wondered what he was and what his abilities were. "Well, what are you waiting for? Hide me too and let's see what they're talking about."

Hunter bit his cheek, debating the risk, but nodded his head and gently touched her shoulder. A cooling sensation rippled over her, and she felt light as air. She looked down and only saw the barest glimmer of her body. *Awesome.*

They walked over to Faria and Darroc, hidden in the shadows of the Forest. In front of them lay the inky stain on the land, the dark magic a permanent fixture. They arrived just in time to hear Faria ream Darroc a new one.

"You are never to touch me or grab me like that again," she hissed at him. "You may be here because of an arrangement that—let me remind you—I never agreed to, but that is not how we do it here. You do not touch without permission. I don't even want you to breathe near me without my permission. Do you understand?"

Lightning crackled overhead. Nellie could hear the shocked murmurs of the guests at the party. Hunter tensed beside her.

"Beautiful," Darroc whispered, admiring Faria's display of magic. "You're right. It has been a long time since I found myself in the presence of such a beautiful female, and you turning me down bruised my ego a bit. I am sorry that I embarrassed you."

"Flattery does nothing for me." She rubbed her hands down the front of her silk skirts then looked down. "I might know a way you can start to make it up to me."

"Anything, lady. Ask and it is yours." Darroc stood with his arms crossed over his chest, and waited for her request. Such a human gesture, Nellie thought.

Hunter stilled next to her, as if he already anticipated what Faria was going to say. "I want you to help me learn this magic." Faria pointed to the ground.

Darroc shifted violet eyes down and back again, saying nothing.

"It calls to me. I feel like I know this. Whatever it is, I want to learn it and then I can figure out a way to stop it. It's destroying the land. We won't be able to plant next year if we can't stop the spread. The dark magic is a thick cloud over everything. Surely you feel it."

Darroc nodded slowly, arms still crossed. "Yes, I can feel it. It is, however, very dark magic. What makes you think I can teach you such a thing? And more than that, you are an elf. You do not have the capacity for wielding magic the way warlocks do."

Faria jutted her chin out and mirrored his stance. "Well, I say I do. Can you help me or not?"

Darroc blinked once, twice. "Yes," he said. "But I must warn you, this is not something I know. I can teach you how I would try to read such a thing but I cannot teach you how to use it."

"Sounds like a starting point. Tomorrow." Faria began the walk back to her party and Nellie and Hunter waited a moment before following, making sure to keep their distance. "Another thing, Darroc. Why are our warlocks running away from you? I would think any warlock not part of this rebellion would be happy to see you. To have leadership."

"I suspect they are suspicious of someone coming forward after so long," he said carefully. "I am certain they will warm up to me, soon."

Faria said nothing after that, and though she kept at least a foot of distance between her and Darroc, they still went back to the party together.

Nellie stopped moving and glanced at Hunter. He gripped a dagger in his left hand, knuckles white against the leather handle, as if he were contemplating assassinating the warlock prince. He looked furious, and mighty. Nellie could see the warrior in him.

"Hey, Rambo," Nellie said. "You thinking of starting something?"

Hunter let out a harsh breath before replacing his weapon. "This is not good. She mentioned to me in the past that the magic called to her, but she hadn't bought it up in so long. I thought she got over it."

"Well, she didn't, Einstein. What will it mean if she reads the dark magic? How can she even do that?" Nellie paced in a small circle, the stress building in her tiny frame. She could only imagine how powerful Faria was without the taint of dark magic, let alone if she embraced it somehow.

"I do not know. I was given minimal information and I am to remain hidden from her for the duration of Darroc's stay. You heard the queen. I'm not to speak with her." His jaw clicked, frustration evident in the way his body shook. He ran his fingers through his hair and muttered to himself in another language.

"Why? When will you explain what you are, what your role is?"

"Because if she sees me, she might get a funny idea in her head." Hunter answered her first question but ignored the other.

"Like what?"

His face turned grim. "Changing fate."

KEEPING AN EYE ON DARROC became a full-time job. Nellie tried her damnedest to stay out of his way for fear of him discovering what she really was. It miffed her that nothing strange happened. He kept to his rooms when he wasn't with Faria. A week ago, she'd seen him ride into town, with the human Callum at his side—the one who Crispin had threatened into service. She thought it entirely too coincidental that Callum now spent time with Darroc.

Anytime Darroc went into Athinia, he was barely gone for more than a few hours and always returned with what appeared to be regular goods: new clothes, books, random trinkets. By outside standards, he was a normal, wealthy prince, enjoying the pleasures Athinia had to offer.

And yet...

Not once had he tried to contact the rebel warlocks, from what Nellie could tell, nor did he speak to any warlocks left at *Mentage*. It was almost suspicious how completely *unsuspicious* he was.

Nellie sighed, feeling the weight of the world pressing in on her chest. She had to do something, had to warn Faria that Darroc was who they had come to fear these past few months. She was going to do it. Right now. Before he taught her to read that dark magic.

She raced out of bed and was just about to leave her suite when the door flew open in a gust of wind.

"Cheese and crackers, Faline!" Nellie clutched at her chest, waiting for her heart to stabilize. She took in her adoptive mother, her frazzled hair, the bags under her eyes. Her rumpled clothes accentuated her exhaustion. It looked like she went a round with a wild boar, and lost. "Why do you look so crazed?"

"I have just been to see the queen, and I bring grave news."

Nellie's stomach coiled. What could be graver than Faria being forced to bond with Darroc for life?

"I haven't slept in a few days," Faline said. It explained why Nellie hadn't seen her for nearly a week since she'd told her about Callum and Darroc. "Now that we are aware of this evil thing Faria is to meld with, I've been trying to narrow down the correct prophecy we needed to focus on, so I decided to meet with old friends of mine from The Council."

"The Council!" Nellie gasped. The Council was an ancient sect of elves who had guarded sensitive information for generations. They were legends. Impossible to find except for those who were in the know. Nellie was awed that Faline was *in the know.*

"The Council long held the belief that Faria was important but perhaps not actually the Chosen. I told Amira what The Council and I had discussed—that we narrowed the prophecies down to what we believe to be the right one. The queen is inclined to agree." Faline pulled an old piece of parchment out of her bag, the words hardly legible for being so faded. "You must show this to Faria."

"What does it say?" Nellie reached for the parchment but Faline held it just out of her reach.

"To put it in the barest terms, Faria and Darroc will have a child. That child is actually the Chosen and will need to be killed by Faria's hand in order to avoid the Final Battle."

Nellie blinked, stunned. If they thought that killing Darroc's child would stop the Final Battle…She let out a bark of laughter. "Nice one, Faline. There are way too many Harry Potter vibes for me."

"This is no joke." Faline looked at Nellie as though she were the one gone crazy. "You must do more than give this to her. You must also tell her what you really are."

"Are you crazy?" Nellie shouted. "She spends all her time with that evil bastard. There is no way."

"Your queen demands it of you. She withheld information from Faria for far too long and it's time that she knew."

Cold dread settled into Nellie's bones. "That could be my death sentence! Not to mention the betrayal she is going to feel after realizing everyone she cared about has been lying to her for months. Or in my case—years!"

"There's more." Faline's eyes bore into her.

Nellie shook her head, disbelief marring her face. "How could there possibly be more than telling Faria that the key to breaking the Prophecy—and defeating Darroc, whom I'm pretty sure she still doesn't suspect—is to kill her future child? What more could there be than the possibility of my murder at revealing who I really am?"

"The queen requests that you join her Royal Guard."

She was getting punked, she knew it. Nellie looked around them, searching for a hidden camera. Hysterical laughter bubbled out of her. She clutched at her stomach, tears streaming down her face. It was too much. It was all too much.

"Everyone thinks I'm a child," Nellie said clutching her stomach, finally gaining control. "And I'm human. What am I supposed to do in an *Elven* Royal Guard?"

"You are a *shapeshifter*, not human. And as I just said, you will tell Faria what you are. And then you will tell Wilhelm and Reed. And Enis. And Johanna. You are to tell no one else."

"No." She would sooner risk walking through the Gate of All Realms and landing on a fire world than expose her secret to so many.

"You will do so and then whatever else your queen asks of you." Faline's face was severe, and Nellie knew that there was nothing she could do to change her mind. "You are her secret weapon."

"Oh, now I'm a secret weapon?" Nellie was overwhelmed. She felt tears of stress and frustration spring to her eyes, and she had the sudden longing for her mother. "I am no weapon! I'm just...me."

"You are a rare, powerful shapeshifter!"

"Hardly," Nelly scoffed. "Rare? Sure, I guess. Powerful? Not a chance."

"Enough, there is no time for this. Find the Captains of the Guard. Show your true self, explain how you can be of use. Make no mention of the true Prophecy."

"Faline—"

"Do not argue with me, girl. War is coming. Faria is in grave danger as are the rest of us. It is time for action."

"Hunter should know about this." She was grasping at straws, looking for any reason to put off the inevitable. "He should be here."

"Hunter does not matter in the end. Faria will end up with Darroc. She will bear his child and if that scroll you carry is correct, Faria must kill her newborn girl. *That* is what matters, or else we are looking at the End of Times. For *everyone*, including your Earth and your precious mate."

Nellie's heart stuttered. "That was low for you, Faline. Do not speak of him."

"Then do not disobey me. Go! Now!" Nellie tripped over her feet as Faline pushed her out of their room. She needed to gather her wits, needed anything to help her comprehend all the information thrust upon her.

Nellie raced down to the barracks of *Mentage*. Though it was late in the evening, there were still few people practicing with each other. It had been a few months since she trained, caught up as she was in figuring out the Prophecy or else going undercover for the queen.

Nellie missed seeing Endo in the practice arena every day. Faline had insisted she train with the other children when she first arrived on Earth. She had been clumsy; she had never tried to use weapons while disguised in her smaller body. Endo led the class of children, correcting their form and encouraging them when they didn't get something quite right. He was sweet, and kind, and those blue eyes of his were the same shade as her mate back on Earth. Seeing Endo was hell, both their demeanors being so similar, but it was nothing compared to knowing that she would never see her mate again. Nellie purposely messed up each week just to have an excuse to be back there, to be near the one who reminded her so much of what she lost. It was torture, but it was all she had.

Now it was torture knowing that Endo was on the wrong side of the battle lines and it was a very real possibility she would never get the chance to tell him how she felt.

Nellie strode across the sandy pit toward the huts at the outer rim of the barracks. That was where Wilhelm and Reed stayed along with the others in the Royal Guard. All four captains stood outside Wil and Reed's hut, which was unusual. Normally at least one of them was by the queen's side. Now, they huddled, rubbing their hands in the cold winter air.

"Hi, Nells," Reed called to her. His leather armor looked new, and it groaned as he raised his arm in salute. "We don't really have time to play tonight. We have orders."

Nellie approached them, not stopping until she was close enough to whisper, taking care not to be overheard by anyone practicing in the pit.

"I am the orders." Nellie tried and failed to smile. "We must go inside, quickly."

Confusion crossed each of their faces, but they didn't hesitate when Wilhelm opened the door. They walked in single file, and Nellie had the overwhelming feeling that she was marching to her own funeral.

The hut was one large room, with stone walls and a dirt floor. There was one window in the front and back, just enough to let light in. The furnishings were bare, only a bed and table with chairs. The fire was low and easily kept the room warm. There was a series of mirrors set up around the windows, but Nellie couldn't gather its purpose without inspecting it further.

And there was no time for that.

She drew a breath and braced herself for what was undoubtedly going to be a bad reaction.

"The queen wants me to inform you that I am to be your secret weapon."

The sound of the crackling fire filled the room.

"Ha," Enis barked out, her canines glinting off the firelight. Enis was small, almost the same size as Nellie in her current form. Bright brown eyes narrowed as she looked at her. "That's funny, Nellie." Something about the way she said it made Nellie feel she didn't find it funny at all.

"Maybe she isn't joking," Johanna said. Her quiet demeanor reflected her voice, her mouth drawn in a tight line. Nellie watched as Johanna's nostrils flared, taking in her scent for any lies. "I do not smell a lie on her. But there is deception."

Enis ripped her dagger from her belt and was behind Nellie within a matter of seconds, the point at her jugular. Wilhelm and Reed stepped closer to her but said nothing. Johanna stepped forward.

"Remove your weapon, Enis," Johanna commanded. Enis complied but did not step away.

Johanna continued scenting her, her eyes narrowed in concentration.

"What is this secret weapon?"

"Come on, Jo," Reed said. "She's a little girl. A human. She cannot be what we have been waiting for." Nellie tried not to be offended but they were right. It was the exact reason she had just given to Faline.

Wilhelm spoke up, his deep voice reverberating in the tiny space. "I don't know…no one knew that we were waiting for word from the queen. It is rare that we are all together. And, no one besides us, the queen and the king know of there even being a secret weapon. Yet, here she is."

He knelt in front of Nellie and placed a comforting hand on her shoulder. His eyes were friendly, though his whole body was taut, ready to spring into action at the first sign of trouble. "Go on, Nellie. Tell us why you are here."

Nellie's heart raced and sweat tickled beneath her armpits. She tried to stamp down on her fear and fill herself with the confidence she needed. There would be no turning back, no way to hide herself after five long years of living in her disguise. Her kind used to be crucified here, so much so that they were now an urban legend to the elves. Doing this might ensure her true death.

But the queen knew what Nellie, and it was the queen Nellie now served. She would do anything to help save Faria.

"I, um, need a bit of space."

As one, they each shifted back a step, leaving her just enough room to change into herself.

Her real self.

"Please, after you see what I am about to do, don't kill me."

"We only kill on the queen's orders," Enis said.

Comforting.

Nellie took a deep breath and concentrated, letting the oxygen renew her. As she pictured her real self in her mind, her skin turned darker, her frame grew almost a foot taller, her curves filled in. Her hair changed from straw to dark with tight curls. She felt the ripple of electricity on her skin as her molecules moved. She slowed the process to not freak them out, so they saw the hair sprouting from her skull and her eyes changing color. She looked down at herself and watched as freckles appeared all over her arms and knew they were on her face as well.

Nellie breathed easier from being in her normal body and relished the strength of her returning muscles.

"*Goddesses above,*" Reed whispered.

Nellie looked at the other three. Their expressions were unreadable. "I'm a shifter," she said into the silence.

"Obviously," Enis said through gritted teeth.

"Nellie," Wilhelm said, taking her in from head to toe. "You…are not a thirteen-year-old."

"Thank you for noticing," Nellie said, rolling her eyes.

"Where are you from?" Reed said, the amazement showing on his face. "How are you here? How do you exist?"

"None of that matters," Johanna said before she could answer. "Do you see what is before us?" She circled around Nellie, taking her in with shrewd calculation. "We have a shifter, and not just one that turns into an animal. She can masquerade as another. Our queen was right to keep you hidden."

"Yeah, I mean, I didn't know she realized what I was until very recently and anyway, I don't know how I can be useful to you all preventing *arma-freaking-geddon*, so if anyone wants to explain, that would be helpful."

"Do you know how rare you are?" Johanna asked.

"Because I can change into whatever I want? Not exactly." Nellie scratched her arm feeling awkward with all the attention. "I only shifted a few times before my clan leader banished me. No one outside my clan knew what I could do. They feared me but I never understood why." That was a sore spot she'd never gotten over. Why was she hated so much? "I don't know how many more like me there are or were, only that normally shifters can shift into one thing, but I can shift into anything."

"There are none other like you," Enis said, shaking her head. "My grandmother was a keeper of legends and aided The Council. She trained Faline to be a keeper, among other things. I'm surprised she didn't tell you."

"Well. We don't exactly sit around talking about what I am, considering the last known shifter in Anestra was crucified." It irked her that they knew more about herself than she did.

"Since you can change into anything—animal or not—you are perfectly designed to infiltrate the enemy," Enis said.

"I will not go near Darroc. He'll catch on to what I am in a heartbeat! No. No way."

"Not him," Wilhelm said. "The others. You can be whoever you want and listen in on them. Figure out what their plans for *Mentage* are and what Darroc ultimately wants with Faria."

"Been there, done that, and I was almost caught! Crispin put a tracking spell on me that the healers were able to break just the other day." She didn't mention that Endo basically knew who and what she was. She was still holding out hope that he would come back to the right side.

Enis grinned at her, but if her glinting canines were meant to put Nellie at ease, they were having the opposite effect. "The queen will demand it of you, anyway. That's why she brought you to us. So we would know to look out for you."

"Faria must be protected at all costs," Reed said, echoing the Queen's foreboding words. "So we will do what we can, regardless of the risk to us. If you are what it takes to keep her protected at all costs, then you *will* do as the queen says."

Nellie let out a long-suffering sigh. "Why couldn't I just be exiled in peace?"

"We do not have time for this banter," Johanna said. "We must strategize now that we know what the queen desires. There is no time to lose. The bonding ceremony will be upon us before we know it."

"Bonding ceremony?" Nellie shouted. "Hell, no. No way is Faria binding herself to that brute. She belongs with Hunter, anyway."

"Hunter?" Enis said. "A human? Impossible." Reed and Wil echoed her sentiments.

So, they don't know that Hunter is different. Interesting.

"We are not here to debate who Princess Faria should be with," Johanna said. "It is time to plan."

They spent the next few hours figuring out the best way to infiltrate the rebels and who she should try to speak to. Nellie already knew it would be Endo. They thought about the benefits of disguising herself as a warlock traveling from far away, ready to fight for the cause. She insisted, however, on going in as herself. She didn't explain it was because she had shared a moment with Endo. Instead, she explained that Endo would be more responsive to a newcomer to Anestra rather than a random warlock turning up out of the blue.

It was late before they finished their plan. Since it seemed that the bonding ceremony would happen in the next week, Nellie would go into Athinia the day before and see if she could find Endo. She was positive he would be there.

She changed back into her thirteen-year-old self before leaving the Captains of the Guard, slipping into the cover of darkness. It had been freeing to be back in her original form for the past few hours, both mentally and physically. Now this younger body felt like a prison.

It was late enough that Faria should have been back in her chambers. Having finished the first of Faline's orders, Nellie steeled herself to finish what she had to do.

She was more terrified than when she'd been banished through the Gate of All Realms. What if Faria was scared of her? What if she felt betrayed? She loved Faria as a sister but to keep something like this from her for years...Faria could be hot-headed and stubborn and might not warm up to the real Nellie right away, if at all. She might never trust her again. Faria and Faline were her family, and Nellie didn't know what she would do if she lost them.

Passing the stables lining the Forest, Nellie was distracted by torchlight flickering in one of the stalls. It was not unusual to find light there, as riders came and went as they pleased, but what was unusual was who she saw there, half hidden in the shadows.

Callum. She hadn't seen him since he had ridden with Darroc into

Athinia a week ago. He brushed the coat of a giant, white stallion that she recognized as belonging to the warlock prince.

Curious, Nellie crept closer to him. His eyes were dark and glazed over as he repeatedly brushed. The methodical *schooooooooop* of the brush and the horse's soft *huff* creeped the hell out of Nellie. No other part of Callum moved, as if he were a reanimated corpse. She wasn't even sure he was breathing.

"Callum," Nellie called out. "What are you doing up so late?"

No response. He didn't look in Nellie's direction or stop what he was doing. He didn't even blink.

Disturbing.

"Callum!" she called again. Still nothing, only his robotic movements. A chill passed over her. What the heck did Darroc do to him?

Nellie backed away and ran across the dark fields, wanting to get as far from there as possible. She had to tell Faline, the queen. Anyone. She shifted into an owl. A screech of pain echoed into the night as her bones shrank and reform quicker than she was used to. She soared into the sky, veering east to make it back inside *Mentage* quicker.

A glowing blue light far below caught her attention before she could fly away.

It was quiet in the fields. There were a few guards patrolling, but none were magic users. There should not be a light where Nellie was looking and yet, there it was. She flew slowly toward it, trying to make out where it was coming from. She froze at what she saw below her.

Faria. The blue light was coming from Faria. But she was not a magic user! Not in the warlock way. Not in the way that would allow her to emit a controlled light from her hands. But there she was, a glow emanating from her. It flickered across her across her face, a look of amazement reflected in that eerie light. Standing next to her hungrily watching her was Darroc. Then Nellie realized where they were.

In the dead zone. On the cursed land.

Panic rose in Nellie as she fought to keep flight. This was worse than anyone thought. Darroc was teaching her dark magic. Was she brainwashed like Callum, too? Was that why the bonding ceremony was happening sooner?

This is all my fault. Even though Queen Amira insisted the two be bonded, she also said Faria must be protected and Nellie hadn't tried hard enough to get to her. She'd spent too much time reading useless prophecies instead of keeping Faria informed. She shouldn't have kept any secrets from her at all. Everything she had done pushed her to this.

She watched the glow die from Faria's hands. The princess accepted a drink from Darroc and a few moments later they began their walk back toward *Mentage*. After a moment, Darroc broke off and went to the stables, to Callum. Nellie desperately wanted to follow him, but Faria was finally alone and it was her only chance to talk to her.

Nellie landed on the ground far enough away that no one would see, and changed back into her thirteen-year-old body, calling out to Faria when the exhausting transformation was complete.

"Faria!" she yelled into the still night.

"Nellie?" Faria turned around, the moon giving off just enough light to see the guilt on her face. "What are you doing out here?"

"Me?" Nellie threw her arms out, indicating the space behind her.

"What are you doing out here? What did I just see?"

"It's okay, Nells. Darroc was teaching me how to read the magic in the ground." The excitement in Faria's voice slammed into her. She was too late.

"Excuse me?" Nellie tried to keep calm. She was sure there was a reasonable explanation.

There had better be.

"I discovered weeks ago that it was calling to me, that dead space, only I didn't know what to make of it. I knew that if I learned how to key onto its frequency that I could learn more of it. Who it came from. It could help us, I know it." She bit her lip and looked away. Nellie couldn't help but feel there was something more she wanted to say.

"You cannot be serious! Can't you see what he's doing to you?"

"First of all, that's none of your damn business. Secondly, Darroc wants to find out who did this just as much as we do. He's a warlock prince and he's powerful. He could help us!"

"I know you aren't that naïve. He is good looking, I'll give you that, but look past that! He is teaching you to read magic. Dark magic, Faria! You are the Chosen One filled with abilities that you haven't even mastered yet. Can you imagine what will happen if you let the darkness in? It will corrupt you!"

"Do not speak of things you don't know," Faria whispered furiously. "You are a child. You cannot possibly know or understand my responsibilities, what this means to me and my people. I will do what it takes to protect them."

"You are killing them! It's right in front of you and you can't even see.

I should have told you weeks ago and for that I accept blame, but you are feeding right into the very evil you want to 'protect' your people from. Have you not realized Darroc's connection to everything? You are the one who knows nothing. Does Hunter know what you are doing? I'm sure he'll feel really great knowing you're sleeping with—"

A slap echoed in the night sky. Nellie's face stung with the contact from Faria's hand.

"Oh, Nellie!" Faria gasped, horrified at what she did.

Nellie touched her face, felt the burn under her hand.

"You are a damned fool, Faria. You have no idea, *none*, of what everyone around you has been doing to try to protect you. You have no idea the risks I have been taking, the secrets I have been keeping. Well, now I know that all you care about is getting closer to the enemy and I can no longer trust you. If you want to go and get yourself killed then you deserve everything coming your way. You did this."

Nellie ran from her then, tears pouring down her face. Damn it all to hell. Maybe she overreacted, but she didn't care. Nellie had never felt so hurt by a loved one before. If Faria wanted to ruin them then who was she to stop her? Maybe it *was* Fate. Faria would bind herself to Darroc. She would bear his child, and everyone would likely die in the coming apocalypse. No one could change Fate and they were fools to try.

"Nellie!" Faria called to her in the distance. She could have caught up to her if she wanted to. She could have stopped Nellie from leaving.

But she didn't.

Nellie wanted to do what the queen said, but revealing herself was not an option, not anymore. Not now that Faria had been compromised.

Now that she had lost her.

Darroc would pay for what he had done. Nellie would likely get killed in the process and die some horrible, painful death but in the end, he would get what he deserved.

NINETEEN

FARIA

The darkness called to her, tempting her, filling her with its alluring persuasion. It would consume her, if she let it.

She never gave in.

Darroc made good on his promise to teach Faria how to read the dark magic in the ground, but she couldn't understand what it meant. She was right—her body did recognize it, but she still couldn't decipher its language.

She had to keep trying.

Maybe then she wouldn't have to marry Darroc for an alliance between their people, for surely that was the only reason her mother would pair the two of them together. To save her land. If she didn't do everything it took to save them then sacrificing what—and who—she really wanted would have been all for nothing.

Faria and Darroc were under the cover of darkness standing at the edge of the blackened ground as they had been for the past few days. It was late, later than she ever stayed out with Hunter and no one was around except for a few guards on patrol. He said it was best to read the magic when there weren't others there to distract her, and she had to agree. She at least didn't want to explain to anyone why she felt the need to be so close to such foul magic.

"Find the seed of power, that burning flame inside where your abilities manifest," Darroc said, staring at her eagerly. He had learned of her abilities through Callum, a human boy who often worked in the kitchens or stables at *Mentage*. Apparently, Callum had asked him what it was like to be so close to someone so powerful, and she felt she had no choice but to admit to having more abilities than the average elf. "Wait until you feel its boundaries and then take from it what you need."

"Is that how it is for warlocks? It isn't the same for elves." She dug deep inside looking for the kernel of magic that made her different.

"We are all cut from the same material from the beginning, and our endings are all the same. We are united in more than that way. Hold your hands over the ground, listen to what it is trying to tell you."

Faria did as he said, shuddering as the magic's oily foulness coated her insides. Whispers echoed in her mind, screams that seemed to never end, yet no matter how much it terrified her, she couldn't move her hands away.

If she got closer, reached deeper, Faria knew she could learn it. If she read what was there maybe she could get rid of it for good, restore the land and protect its future vitality. At the very least she could say she had done all she could to help her people. Desperation made her blood thrum as she searched in every hidden chamber inside herself.

"Open your eyes."

An eerie blue light emanated from Faria's hands, hovering just above the ground. "What is that?" she breathed.

"It is the magic you created from the well inside you," Darroc responded. His eyes bore into her, devouring her. She suddenly felt naked, exposed down to her core, and turned away from him. The intimacy he tried to share with her made her nauseous. She missed being alone with Hunter. He made her feel free. Now she was with the wrong male who made her feel trapped, on display for his pleasure.

"Impossible. Elves don't create magic the way warlocks do. They simply have it, the way they have blood and need oxygen to breathe."

"Indeed, they don't." Darroc's violet eyes shone against the light she provided. "What are you, then?"

"I am nothing." Faria shrugged. "Just Faria."

"I had heard whispers of you being the Chosen from the farthest reaches of Wendorre and beyond. I never really understood what made everyone so sure, until now."

It shouldn't have shocked Faria. Though they had not spoken about it, there would be no reason for him not to know that she was special. Hearing the words come from his mouth unnerved her. "Warlocks know of the Prophecy? I thought that was an elven thing."

Darroc slid closer to her, the glow from her orb stretching his features into something more sinister looking. "It's an 'everyone' thing. We have our own versions, of course. But I wondered what it was about you that made you the One. Looks like I have my answer."

"You have no answer," Faria said, shifting back a step. "I told you, there is nothing special about me."

"What else can you do? What other abilities do you have?"

His incessant pestering was starting to irritate Faria. He had been there little more than one week; that he thought she should confide in such a private thing was laughable. "Nothing."

"I can tell you are lying. You will need to be truthful with me if we are to spend our lives together."

She had the sudden urge to slap the smug smile off his face. "First of all, I have not agreed to bonding with you. Secondly, what I can or cannot do is not your business. Thirdly, I am nothing but elf so I suggest you back off before I decide to set you on fire." Sparks shot from her fingertips, emphasizing her threat. Seriously, the nerve of him. "And if you're so caught up in honesty, *Darroc*, then why don't you tell me why you haven't called your people to you? Where have you been all these years while we took care of them? Why hasn't Wendorre's power restored if you, a Royal, harness their power? What is it that you are hiding from me, huh?"

He didn't answer and instead removed a bottle of fermented rice drink. It was a warlock invention— or so he claimed, when he first shared it with her days ago—to help restore her energy after manipulating magic the way warlocks do. She choked back a gulp, though her energy levels felt fine, and chucked the bottle back at him.

The darkness thrummed as he stared at Faria. She felt it chipping away at her as if it were sentient and it wanted in. It almost begged her accept its emptiness, but she knew she would not. It felt as though the oil tried to sludge her veins and she had the impression Darroc knew more about the darkness than he led her to believe.

"You, my little *princess*, are fiery tonight, aren't you?" The blue light faded as he walked in circles around her. "We will be together; of that I am sure. Your mother and I have already decided when. Secondly, your abilities are very much my business and will be even more so once you bear my child. Thirdly, you cannot possibly begin to understand warlock politics, nor do I have the time to explain them to you right now." He turned on his heel and made his way in the direction of the stables. "I am off for a few days. We shall perform the ceremony when I return."

He strode away, leaving Faria feeling colder and emptier than ever.

The night sky pressed in on her. Her throat closed and the more she tried to breathe in air, to give her lungs the relief they needed, the harder it was to get her body to obey her. She pulled at her hair, walking in circles. She inhaled for five counts and exhaled slowly through her nose before she completely drowned in her feelings.

Outrage consumed her as once again Faria felt her life slip out of her control. Not only did she have to do the binding ceremony with someone she didn't love or even *like*, but she couldn't even choose when it was to happen? Thunder rumbled overhead and it was all she could do to hold the weather at bay. Seeking out her mother, no matter how late it was, was the only way to get answers.

How dare she! Faria couldn't be with who she wanted because of *rules*. She couldn't decide with whom she would bond with because of the *Fates*. Unbelievable. It was hard enough keeping her emotions in check so her abilities wouldn't cause an earthquake or something worse. If one more thing happened out of her control, she felt she might actually cleave the world in two.

She should have been relieved that she kept her powers in check when Nellie confronted her, but instead she felt hollow inside. When Nellie accused her of *sleeping* with the enemy and when she said she was a fool for what she was trying to do, red descended over her vision. Her palm still ached with the force of that slap. She couldn't control the anger she felt, no matter that Nellie was a young girl, her *sister* for goodness's sake. She'd taken the brunt of her frustrations out on her. For the loss of control she had in her life. As she watched Nellie run away from her, Faria knew something broke between them, perhaps beyond repair.

Shame burned through her as Faria entered the Spring Garden. It was a different atmosphere this late; various scents and phosphorescent lights around different shrubs and flowers shone where they were hidden in the daylight. Normally Faria would sit and bask in the flavors of the night, but she didn't deserve that pleasure now.

She stalked toward the fountain in the middle of the garden, intending to veer right toward her wing of *Mentage* when she felt eyes on her.

Seated under the stone phoenix sat the queen.

Faria's heart skipped a beat and her throat dried. She hadn't had time to decide if her mother was on her side or not, but she couldn't turn away from her now that she was spotted.

"Mother," Faria said, bowing her head. "I didn't expect to see you here this late."

"Where is our guest?"

"I don't know, he said he will return in a few days for our *ceremony*,"

Faria replied, staring her mother down in silent demand for an answer.

"Johanna is on duty tonight. She will follow him." Sweat glistened along the queen's brow though the air was crisp. "We need to talk."

"Am I finally going to get some answers?" Faria crossed her arms, preparing to defend herself from what her mother would say.

The queen seemed to wait, considering her words. "It is the greatest burden, to be queen," she said, dragging her fingers across the jade edge she sat upon. "It's one thing to know that you will become queen, but it is an entirely other thing to embrace the role."

Her mother shifted, sitting up straighter, and Faria did the same. Her mother never really spoke of her feelings and to do so now felt ominous and made her uneasy.

"There are things you must know and even more I cannot begin to explain to you." She held up her hand before Faria could protest. "Not because I don't want to, but because it is forbidden."

"Another rule that I have to just accept?" Faria couldn't keep the bitterness from her voice.

"Yes. I want to tell you what to expect from the trials once you are to become queen."

That was unexpected. The trials were what every queen must suffer through in order to prove their worthiness of running the Queendom. "Tell me of the trials? But you cannot! It's—"

"Against the rules?" She finished for her, raising a brow. "So, you'll only follow the rules that you want to follow? That will not make for a fair ruler."

"That isn't what I meant."

"Isn't it?" The queen sighed. "I do not have it in me to argue with you now and even if I did, there is no time. The trials. You are right in saying that I cannot tell you all of them, but I can tell you that at one point you will be shown the future."

"The future?" No one could know the future.

"I cannot tell you more." She adjusted the cloak wrapped around her. "The future is shown to all future queens. There is no way to change it, no way to know how that particular future will come to be. It just…is. Your strength and resolve to be leader and queen will be tested, as will your faith in all the goddesses above." She shook her head. "I accepted the crown knowing what would become of me, of *Mentage*, of all Anestra. Even you."

"So, you know how to stop this warlock rebellion?"

"I already put that in motion by summoning Darroc here."

"And bonding with him is the only way?" Faria felt any hope she might have had sputter from her.

The queen shrugged her shoulders. "I do not know. I could not see past the time that I am to Fade."

Faria was too angry to register anything other than she summoned Darroc on purpose, knowing he would be a catalyst of some sort. "You are using me, Mother. You are using me to start this war."

"No, I am taking the offensive. Bring evil here, watch what he does, learn the enemy."

"So, you admit that he is definitely an enemy?" Faria asked through gritted teeth. "I am not a battle strategy! I am your daughter."

"Please understand, Faria. I have tried to do what was best for you."

"How? There is war on our doorstep, and you have hardly prepared me for it. I have these abilities…this power I feel inside me. You knew I was the Chosen and didn't tell me what that meant. Why?"

"If you had listened to Faline's lessons, you would be more prepared," the queen responded. "I have done all I can to protect you."

"But you're still making me go through with the ceremony? There is something off with him, Mother. I asked him to teach me to read the magic in the ground and—"

"You what?" The queen's face paled.

"It calls to me. I thought if I could somehow read it, then I can control it or learn who did it. But it was too creepy and the way he was looking at me…I am not entirely sure he isn't a monster. Please, don't make me do this."

The queen reached her hand out and trailed her fingers along Faria's jaw. She stood. "My daughter, one day soon, you will understand all that I have done to try to protect you. Everything that was within my bounds without consequence. But hear me—the ceremony will happen. It is destined, just as surely as you are destined to save us. I cannot prevent this."

"Mother, please." Faria's voice broke. "Please don't make me do this."

But she walked away, without a backward glance. Faria had no Nellie, no Hunter, and now her own mother wasn't even on her side. Never in her life had she felt so alone.

TWENTY

NELLIE

The cobbled streets bustled with activity; shopkeepers and restaurants set up outdoor stalls to entice guests to spend a bit of coin, while horses clomped down the patchy dirt road. The spice of roasting food and manure perfumed the air. There were hundreds of all races bouncing from shop to shop, holding hand pies and fresh loaves of elven bread, bundled against the cold. Anestra hadn't seen this much activity since the queen's coronation decades ago, and Nellie hadn't seen this much life in Athinia since Faria's birthday. Even then, that was nothing compared to this.

The air was ripe with energy for tomorrow's festivities. Clay pots were decorated in striking silver and purple, the royals' colors, and the letters F and D were monogrammed on linens, tunics, and even dishes. Nellie felt like it was the British Royal Wedding all over again and kept wondering to herself when a news crew would pop out of the woodwork to interview the guests.

The smell of roasted and grilled meats reminded her how hungry she was. She couldn't remember the last time she'd had a meal, having spent the past few days reviewing her orders. The temptation of eating the savory spiced meat on a stick again was almost enough to distract her from her mission.

Though the various shop stalls called her name, particularly the iridescent silk scarves that reminded her of fine Asian silk, Nellie was on a time restraint. She wandered the streets as herself and though the tracking spell Crispin laid on her seemed to be gone, she still wasn't sure if he were hiding among the crowd. Even though there were dozens of soldiers and guards patrolling the town, Crispin still knew what Nellie looked like and could easily lay another on her without her knowing.

It was risky. Extremely risky.

Nellie hurried forward, tucking her warm fleece cloak tighter to her. She avoided eye contact of almost every vendor that surrounded her, determined to get her business over with.

Nellie's skin thrummed as she approached Taps, the tavern Johanna said was usually filled with warlocks. She felt certain that she would find Endo there, possibly with others who had turned against the queen.

The scent of various perfumes and body odor mixed with ripe air assaulted her nose and made Nellie's eyes water as she opened the door, escaping the winter chill behind her. She waited for the floating black spots in front of her eyes to recede as she adjusted to the darkened room.

A fire roared directly across from the door, accounting for most of the light in the tavern. Thick wood beams crossed over in high arches in the ceiling while grand iron chandeliers filled with lit candles hung down, and a thick oak bar took up the entire right side of the room. Sconces were lit every few feet along the perimeter, with darkened booths toward the back. The tavern was filled to the brim with visitors from all over; elves, humans, dwarves, even some who looked suspiciously like Fae, though they hadn't been seen in Anestra since the Great War a millennia ago. There were no bar stools available and most of the space was standing room only.

Nellie scanned the room for any sign of Endo, noting the undercover guards the king had ordered to the tavern. She took care not to look too long so as not to alert Endo to anything odd, should he see her. She almost gave up when she spotted his figure next to a group of other warlocks laughing over a pint.

Bingo.

She visually searched Endo for weapons, and okay, to check him out. He stood tall and his bright eyes glinted in the torch light. He wore a red tunic and worn leather pants and his dark shaggy hair hung just below his ears. When he looked her way, his eyes widened a fraction. She waved and scooted in between him and the bar, keeping her back to the wall so she could see the whole room. No sense in risking anyone sneaking up on her.

"What are you doing here?" Endo whispered in her ear. "We shouldn't be seen together."

"I know. Are Crispin and Smyth here?" She signaled to the barkeep for a shot of whatever was closest to her.

"No, but it is still a risk."

The barkeep laid out a glass and poured her a strong drink made of rye. She turned back to Endo. "I had to see you. The ceremony is tomorrow."

Endo's mouth drew tight. "I know what tomorrow is." He sighed. "I missed you."

Butterflies ate at her. "I've missed you too," she whispered. "But I need to know, Endo. I need to know what type of danger we are in."

Endo sipped his drink. She watched him swallow, her eyes lingering a moment too long on his exposed neck. She needed to get it together. "There is no danger to worry about tomorrow."

She leaned closer to him and breathed in his cool scent of wood spice and ale blended together. "What can you tell me?"

He tucked a loose curl behind her ear then trailed his fingers down her arm. Goosebumps erupted in their wake. He leaned in, his voice barely audible over the raucous sound of the bar. "There will be no war, as long as everything goes smoothly. Phase one begins tomorrow. I am not certain what that means, but there will be peace talks soon after, and with any luck we can return to Wendorre within the next ten months."

"Ten months? That's oddly specific."

"That's how long he'll need and we'll have time to gather our numbers as well. He has friends in other realms and he's been coordinating with them to make sure they don't come too soon."

"Ah," Nellie said, trying to keep the alarm out of her voice. "If there is no war then why is he gathering friends?"

Endo shrugged and plunked down his glass, getting ready to leave. "I imagine they're coming with us to Wendorre. Not sure, just know they'll be here in ten months."

"But what could possibly take ten months…." Nellie's voice trailed off. *No!* Her heart stopped then continued again.

"There will be no war. It will not come to that." She was anything but reassured by his words. "But, please, do not go looking for trouble. If he figures out what you are…"

"I know," Nellie said. "I'm being careful." She took one last look at him before she turned to leave. He grabbed her elbow, stopping her. His face was mere inches from hers, and he hesitated only a second before he placed the briefest of kisses on her lips.

It was the best three seconds of her life.

"It isn't too late to come back, Endo. I refuse to believe that you think he's here for the benefit of the warlocks. She is a benevolent queen. You can come back."

He shook his head. "Remember what I said."

Nellie ran out, afraid to spend a moment longer with him. She really couldn't risk anyone seeing the two of them together. Instead, she focused on the information she would bring back to the Royal Guard and the queen.

It was dusk when she found herself on the main road. She watched lanterns and flags sway in the breeze and lutes strum out into streets. Though it was freezing, most of Anestra's citizens had enough alcohol in them to keep them warm until the summer and hardly noticed when a heavy wind picked up.

Nellie passed the store vendors selling their wares, and this time the smell of the grilled meats turned her stomach sour. It was too much to process. Her feelings for Endo were complicated and she knew there was nothing she could do. If he didn't want to come back, if he didn't want to be with her, then she could not force him. Her insides were knotted and every breath felt like drowning.

She was halfway back to *Mentage* when she remembered what else Endo had revealed. Ten months, and it started tomorrow. There was only one reason that Nellie could think Darroc would wait ten months.

Nellie knew it was all part of the Prophecy, but it still made her blood run cold. She had no idea how she could protect Faria from that monster. How she could stop him from impregnating her. How she could stop his friends from other realms coming to help in their War. Who were those friends anyway?

Nellie wished she could call for back up, too.

The iron gate loomed ahead and Nellie found Enis waiting for her in the shadows. They entered through a secret entrance, careful to avoid being seen, just in case Darroc had spies they weren't aware of.

"Did you find anything out?" Enis said as they approached the Council Room. Johanna, Wilhelm and Reed were there as well. Nellie nodded her head, her curls bouncing into her eyes. She didn't want to say anything until they were safe in the room.

Reed knocked twice and heard a clear, "Enter," before opening the doors.

Queen Amira stood across the doorway, her back held straight though her eyebrows were furrowed with worry. She looked beautiful, Nellie thought, with her dark skin and long braids trailing down her back. She was dressed in leather riding pants and a dark shirt tucked in at the waist, accentuating her curves. She looked fierce in the firelight, and every bit of the queen Anestra needed. King Dennison sat next to her in his usual cloth tunic and dark pants, his hair braided as well. The firelight reflected off his pale skin, making his features seem sharper than normal. There was no hint of his usual smile on his face.

"It begins tomorrow," Nellie said without preamble. "After the bonding ceremony. Endo did not say what it was. I'm not sure he knows, he just said he knows it as phase one."

"So soon," the king gasped, gripping the arm of his chair. He looked back at the queen. "Though we spent the past few weeks gathering intel, this is very short notice to prepare for this *Phase One*."

The queen stared at Nellie, her intelligent eyes missing nothing. "What else?" she asked.

Nellie took a deep breath. "In ten months, he will make his move." She looked deep in the queen's eyes, willing her to understand what she didn't want to say. "In ten months, his plan will be ready. And friends from other realms will join him to start the war."

"Ten months?" Wilhelm said. "That's oddly specific."

Nellie didn't look into the faces of the other females, but it seemed the queen had caught on to what she was saying, as well as the king.

"No," the king said. "We will stop it."

Queen Amira glanced at her husband. "We cannot. This is Fate. This is how it must happen."

"Um, pardon, Your Majesty," said Reed. "What is the significance of ten months? We should be happy we have more time to call more forces to us, shouldn't we?"

It was Johanna that responded. "Faria will give birth in ten months. That is why he is waiting. To guarantee his child. Then he will attack and most likely leave with her."

The fire crackled in the silence. As the breaking of logs burned to ashes, so too did Nellie's resolve. Despite the warmth from the flames, the room felt frozen. No one dared to breathe.

Nellie couldn't take it anymore and was about to break the silence when a deep gong sounded within the Council Room. Immediately, the Royal Guard had their weapons out, and the king went to stand by them as their leader, his own bow appearing out of nowhere.

Seconds passed but nothing happened. As one, the Royal Guard strode to the door to check the grounds, the king leading the way.

"What was that?" Nellie asked the queen. She felt as though her skin were crawling with ants.

"I do not know. It felt like a change not just in atmosphere, but into the fabric of life. I must think on what this means."

Nellie recognized the dismissal and left the room. She didn't know where to go from here. Faline was likely already in bed, Faria and her were no longer on speaking terms, and she had no idea how to summon Hunter to give him an update.

Queen Amira was wrong to make her Faria's secret weapon.

She felt completely useless. She still hadn't told Hunter what Faline's discovery about the Prophecy was and she felt it was important for him to know. How could she protect Faria? How could she protect her new home?

Where would she go once war came? Would she stay and fight? Would she even survive?

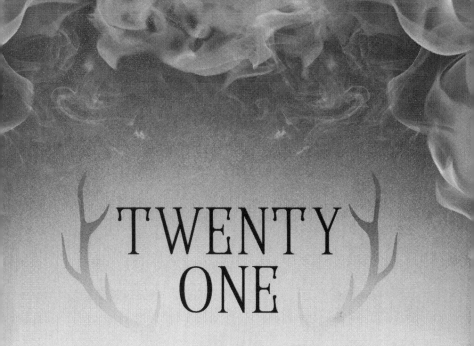

TWENTY ONE

FARIA

Stupid. Impossible. Completely unfair.

The *thunk* of weapons reverberated as Faria continued chucking one after another at the surrounding trees. Scorched grass and dead flowers lay at her feet. Where once wildflowers bloomed in her wake, now was blackened earth.

Faria wiped the sweat dripping from her brow, tears falling despite her best efforts to keep them at bay. She had learned long ago that crying got her nowhere but now the tears felt cathartic. Foolish, still, but cathartic.

Stupid, stupid girl.

Though she knew she would complete a bonding ceremony one day,

Faria had never dwelled on it much before, and now that it was upon her, she just couldn't grasp it. She felt as though her life was a marionette, the strings pulled by an almighty puppeteer; that she was watching the heartbreak of her life happen to someone that wasn't her. Somewhere deep down she had hoped to find her true mate, however rare, and now it wouldn't matter.

She no longer had Nellie. She no longer had Hunter. She no longer had her mother.

The entirety of her life was spinning out of control and she cursed the forces pulling her strings. It was the Fates. It was the Prophecy. It was the impending war. It was the stupid, impossible male she couldn't stop thinking about though she hadn't spoken to him in weeks.

She screamed at the sky, arms out, begging her frustration to leave her. Watching the birds take flight in fear gave her small satisfaction. At least she controlled something.

Storm clouds rolled into the night, covering the shine of the moon in the meadow. Lightning streaked, brightening the Forest in short bursts. Her emotions were tumultuous; she felt she could flood the continent with a single thought.

If only she could run away. To just leave, start over somewhere else where they didn't know her name. Forget that she was a princess. Forget that her people might die depending on her next move. Forget that she would never have a life filled with love, only settled acceptance.

But she would never abandon her duty or her people, especially not with an impending war, and especially not while Darroc wormed his way into *Mentage*, learning its secrets. She would never abandon her people to him.

Faria glanced around the meadow. It was where she had practiced with Hunter every day for two months. The one where he had let down his guard and made her feel that she was more than what her birthright told her. Being there, away from Darroc, allowed her to grieve and take a moment to feel sorry for herself, to properly break down before she had to build a wall for tomorrow. A fortress to protect her mind and her heart.

A rustle of brush stilled her breath, along with a breeze carrying with it the all too familiar scent of earth and spice and everything she longed for in this life and the next. Her stomach bottomed out while her heart beat double time. She swallowed, trying to rid her throat of the sand that had lodged itself there. After weeks of not seeing him, Faria dared not hope he was there now, but it was impossible not to recognize the scent that called to her. The one she knew breathed new life into her.

"Lady Faria." His velvet voice drifted over to her, the weird distortion of the meadow making it seem as though he spoke in her ear, its caress sending shivers down her neck. Faria clenched her fists, steeling herself before she looked over her shoulder. Her heart forgot how to beat.

Faria scoffed at his attempt at being formal again. The last time she'd seen him, he'd thrown her against a tree, grinding into her, demanding she submit to him. Now he seemed to think that formality would draw some kind of line. As if a line hadn't already been crossed. It was offensive.

Breathing was near impossible with how much she longed to foolishly hurl herself in his arms. Then anger took over—anger at seeing him now, after he had so cruelly reminded her that he would never be an option for her. She was not a pathetic girl pining over a silly crush. She was a queen.

She flung out a hand toward him, bending the air to her will as she threw a punch in his direction. If it were anyone else, it would have knocked them off their feet, but he was not anyone else. He deflected her attack as easily as swatting a fly.

Hunter stepped out from the shadows and despite her rage, she took an infuriating moment to admire him. He seemed ready for battle in black leather armor, weapons glinting from pockets both seen and unseen. His skin was golden even in the cloudy night, and his green eyes were fiercely luminescent. His presence was massive, as if he took up twice the number of molecules necessary, demanding more energy and space than the average male.

And he was anything but average.

Stupid, stupid girl.

"What are you doing here, Hunter?" She turned away, resuming her attack on the trees. She didn't trust what she would do if she kept looking at him.

"I felt your distress." She sensed him inching closer as if she were a bomb about to explode. Good. He should be worried.

"Oh really? Great. That's nice. I've been in distress for weeks and you weren't here. Suddenly you care?"

"There are rules—"

"Screw the damned rules!" Lightning struck the ground. "I am so tired of the rules! It is because of those *rules* that I have to bond with that monster tomorrow. That I need to make this desperate attempt to save my people because nothing else will work." Faria flung dagger after dagger at the trees beyond, watching as they turned to ice mid-air, each thunk accentuating her words.

Hunter's face paled and he took a step closer. "The ceremony is tomorrow?"

She didn't care that he was shaken with the news. The winter air was crisp and Faria could see her breath with each exhale, but all she felt was heat.

"As if you didn't know," she said, brandishing a sword from her back and resuming her assault on whatever nature surrounded her.

The silence from Hunter was enough. Even if he didn't know, he had nothing to say about it. Nothing that would matter. He reached for her as if to touch her. As if he could still. "I did not. I thought..."

"I don't care what you thought, and unless you have a way to get me out of this mess and still save my people, then please leave me alone."

"Faria." He walked closer, though she gave off enough energy to suck the life out of anything dumb enough to get in her way. "There are things I cannot tell you. I am forbidden to."

She clenched her teeth. "What a shocker."

"Please." He grabbed her hand and pried her fingers from around the hilt of the sword. The sound of it hitting the ground echoed in the silence. He pulled her to face him and like a fool, she let him.

Stupid, stupid girl.

The air in the Forest changed, becoming charged as it would before a lightning storm. The hair on the back of Faria's neck tingled and gooseflesh erupted down her arms. For the first time, Faria looked deep into his eyes and gasped at what she saw. Instead of the human he pretended to be, she saw him for what he really was.

His tan skin was deeper and inked markings she never saw before writhed along his skin, as if they were alive. His eyes shone with that almighty light and she could have sworn she saw his canines poke out from between his lips. It felt as if his essence expanded, taking up more space—no, demanding more from the space around him. She never saw anything more beautiful, or more frightening.

He stared at her and it felt as if he were laying her soul bare. Indeed, a breeze whispered against her, sending a sweet chill down her spine. It smelled of him, of ocean and spiced wood, but also of oranges and mountain air and fresh rain. He smelled of life while promising death. He was formidable in every sense of the word, and Faria had a feeling that whatever version he showed wasn't his entire true self, as if he were still muting parts of himself from her. That never ending humming in the glen felt more alive, as if the source of it were responding to the magic it felt before her.

Of the Val.

The fabled, mysterious, legendary, extinct Val, protectors of the Elven Royal Bloodline.

Faria realized the charged energy she felt was not an impending storm, but him. It was enough to weaken her knees. She felt her own energy respond, suffocating in the power of what he awoke inside of her. She took a moment to let it ripple over her skin.

"Um…Hunter?" Faria's voice cracked embarrassingly with awe, her anger long forgotten.

He stood, breathing heavily as if the transformation pained him.

The symphony of feeling that ran through her reminded her of the first time he had brought her to this part of the Forest, where she could smell things that weren't there, where her senses grew stronger and her abilities manifested. Everything he exuded was everything her body thrived on, what she needed to survive. How did she possibly breathe this long without him, what he was beside her?

His nostrils flared and she knew he felt something similar. He looked at her with more intensity and hunger than she had ever seen.

"What are you?" Faria whispered, daring to reach out a hand to touch his face, though she already knew.

"Something that should no longer exist." His voice was gruff, deeper, and more melodic, the baritone vibrating through her blood.

"You think?" she exclaimed. "Since when?" His skin was soft though she felt the beginning of stubble tickle her fingertips.

"Always."

"And you are showing me this now because…?" Because he would save her? Protect her? Because though she was in a world of trouble, he was here to save the day?

"It wasn't me. There is something happening tonight. The moon. The energy of your powers, something that forced the change in me. The Elders will not be pleased."

Faria had no idea how to respond to that.

She stared at him and marveled at his beauty, at his strength, at how there was an honest-to-goddess legend standing in front of her. It dawned on her that her life the past few months had been filling up with legends. First with her being the Chosen One, then with Darroc revealing himself to be warlock royalty, then Hunter being Val. Suddenly the answer she had been looking for became clear.

"You are the answer. You are Val! You can defeat the evil, save us, and the ceremony need never happen. You're my savior!"

"No." He shook his head once with a sharp cut to the right, negating her excitement.

"I hate to break it to you, but I'm pretty sure that's in your job description."

"No. I am not a warrior Val, not anymore. I no longer have access to the powers that once made me a formidable soldier. I am only Protector. I don't have the abilities to fight your evil. I am simply here to keep you alive. I cannot interfere with the Fates."

Again, with the Fates. "Well, based on what I'm seeing from you now, I'd like to think that it was the cursed Fates that allowed you to show yourself to me." Faria stared hard at him, willing him to agree with her. She needed him on her side but more than that, she just needed *him.* He wasn't human and it didn't escape her notice that they would make a great pairing, one that even the queen wouldn't be able to dispute.

"No, it is the magic. The Forest. The moon. Something calls to me."

He quieted, listening as Faria did the same. The Forest was alive around them. The trees, the water, the animals—everything was louder, clearer, singing as though in complete harmony with each other, with the earth they stood upon. It was peaceful and joyous and not at all like anything she had ever heard. As if the Forest were one sentient being and it reveled in his presence, in what was happening between them.

But then Faria remembered what *was* happening and despite what she felt, she still had a duty to fulfill tomorrow. There was no way around that.

The thought of Darroc touching her, of carrying on his wretched bloodline through her, was enough to make her want to vomit. Though her blood had responded to Darroc's power, her heart had not.

"What is it?" Hunter asked, sensing her change in emotion. He reached for the dagger now gripped in her hand, the handle starting to melt around her fingers. She hardly noticed.

"I can't bond with him. I can't have a child with him. My girl cannot have him as a father. The thought of him touching me..." She swallowed the bile that crept up her throat, unable to continue. She could not. She refused to play into what he wanted from her.

Hunter cupped her face, the gesture gentler than any she had experienced from him. He started to say something then changed his mind, his mouth clamped in a grim line.

"What?" Faria asked. She couldn't believe after weeks of missing him he was finally here with her, that she knew what he was. As Nellie would say, the Fates finally had thrown her a freaking bone and she wasn't going to let it go.

"I have come to tell you that I will be gone."

Well, that wasn't what she wanted to hear. "What?" her breath froze in her lungs.

"I am leaving, on a mission, Lady Faria. The Elders demand it. I have protected you. I have gotten you this far." He took a half step backward, placing his hands behind him. As if he were already ridding himself of her. As if it were so easy for him to do so.

"There was nothing to protect me from, then. Tomorrow and every day after is what I need protection from." She closed the space he tried to make between them, baring her teeth in his face.

"I have taught you everything that I was allowed to."

"He is a warlock prince, Hunter." Faria threw her hands in the air, exasperated. "I don't know how to use magic against him. I won't be able to stop what he does to me or how he uses it. My abilities aren't like his."

"I don't know the depths of his magic, nor do I have the ability to use all of mine. I can't teach you how to stop it. I have made you strong enough to defend yourself if he does use it against you."

Faria scoffed. "You're an idiot. Stupid, naïve Val soldier."

"Prince."

"Excuse me?" How cruel did the Fates have to be to send a prince to an elven princess, and yet she had to be with the wrong one. Maybe she hadn't heard right.

"I am a Val prince."

Faria's mouth dropped in shock but she quickly recovered, refusing to allow him the satisfaction of surprise. It did affect her, though. It was one thing to be Val, to have the Val not just be a fable but to be a prince…she couldn't wrap her head around it. She didn't remember ever learning of him during her lessons with Faline. The only image of the last Val prince left in existence as far as she knew was her favorite tapestry hanging in *Mentage*.

"Well, *Prince*." Faria stepped close enough that she needed to tilt her head up to look at him, leaving barely an inch of space between them. The electricity in the air fueled her anger. "I am the future queen. You are my protector and I forbid you from leaving me." She felt the energy of her emotions, a tidal wave she could no longer hold back. All of her frustration at having the weight of the world on her shoulders at only eighteen years old supplied her outburst. At how unfair it was to have to marry out of necessity, not love. To have to love someone who would never be with her. At the Fates for being so callous, so cruel for allowing her to see the prince she could never have. She slammed her palms against him, clawing at him, trying to draw blood. She wanted him to do something. To care.

Hunter simply stood there, taking the brunt of her anger. Finally, he let out a low growl and grabbed her wrists, preventing her from causing further harm to either of them. She breathed heavily, tears flowing down her face, and cursed herself for being so emotional, for allowing any male to incite such fury in her. She gasped for air and surveyed the damage she had done to him. He healed almost immediately, though the bruising of his skin took several moments longer. Blood trickled down his chin and even that was abnormal, the red glinting with silver. More proof that he was different, that he was leaving. It only increased her sorrow and the lump in her throat expanded.

"Hunter," Faria cried, pride be damned. If he was leaving, she might as well say what she wanted to. "I can't be with Darroc. The thought of him touching me…I will never love him. The way I feel for you… I hoped to change our laws in time. Hoped my mother would see reason, or maybe even hoped…" she trailed off before she could finish her thought. Hoped for what? That a true mate bond would appear, meaning they were two pieces of the same soul that found each other in this life? "I want you to see me as more than just your future queen."

His face was pained, his mouth clenched tight. His hands, still clasped around her wrists, eased their grip. He took a step back and worked his jaw, breathing in before speaking again. "I must go, Faria. The Elders command it. I cannot deny their compulsion."

"Why must they command it? Don't they know I'm in danger?"

"I can't say."

"WHY?" Her voice echoed in the meadow, quickly drowned by the frenzy of animals. The wind picked up speed and thunder crashed. Though she did not feel it, ice pelted the canopy of trees from above. She knew she was having a tantrum, knew she must have looked ridiculous and was not giving him any compelling reason to stay.

Hunter stepped back again, his face carefully blank, but gave no response. His body was taut as if the commotion around them affected him. Energy bounced off him, calling to the powers inside her. Faria tried her hardest to ignore it, to ignore what she wished he would feel or say or do to her.

"So that's it? I pour my heart out to you and nothing? I tell you I'm in grave danger and nothing? I tell you I can't stand the thought of him touching me and nothing? I'm doing this to stop a war and here you are, a *Val*, a soldier created for elves by the Fae, and the only thing you have to say is that you're leaving?"

Hunter's eyes shifted to the side, shaking his head. At least he had the decency to look guilty but it infuriated her to no end that he wouldn't answer her.

"If that's it then just leave, Hunter." She was seething and falling apart, watching pieces of her heart trickle away.

"I've been trying."

Faria noticed then that his body vibrated slightly and sweat had broken out down his neck. "What do you mean?" He looked pained and she almost felt bad. Almost.

"Something is keeping me here. The Elders, their call is so strong it hurts my bones, but I'm stuck here, unable to heed their demand."

Faria closed the gap between them. Their breath mingled in the cool air as she touched his face. His cheek pushed against her hand, the warmth of it spreading through her. "What is keeping you here?"

His face was fierce, his whisper both a defiance and acceptance. "You."

A break in the clouds revealed the full moon, shining brighter than Faria had ever seen. The glow illuminated his face, and the halo of light in his eyes gleamed. The booming sounds of nature faded to a simmer in the background but it was nothing compared to what Faria felt inside.

She couldn't have walked away from him then, even if she wanted to.

Faria grabbed the back of Hunter's neck and paused just a moment, waiting for permission, and when he didn't object, she kissed him fiercely— before whatever magic kept him here took him away from her. He pulled her to him, melding their bodies together, refusing to let a whisper of air get between them.

A ring of fire erupted, surrounding them in a rainbow of colors. Blue, purple, green. Over and over again it changed. The heat danced across them. It felt as though it were a part of them, a manifestation of what they felt inside. The sounds of the Forest exploded into a deafening symphony. Hunter pulled away from her, looking down at her swollen lips then back into her eyes.

"Why did you stop? Faria asked, breathless.

"I'm not allowed to feel what I am feeling, Faria. Nothing beyond what a protector should feel and yet, everything is alive inside of me. For months I had tried to deny it. Being around you clouded my vision and every day when we were apart, I felt as though the floor slipped from under me. I breathe, and it is you giving me life." He ran his hands down her back, tightening at her waist. "Every look you give me scorches me, twisting my insides and even now, I am on fire. With you, every second I am on fire."

He kissed her then, possessively, not giving her a chance to respond. She couldn't stop herself from trying to touch every part of him, to memorize this moment, this feeling. The fire surrounding them rose higher, its light a brilliant emerald. The power that emanated from it was extraordinary, as if it were the true source of magic in the land.

Their bodies were magnets for each other and without another thought, Faria tore at his clothes and Hunter at hers, his mouth covering every inch of skin. She knew then: she knew what it was like to breathe underwater because she was doing it. She was drowning in him, in his essence, and he kept her alive. Everything she gave, he took willingly.

She stepped back to admire his body, the writhing tattoos that spread down his arms and across his abdomen. She licked the planes of his stomach slowly, his stuttering breath letting her know how she affected him. She traveled lower, wanting to show him how much he affected her, but he grabbed her waist, lifting her as she wrapped her legs around him.

"It is I who must worship you, my Princess."

His words were her undoing and she allowed him to pray to her body in every way he knew how. She knew time was running out, knew whatever magic kept him with her would not last and she wanted to take advantage of every moment they had before it was gone.

The humming of the meadow crescendoed as if it, too, knew time ran short.

"What is happening?" Faria asked.

"I don't know. Do you want to stop?" He hovered just over her entrance and his muscles strained as though it took every inch of power he had to stop himself from touching her.

Did she want him to stop? Was he crazy? He was no more than a breath away from her and she felt as though she were dying. She needed him as much as she could tell he needed her.

"I thought this was forbidden," Faria said.

"It is."

She didn't hesitate. "Don't stop."

The pull she felt for him amplified, as did the sounds of the forest. Wind raked through the trees, though they were protected by their ever-brightening fire. She quickly flipped him and straddled his hips, claiming and possessing him with everything she had in every way she could, and he for her. She poured every ounce of love she had into him, the very essence of her soul open for him to take.

A flash of light exploded, illuminating the fields with wildflowers. Every scorched area from Faria's earlier outburst was lush and green and overgrown. As their passion died down, the flames did as well, silence in its wake.

A sound like a gong ringing echoed in the stillness and Faria started to feel different. Her whole body thrummed. More than just her flesh. It was deeper, on a molecular level. She glanced at Hunter. His eyes were filled with wonder. She felt all his emotions; love, affection, and heartbreak.

"What is that?"

"That is the sound of Fate changing."

A pained scream echoed in the night and it took Faria a moment to realize it came from Hunter. His body convulsed on the ground, the tendons in his neck protruding against the strain. His tattoos froze and stood out in stark contrast to his pale skin. Panicking, Faria tried to grab hold of him but he shifted between being a solid mass and transparent, quickly losing any form. It was impossible to hold onto anything tangible.

"Hunter!"

"I am being summoned," he said through clenched teeth. "I will be punished, Faria. I'm so sorry."

"Hunter, wait!"

He yelled again, looking at her as she tried desperately to keep him there. Her hand snagged on his rope necklace, her hand clasping over the gold coin that dangled from it. Faria had more questions, more things she wanted to say, and what about tomorrow? The ceremony had to be called off. She couldn't possibly bond with Darroc now that she'd given herself to Hunter.

"I love—"

But he was gone.

TWENTY TWO

FARIA

There was a time, when she was young, that Faria had believed in the good of the world. She felt happily repressed in her cocoon in Anestra, surrounded by her people who were all like extended family to her. Though she often felt lonely, she knew she was loved beyond belief by her father and her land comforted her as she nurtured her budding gifts. Any frustrations Faria had she put toward practicing in the arena; increasing her aim with her bow, striking down potential foes with her sword, throwing dagger upon dagger through the targets she pictured to be her enemies' hearts. She embraced the bloodthirsty feelings that surrounded her, if only for those moments, because she knew it would increase her and her peoples' chances for survival, should the need arise.

She would leave the arena and either have breakfast with her father as the sun rose, or help the workers in the field until she was near exhaustion and ready for her lessons with Faline. She believed she would be fit to rule one day after her mother Faded, and though it would be many centuries away, she felt she cultivated her relationships well enough to be able to take over when the time came.

She felt none of that, now.

Standing outside in the frigid, blustery morning, the sun fought with thick clouds for domination, an eerie representation of the war Faria battled inside herself. Elegant silver lace and silk wrapped around her in the form of skirts and bodice. Around her wrist was Hunter's necklace, the only thing she was able to grab as he disappeared from her. It was hidden under sparkling sleeves that twined around her arms, eclipsed in a point above her middle fingers, caging her in. A white antler crown gilded in silver that came to a sharp peak rested on the center of her forehead.

Though her legs threatened to give out, she stood firm, refusing to show an ounce of hesitation. Her slippered feet became increasingly sweaty the longer they stood on the grounds of *Mentage*, a few feet away from the inky scorched land.

The sinking feeling amplified in the pit of her stomach the closer it came to say the binding vows. Queen Amira presided over the ceremony as was tradition. Several warlocks and elves worked in harmony to build a wall of wind around the guests to keep the winter chill away. Faria could have done it herself if she wasn't caught in her despair. Darroc stood across from her dressed in black and silver, his violet eyes devouring every inch of skin her dress exposed. He oozed charm but she saw the cruel arrogance in the curve of his lips.

Her mother raised her hands and Faria felt a *thrum* vibrate in her blood. The binding magic activated. She didn't hear the words in the old language her mother spoke. She didn't feel Darroc grip her fingertips, eager to complete the ceremony. She retreated inside herself, hiding behind the wall she built in her mind to deal with this new reality set before her.

There had to be some way around this. Something she could say or do to make it so it wasn't permanent. So that it wasn't her soul she was giving away.

So that the Fates would change their mind about who They thought she was meant to be with.

Screaming inside. She was screaming and drowning and burning and there was nothing anyone could do to help her.

This is for my people. This is for my people.

The mantra replayed over again.

I am doing this for my people.

Then why did it feel so wrong?

Though it was just after noon, the sky had darkened, and she knew she needed to get her emotions centered before she lost complete control over her powers. The threat of storm rendered the air.

She thought of Hunter. The curve of his lips. His fingertips across her bare skin. The way one curl fell across his forehead when they sparred. The way his jaw clicked when he was frustrated.

If only she could see him. If only the person standing across from her wasn't the wrong prince. If only those violet eyes were emerald and the hand holding hers wasn't the wrong fit and the words leaving his mouth were from the one she loved.

If only, if only if only.

Thunder rumbled as murmurs rose from the onlookers. Nearly every able-bodied person from Anestra was in attendance. Pressure built in her chest. Her breath quickened. The earth shook beneath her, tiny pebbles quivering against her feet.

Faria looked at her mother in a silent plea. A warning flashed in the queen's eyes as Faria reached out with everything she had to stop this, to find another way. But there wasn't one.

Faria glanced toward her father, seated in the front row. He was dressed in black, sitting rigidly, his face even more pale than usual and decorated with concern. He didn't want this, Faria could see that, but he did nothing. Rows of guards stood at attention around the guests and even more crowded the stone wall in the distance that surrounded *Mentage*. All of that protection, but none that could protect her from her fate.

So, when Faria said the words that bound her and Darroc—the words that claimed she had chosen this, that she accepted his pledge—it was not him that she accepted in her mind or her heart. As she closed her eyes and said those damning words it was a different smile she was picturing, a different touch she was feeling, a different prince she was marrying.

Her mother placed a hand over their clasped fingers and a violet light encircled them. The queen whispered low and the light flashed green. Faria felt a thread wind through her, tugging in her core.

Cheers erupted around them and the whooshing of wind brought her back to reality. She opened her eyes to rain falling and evaporating before it could reach them. She knew it was because of her mother that they weren't drenched. That one act the queen could do to help soothe her. Her only metaphoric way to wipe the tears she felt building inside.

The only time Faria felt the queen might love her.

She looked at Darroc just before he smashed his lips to hers. It took everything in her to stay still, to not strike lightning upon him for daring to touch her without permission. He smiled fiercely and waved at the crowd, but she knew it was just an act, just as he knew she was putting on a show, too. Smiling through the tears, Faria glanced back at her mother who nodded before walking away, taking the rain with her.

IT WAS AS GRAND A feast as Faria had ever seen with platters filled with spiced nuts and grain mixed with fruits for the elves, roasted meats for the humans and warlocks. Towers of desserts tempted the guests. The Great Hall had been transformed with silks draped from the ceilings and doorways. Flowers were interspersed between the mountainous platters of food, and twinkling lights hovered above the guests. It seemed like every musician in Anestra was there, playing tunes to everyone's enjoyment.

It was done.

Faria smiled at her future subjects. What she sacrificed was nothing compared to what they would feel if their lives were forfeit in a war over her stubbornness. She tamped down on her breaking heart as she reminded herself of all she had saved because of this alliance.

It sickened her that she had to share her land, her people with him. When Darroc raked his eyes down her body as a predator played with its prey, she realized what it was that frightened her so.

He looked at her with victory. Like something that was conquered. Like he had won.

Unease settled in her, and suddenly Faria wasn't so sure the alliance was the key to saving her people. Was she really so naïve? Was her mother?

Darroc stalked over to Faria, wine goblet in hand, his silver silks flowing about him in his gait. He grabbed her waist and yanked her closer to him, close enough that she could smell the stench of alcohol on his breath and something else, something rotting underneath.

He sniffed her neck, which might have looked intimate to onlookers, but it was more than that. It was possessive, as though he could rip her throat out and enjoy every second of it.

"You smell of him."

Bile rose in her throat. He couldn't possibly know Hunter, or what they had done together.

She managed a smile and allowed him to lead her to the middle of the ballroom. The sea of people parted to let them through, yelling well wishes their way. The musicians slowed their tempo as they saw them approach and a sweet melody began to play. Faria tried to focus on the rhythm, the feel of her beautiful silver lace skirts swishing around her bare legs, the feel of her corseted top caging her in—anything other than who she touched. Who gripped his sweaty hand tightly in hers.

Faria's stomach clenched and her heart clamored in her chest, wondering if maybe it were possible that she bonded not with him, but with someone else. With the other prince. She should have felt Darroc's life pulsing with hers, his heart beating as hers did. It was part of the magic of the binding ceremony, but there was nothing but emptiness when it came to him. And yet, a connection was made somewhere. The thread that formed during the ceremony pulled at her, tugging her in another direction. She knew it was impossible but maybe…

"So, tell me, my sweet, why on our day of celebration do you smell of another male?" Darroc whispered, his reeking breath heating her cheek.

"I don't know what you're talking about," Faria said, leaning as far back away from him as she could without it being obvious. She smiled at the onlookers, keeping an eye open for anyone to help her.

But after Hunter's disappearance and what she had done to Nellie, she had no one.

A movement in the shadows next to the open balcony door distracted Faria but it was too dark there to see clearly. It must have been a trick of the light.

Darroc twirled her, keeping in time with the beat, but her eyes kept hopelessly shifting back to that spot in the shadows, willing her vision to clear, willing who she wished to be there to make himself known.

An unfamiliar girl glided her way along the stone wall, toward the spot Faria so desperately kept her eyes glued to. Her brown hair and lightly tanned skin blended in with the darkness, but those eyes almost shone with ethereal light. Who was this person?

Wilhelm, standing closest to the balcony, looked at the girl and snorted before looking away. It was clear he recognized her but why didn't Faria? Granted, there were many people there that she had only met briefly, but she would have recognized her. She absolutely striking. If Wilhelm knew her then she must have visited *Mentage* several times before. Had Faria been so caught up in her problems that she failed to see they had someone new staying with them? What else had she let slip by her?

The girl had something in her hand, mostly hidden in her teal velvet skirts. The bodice of her dress went up to her neck, seemingly holding her in position, while little crystals reflected off the firelight from the sconces nearby. She glanced in Faria's direction, though it wasn't her she was looking at, but rather her dance partner, who unfortunately was preoccupied with Faria's body. The girl stiffened as she watched Darroc's hand move up to grasp Faria's neck, turning her head to face him.

"There is nothing left behind you, *Princess* Faria," Darroc sneered. "Your future is right here. It has you in its grasp. Do you dare ignore it?"

Faria looked at him then, really looked at him, despite the fear that tried and failed to rise in her. Her body was too caught up in the war over heartbreak and anger to allow fear any room. She scented him, as she had been doing since he first arrived. That smell was off, that wrongness was stronger, and the violet of his eyes was not so vibrant now. His fingertips, still gripping her neck, felt calloused and as though claws were trying to fight their way out.

How dare he think to put his hands on her. To threaten her. The impulse to set him on fire was nearly uncontrollable. Faria said as quietly and clearly as she could, "I don't know your agenda, Darroc, nor do I know what you really are. But this ceremony was for my people. Everything I am doing is for them. I will save them, I will retain this land, and I will find a way to break the vow that I accepted. You will not be here long, even if it takes my dying breath."

He threw his head back and laughed, loud and boisterous, playing off

Faria's words as if it were a joke.

"No," he said as he calmed down. "That is where you are wrong. Everything is happening exactly as it was predicted it would, and soon, the Prophecy will be fulfilled. Soon, everything that I had planned on centuries ago will finally come to fruition." His eyes slowly devoured her body before resting on her womb.

The song ended and Faria stepped away from him, eyes narrowed. What was she missing? Why was he staring at her like that? It sickened her to be so close to him, let alone touch him.

"The Prophecy involves a child," Faria whispered furiously at him. "And trust me, I am not letting you anywhere near me to let *that* happen."

His face darkened but that rapacious smile stayed in place. "No need for all of that." He leaned in closer and whispered in her ear words that made her stomach jump into her throat. "I've spent a long time learning to create life where there is none. A certain warlock drink to restore energy might not have been exactly what I claimed. The second you bound yourself to me the damage was done. You are with child, and it *is* mine."

Faria scoffed, hardly daring to believe his words but he had no reason to lie to her, not anymore. He thought himself a god? To create life? Was he joking?

No. There was no way that she was pregnant, let alone with *his* child. Absolutely not.

And yet, the victory laid out so plainly on his face said otherwise. Faria had to speak to her mother, immediately.

Callum tapped Darroc on the shoulder, much to his chagrin, and in his distraction, Faria looked for the queen. She found her staring at the shadowed area Faria had watched earlier, brows furrowed in concentration.

That girl was still there, handing a scroll over into the darkness. She nodded and headed outside onto the balcony. Though his back was to her, the person the girl was with was him. Faria would recognize him anywhere.

Hunter. She thought he was called away, that he would be punished. Why was he here?

Dressed all in black, armed to the teeth with a bow, daggers, knives, a quiver of arrows, an axe hanging from his waist.

Faria glanced quickly around the room though no one looked his way. No one except that girl she didn't know, and her mother. The queen didn't acknowledge him, but her rigid attention on that corner let Faria know she was fully aware of his presence.

The whole time, he was there. Did he hear what Darroc said to her? Did the Val have that keen of abilities?

Did he know that Faria was with child, and it was not his, but Darroc's?

The girl looked back at her as Faria reached out again with her senses, trying to scent or feel who she was. She felt familiar, in a way, as if she knew her energy. Still, Faria did not recognize her. The girl gave a sad smile as she reached for Hunter and wrapped her arm around his, drawing him closer to her.

His back stiffened, though he made no effort to remove her. After all that had happened between them, everything they said and done just hours ago, he stood there with someone else. After all she had sacrificed, every painful feeling of betrayal, rejection and loss she had to stamp down on, he dared to show up here and reveal himself to her, with someone else?

A sharp pain ripped through the pit of Faria's stomach straight to her heart. More than jealousy, more than the compelling need to do the girl physical harm, to take her hand off what was hers, Faria felt a burning sensation that nearly brought her to her knees. As though a thread were pulled taut, slicing through her soul. The queen whipped her head to Faria the same time Hunter did, both completely attuned to her every move.

A rumble shook the windows and a sudden storm thrashed outside. The floor trembled beneath them as guests gasped, trying to regain their footing. Faria looked to her mother, silently pleading for some sort of help, some stability. The storm outside calmed to a gentle rain. The king sidled up next to the queen, anguish on his face. He reached his arm to Faria but slowly dropped it back to his side.

Faria moved her attention back to Hunter, still standing in the shadows just outside the balcony. And though she tried not to, a quiet sob escaped her, in a crowd full of boisterous people celebrating what should be the happiest day of her life. He simply stared. His face half hidden, revealing almost nothing as his eyes searched her face, her body. From across the room Faria watched as his jaw clicked. She knew every inch of that body, every muscle that moved, and she could see his heart beating as his vein pulsed in time with her own. She knew that it was taking everything in him to not come her way.

Their eyes met and the sconces on the walls flared blue, then purple. The crowd clapped; they thought it was being done for their entertainment. Then green—that blessed emerald green of their shared power—flared just for a moment before it was gone, replaced by ordinary fire.

The floor slipped from beneath her feet as Faria realized their connection had been severed. Where she once felt his life, the love in his eyes, there was nothing but an empty echo. She gasped and clutched at her chest, reeling from the realization that something cruel, perhaps the Fates, had caused this to happen. Hunter turned away, putting his arm around that girl Faria didn't know. Jealousy and anger and heartbreak erupted as he led her away into the darkness.

Her vision swam until she saw nothing, anymore.

TWENTY THREE

FARIA

•TWO MONTHS LATER•

S he kneeled on the frozen ground, eyes closed, trying to train her mind to focus on anything other than the life she grew inside her.

Too often, she thought about ending the pregnancy, but she knew this was likely her only opportunity to continue the Agostonna line. For the good of her Queendom, she would bear this child.

A wind tore through the empty field, but Faria did not shiver. She wore nothing more than a simple dress, her feet bare. The fire in her blood kept her warm. Kept her numb.

She had not seen Darroc in weeks. She had no idea what he was up to. She left it to her mother to figure out. Her role was finished. The

Chosen One was with child. It was all she was good for.

Faria and Darroc maintained their own wings at *Mentage*, not caring what anyone thought of it. She refused to be with him, and he insisted she would come around when she was ready.

She would never be ready.

Thanks to Faline, Faria knew that the queen and king were keeping Nellie busy on missions. She didn't ask what that meant. She no longer cared.

She found she couldn't be bothered to care about anything, anymore.

TWENTY FOUR

NELLIE

◆FOUR MONTHS LATER◆

The Barren Plain stretched before them, desolate, hot, dusty. She had been traveling the roads of Anestra for weeks along with Johanna, trying to find evidence of the "friends" of Darroc that Endo promised would be coming.

Anestra was beautiful, filled with lush valleys, forests of golden leaves, fruit she had never seen before, and winding rivers filled with rainbow fish. The villages they visited were well-advanced, Nellie thought, for not having electricity or modern technology. Most of the villagers kept large houses, each with their own yards and gardens, and the towns boasted small shops and farmer's markets every weekend for the townspeople to share their bounty. There were a few temples, usually devoted to the three goddesses, though Nellie knew many of these villages were filled with people from Earth. Children ran in the streets when they weren't in school. Everyone seemed happy.

No matter where they went, no matter who they met, they never came across anyone displeased with the queen, nor anyone who complained of the Queendom at large. The townspeople aired their grievances when they traveled to *Mentage* every few months, and that seemed to be enough.

Nellie couldn't understand, then, why there was ever dissent among the warlocks. Darroc had claimed he needed a warlock queen for his peoples' power to be restored. Faria was their queen now, and nothing had changed. The evidence showed that Darroc had lied to them, yet still…

Though they found no true evidence, they did happen across a group of warlocks along the edge of the Barren Plain. They looked young, though Nellie knew they were likely decades older than her.

"What business brings you here?" Johanna asked without preamble. Though she had eternal patience, Nellie knew Johanna was just as frustrated as she was at finding nothing to help them.

"We are to meet with our brethren," a bearded man said. "They stay near the Caranek Peaks."

Nellie had remembered what Endo had said, about how he had tried to find a way through the impassable mountain range months ago. That was where Wil and Reed were headed as soon as Nellie and Johanna returned home.

"What are their names?" Johanna asked. "Perhaps we know of them."

The three males seemed to be sizing up Johanna and Nellie, but they were wise enough not to start trouble. "My nephew moved here years ago, works at *Mentage*. Name's Endo."

Nellie tried to keep her face blank. "Endo has not been seen in quite some time." She felt a sinking sensation in the pit of her stomach. She still hoped he would turn up, hoped he would come back to the right side. Instead, it seems like he had called in reinforcements.

"I see," the bearded man said. The three exchanged another long look.

Nellie was growing restless. She was dirty, cranky, and wanted to return home with something useful. "Have you seen or heard of anything suspicious on your travels?" she asked.

"We heard that some months ago a phoenix was seen flying north, if that's what you mean by suspicious."

Nellie tried and failed to keep from rolling her eyes. "No, fairy tales are not what I meant." She shoved Johanna. "Let's be on our way."

They all nodded to each other and when she was sure they were out of hearing range, Nellie asked, "Do you think they are here for reinforcements? Or perhaps Endo sought help for the side of good?"

"I doubt only three warlocks are what Darroc needs to build his army, and I am more than positive they were not the 'friends' we were to look for. I didn't detect deception from them. The phoenix is what I'm interested in."

"Why?" Nellie asked. "They are only legends."

Johanna laid her dark eyes upon Nellie. "So are you."

Touché.

"Wil and Reed heard Darroc tell Faria a story about a phoenix. How the king turned his wife into one and she left, taking their power with her.

Seems a little coincidental that there were rumors of a sighting."

"Or perhaps they are just rumors meant to entice more warlocks to come and stand against the queen," Nellie said.

It was growing dark and she was tired of endless roads and sleeping on the ground. They had turned away from the Barren Plain miles ago and were just leaving a copse of trees when they came to a farm overrun with weeds. Chunks of dusty dirt covered overgrown fields and Nellie could just make out the remnants of a burnt cottage in the distance. It felt strange there, oily. It reminded her of the darkness that inhabited the edge of the Forest of the Dawn.

It reminded her of Darroc.

"What do you think happened here?" Nellie asked.

Johanna's mouth was tight as she took off her pack and leaned against a tree trunk, careful not to cross the hidden demarcation line. "It seems as though the warlock prince made a stop on his way to *Mentage*."

Nellie rolled out a mat and laid her sleeping bag on top of it. "At least we'll have something to tell the queen," she said.

The panic of the end-of-the-world pressure struck her again, carrying her into a fitful sleep.

TWENTY FIVE

FARIA

◆SIX MONTHS LATER◆

"**F**aria, you must get out of bed."

She rolled over, ignoring her mother's voice. The queen had never cared to visit her chambers until recently. For Faria, it was too late.

"Summer solstice is almost upon us. You will be expected at the celebration."

Celebration. She nearly laughed except that she'd forgotten how to make those muscles work. There was nothing to celebrate. The dark stain on the land was successful in ruining any hope of a bountiful harvest for the year. They had planted new fields, a maid had told her. But it would be a tight winter.

The baby inside her kicked her ribcage, as if she were telling Faria she wanted to get out of bed sometime today, too. Faria didn't care.

There was a darkness in her, put there by Darroc. She could feel it. Whenever he deigned to see her, which was rare, he did so only to check on the progress of the baby. The growth of her belly. He cared little if Faria ate, if she went outside, if she bathed, so long as she did the bare minimum to keep their child alive.

Their baby did not move when he was there, as if she blamed her father for how he had deceived her mother.

She didn't know why Darroc was still allowed at *Mentage*. She wondered sometimes why he didn't bring her to Wendorre. She was their queen, wasn't she? It didn't matter. She was content to stay in her rooms until she Faded into the beyond.

Faria rested a hand on her belly, smoothing it in loving circles, humming a soothing tune.

She would get out of bed when she was ready.

But not today.

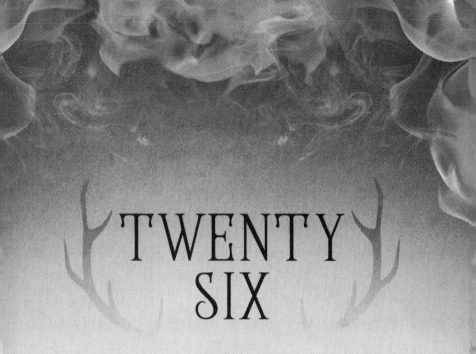

TWENTY SIX

NELLIE

◆EIGHT MONTHS LATER◆

She crossed her arms over her chest, refusing to budge. "I am going to see Faria."

Faline shook her head. "You must not. She is too fragile. If she realizes who you are, who knows what she will do. Who knows how her powers have festered?"

"There has been no sign of her using her powers for months," Nellie said through clenched teeth. "She has, thankfully, started volunteering again in Athinia, but she is wandering the Spring Garden as if she were nothing more than a ghost. She needs me."

"What she needs is for you to finish your assignment."

King Dennison had given Nellie one final task, which was to see once again if she could find Endo in Athinia. Their searches within the far reaches of Anestra resulted in nothing useful. They had even reached out to dwarven leader, Thuul, but he assured them no human, warlock, or elf were in their mountain city.

The king, meanwhile, was busy gathering and training people constantly flooding into Athinia. Nellie and Johanna had spread word once they reached Mercy Bay that the king called for help. It was a gamble, since they still didn't know Darroc's plan or who he might have made alliances with, but it was one they had to take.

"I will go into Athinia," Nellie promised. "But I am tired of sneaking into Faria's room dressed up as a cleaner or cook to deliver food to her. I want to hold her, to lay down with her, to talk about her fears, to see where her powers are, see if she is at all mentally capable to handle what is to come."

"You cannot," Faline said, "because she still does not know that she must kill her child."

Nellie froze. She felt something akin to rage start to boil under her skin. "Whose idea was it to keep that from her?"

Faline's silence was answer enough. The queen, of course, no doubt because it would be the last remaining push over the edge before Faria shattered her mind.

"Where am I to meet Hunter?" He was going to remain invisible, keeping an eye out for anyone they identified as problematic while she focused on Endo. It was their last attempt at gleaning any information they could. Darroc left for months at a time and when he did show up, he seemed to disappear after seeing Faria in her room. They had done all they could to prepare for whatever war he brought to them, without causing a panic throughout the realm. Only those in the guard understood the danger Anestra was in.

They had nearly one thousand capable and ready-to-fight soldiers, weapon wielders and magic users alike—not counting civilians they could call on if needed. Yet, Nellie had the sneaking suspicion it still wouldn't be enough.

"Outside the tapestry of the Val," Faline replied. She had been dumbfounded when Hunter admitted to Nellie and the queen what he was and spent weeks in complete awe of him. Now, Nellie almost snorted. How vain of him to wait for her outside a picture of himself.

She left her rooms and up a staircase leading to Faria's section of *Mentage*. Wildflowers filled the vases on little tables lining the hallway. Someone had thought to change the curtains hanging from the windows to a light blue. Nothing seemed amiss. It was all perfectly orchestrated so that rumors of Faria's health did not spread.

Nellie found herself standing outside Faria's room. It was risky, but she doubted Faria would open the door.

A shoulder brushed against hers, his electric presence causing her arm hair to rise with static.

"You shouldn't be here," she murmured.

"I stand out here, every day, invisible, hoping to catch a glimpse of her." He clenched his jaw. "I hate these rules. It doesn't feel right. I feel a pull to her, but I cannot heed its call."

"It's called love, and it's because you're being cock-blocked by Darroc the A-hole."

"It is deeper than that, Nellie." Hunter ran his fingers through his hair. "I can't describe it. I can feel her feelings. My dreams are hers. Every time I try to see her, the Elders yank me away."

"Have they explained why they're controlling your every move?"

He shook his head. "They don't trust me or what I would do. I worry if I cross a line, they'll send me away."

Nellie raised a brow. Hunter hadn't explained who the Elders were, other than his guardians. He had told her almost nothing about himself, but mentioned a few times that parts of his memory are gone, along with access to parts of his magic.

"Let's go," he said, "before I kidnap her and risk starting this war before any of us are ready."

Their time in Athinia proved fruitless and Nellie had the distinct impression that they were out of time.

TWENTY SEVEN

FARIA

·TEN MONTHS LATER·

Her waters broke near midnight.

Blinding white hot pain erupted through her womb. Darroc was on his way back from the edge of Anestra, where he last told Faria he was meeting with friends. She hadn't seen him in weeks. She knew he would be there soon. The dark magic he used to impregnate her created a tether between them. She could sense him as strongly as she could feel her baby girl trying to make her way into the world.

Whatever evil hell he implanted in her pulsed as sure as her heartbeat. Faria's child was not evil, of that she was sure, but something about her was.

Darroc had explained to her how it happened. She had sat in a chair, staring out her bedroom window. Spring had just begun. He wove such terrible stories about how he experimented throughout the past several centuries on countless species. How he created new species in the process, trying to find a way to grow warlock babies. He didn't go into all the details and she didn't want him to. What he told her was enough to cause her nightmares for weeks. Who knew how many innocent people he had butchered in the process? Faria could only imagine what kind of black magic he had performed to sacrifice so many people in his quest for total domination.

Because that was what it was. That was why he inserted himself so firmly within *Mentage*, why he was so willing to teach her his magic. Why he innocently gave her a potion masquerading as a drink to restore her energy, counting on her naïveté in the days leading up to the ceremony. Sealing it with a kiss was as if they had lain together. It affirmed the bond he needed to create life within her.

Faria should have seen it coming. He as good as told it to her on the first day they met. He needed a warlock queen to restart his race's power. And there she was. Warlock queen for ten months and him their new king, and yet still, their power had not been restored. Not until she gave birth, he assured her.

Faria wished she could set him on fire.

She hadn't seen nor heard of Nellie in those ten months, either. She never had the chance to apologize to her. Faline had assured her Nellie just needed time, but eventually, Faria gave up.

Faria had plenty to catch up on, after she decided to partake in the summer solstice activities. She had visited the sick in Athinia most days in the summer as she felt kindred to them, needing to overcome a foreign invader in their bodies. She had even spent time with her mother. She couldn't tell if the queen had taken pity on her or perhaps she had felt true remorse for needing to follow through with what the Fates decided for her. Either way, Faria appreciated it, even if it changed nothing.

Hunter was gone as well. After everything he admitted to her. After what there had been between them. Faria felt used up, abandoned, and furious.

She had asked Wil and Reed to train with her, needing a release for her emotions. The loving looks they had passed each other and the way they had teased each other broke Faria's heart even more. She used it to fuel her energy until her belly was too swollen to continue.

Another current of pain ripped through her as the baby readied her descent. It was just another pain to add to the growing list.

The queen entered Faria's room with two of her chambermaids and Faline, each of them looking as worried as she should have felt.

"Faria, it is almost time." Her mother rubbed a cold cloth over her face and down her neck. "We will be here the whole time."

Faline gave the queen's hand a subtle squeeze, her face dire.

"Where is Darroc?"

"He will not enter here," her mother answered. "It is customary for the females to remain alone until the babe is cleaned and fed. You do not need him here."

"I didn't want him here at all," Faria said through clenched teeth. Breathing heavily, she thought of what names she could use for her child to distract herself from what was to come, but it was no use. The baby was about to make her appearance.

The chambermaids busied themselves getting cloth and water ready while her mother stayed next to her, eyebrows knitted, mouth drawn in a frown. Faria noticed the fine lines on her cheeks and around her eyes and wondered when her mother had started to age.

"I am sorry for this, my daughter. If there were any other way, anything else, I swear I would have found it."

She swatted her mother's hand away from her cheek. "What are you talking about?"

Her mother exchanged a look with Faline, who shook her head quickly before busying herself laying cloths under Faria's legs.

"What is it that I don't know?"

"Nothing, child." Faline patted her hair. "When you are ready to push, do so. Your body will know what to do."

Faria didn't have to wait much longer before Faline's words proved truthful. The pain was excruciating as her body ripped open, and though her abilities lay dormant, her healing gift seemed better than ever. It flared to life, disorienting her with its rush of cool healing. Once the babe was out, Faria felt her body already begin to repair the damage that was done.

The fog in Faria's brain was punctured by the sweet harmony of the baby crying. She tried to see her daughter, but the queen's back was in the way.

"What is it?" Faria wiped the sweat from her neck and held out her arms. "I want to hold her. Let me see her."

But it was Faline's response that surprised her the most. "What have you done, child?" The fear in Faline's eyes amplified Faria's own emotions, setting the fireplace in the corner blazing. It seemed her gifts were back in full force now that the baby was born.

"What are you talking about?" Faria looked at her mother who still held the baby. "Give her to me."

"It is a male," the queen said with a mixture of awe and trepidation. "It is—impossibly—a male."

Faria's heart dropped. Whatever spell Darroc cast on her must have changed her, changed the very core of how their line continued. The firstborn was always a female. No exceptions.

"Oh gods, he did this," she whispered, her voice shaking on the verge of hysteria. "He cast a spell on me. Told me the child was the key to everything."

The queen's gaze cut to Faline and nodded her head once. Faline's eyes shone but she nodded back and ran out of the room.

"Where is she going?" Panic threatened to take over and the sconces on the wall flickered on and off with Faria's erratic breathing. "What is happening, Mother?"

Queen Amira turned to Faria, eyes shining with tears, but still, she did not hand over the baby. "Darroc will be here any moment. Quickly, child. You must do as I say." Tears escaped her eyes and her bottom lip quivered. "We believed the answer to everything was to kill the child. We thought we found…but that has now changed, now that it is obvious what this is. I don't know the right answer anymore. I wasn't shown this." The queen was frantic, trying to get the words out.

Still, she did not hand over the baby. Her grip tightened on him.

"Mother. You will not kill him." The air in the room dropped to a frigid degree and while Faria and her child could breathe fine, the queen started to struggle.

"No, I don't think we can, now," Queen Amira squeezed the words out. Faria released the cold in the air with a thought and the fires flared back to life. "Faria, you are Fae-blessed. I was never allowed to tell you. It helped ensure you were the Chosen, to ensure the Prophecy came true. A Fae visited me on the night you were born and explained the best way I could protect you and your new abilities." Tears slid down her cheeks. "I used the blood from that night to protect this land, to create a shield so that no harm would come to you until my dying breath."

The queen went to a bag of supplies on the floor and pulled out a vial of clear liquid. Faria recognized it as Elixir of Life, a potion filled with all nutrition a baby needed in their first few days. It was given only if the mother was unfit to care for the child. Faria watched as the queen placed three drops in the baby's mouth, satiating his hunger. Faria's unease increased.

"None of this is making sense. Fae? They haven't been here in nearly a millennium."

"That is not true, and I don't have time to explain it now. I'm so sorry I've kept all this from you. Take the boy, go straight into the Forest. Are you healed enough now?"

Faria nodded. She was sore, and exhausted beyond belief, but no longer torn. Her adrenaline spiked, realizing what her mother asked of her.

The queen lay the baby down in his prepared crib. Faria watched as her mother prepared a bag filled with linen and food, along with a sealed envelope. She picked up the baby again and turned back to Faria.

"Take him and run, quickly. Do not stop until you get to the meadow. You will not see me again." She pressed the satchel into Faria's hand and hugged her fiercely, breathing her in. The queen ran a single finger down the baby's cheek, and that action broke the dam of panic Faria tried hard to keep at bay.

"What do you mean, Mother? Why won't I see you again?"

Queen Amira held Faria's shoulders in place and looked into her eyes. "The protection spell will end when my life does. You will know when that happens. Get that child to safety. Darroc cannot have him. It is imperative that you listen to me. Leave Anestra if you must."

"I will not abandon my people."

"Don't worry about them. Your son is your first priority now." The queen helped ease Faria out of bed, pushing her toward the door.

Faria hitched a breath. Though she had advanced healing, she was not prepared to do any type of physical activity too soon. "He will find me Mother, I know it. There is something in me. He always knows where I am just as I know he will arrive at any moment."

"Leave now, Faria. This is what must be done."

"But father—"

"He is readying our armies, prepared to protect and lead *Mentage* until you return." She gathered up the stained sheets and tossed them into the fire. "Your father knows what to do. I love you, my daughter. Go, now!"

Faria scrambled through the door, ignoring the pulsing ache from giving birth. She gritted her teeth, willing herself to feel stronger with every step she took. The queen pushed her down one of the secret corridors that led directly outside, opposite the stables. Then she flew out into the night.

The fear of Darroc's arrival fueled her adrenaline and Faria ran faster than she ever had before. She refused to look back, refused to take one last glance at what she was leaving behind. It was only minutes before she reached the meadow, giving herself a moment to catch her breath.

The moonlight trickled down in between the canopy above, spreading shadows out like long fingers tickling the grass below.

Panic swelled. Darroc would undoubtedly find them. The spell he had placed on her was still there. She could feel it like a phantom limb. This would be the start of the very war they wanted to avoid, but the queen had insisted. There were so many things her mother never told her.

And Faria was never going to see her again. The queen was going to die protecting her.

But what was there to protect her from? Darroc was expecting a daughter, not a son. Why flee him? Maybe it would have deterred him from his plans.

She finally looked down at her baby in wonderment and love filled her. His dark hair and round face looked angelic in the night. His ears were slightly pointed, though Faria's were round, and his nose was a tiny button. His eyes were closed, resting amid the chaos from the past several minutes. His skin was pink now but would soon turn tan as Faria's was. He was beautiful.

A gentle breeze shifted through the meadow and a familiar scent encased her, one of ocean and rain and the air she breathed. It had been ten impossible months since she last enjoyed that scent, her heart shattering all over again with the memories it brought.

He approached on silent feet and fell to his knees before her, head bowed. Every inch she could see was covered in weapons. He looked ready for battle.

"Faria," he breathed. "Please forgive me."

"For what, exactly? For abandoning me, not bothering to come around for months, not explaining yourself, or not saving me from that absolute monster?"

"Yes, all of it. I was sent to another realm and the rules—"

"I have had enough of the rules, Hunter." She felt her anger at him pour out of her. "I don't care about anything except getting my son to safety. Will you help me? Is that why you are here?"

His head shot up. "Son?" Hunter searched Faria's eyes, questioning. "Are you certain?"

"Yes."

Hunter opened and closed his mouth several times before saying, "May I hold him?" He held his breath, waiting for her answer.

Faria handed her son over, watching Hunter's face fill with joyous light. "I did not think it was possible," he breathed.

It was distracting, the way Hunter looked holding her child. As if a piece she was missing was suddenly filled again. She ached over their situation. He was not her partner and that was not his child. Once again, the Fates were unbelievably cruel to give Faria this moment.

"What didn't you think was possible?" she asked.

He ran his finger down the length of the babe's cheek and whispered something in a language Faria didn't recognize. Suddenly, the baby opened his shockingly emerald eyes with a golden halo circling the center. They were the mirror image of the pair staring back at him. Faria's breathing came in short bursts, dizziness threatening to take over. It couldn't be.

Hunter stared down at the boy, rocking him gently.

It was not Darroc's offspring she had been carrying for the past ten months.

It was Hunter's.

TWENTY EIGHT

NELLIE

S ilence wrapped around them as the Royal Guard sat at a table in the Great Hall. All were dressed for battle, waiting for the signal that would undoubtedly start the war.

The child sacrifice.

Nellie felt so strongly for Faria, for not knowing that her daughter had to die, effectively ending the future of the Agostonna line for the sake of staving off the Final Battle. She didn't understand why the queen kept Faria in the dark, nor why she wasn't allowed to see her. Too much time was spent worrying that Faria would have a psychotic breakdown and not enough time was spent trusting her to do the right thing. Instead, when

Faria found out, she would likely feel hurt and betrayed that everyone knew more about her life and future than she did.

Not being there for Faria had been frustrating, especially because when she did explore the depths of Anestra, Nellie mostly came back with nothing. She knew the missions were important, but she would have rather spent her time showing Faria her true self and groveling for her forgiveness for months after.

A stirring in the hallway rippled toward them in the form of whispers; hushed, excited voices echoed in the quiet room, bringing everyone to attention, the untouched food all but forgotten.

It is a boy!

"A boy?" Wilhelm said, pushing away his plate. Johanna jumped to her feet while Enis pushed away from her place against the wall. "That cannot be."

"Nellie!" Faline burst into the hall, breathless.

"What's happening, Faline?" Nellie said. "Is it done?"

"Everyone, assume your positions!" Faline shouted. Organized chaos ensued as scores of elves, humans, and even a few warlocks trickled out from areas Nellie couldn't see and ran to their positions around *Mentage*.

King Dennison stormed in, quiver of arrows strapped to his back, his bow at his side. On his belt were several daggers and bottles filled with various liquids, no doubt to light the arrows on fire if need be. Though his ability was accuracy, he couldn't manipulate elements like his daughter. He was dressed head to toe in thick leathers and at his helm was a pointed silver band. He looked every bit the warrior a King of Anestra was meant to be.

"Faline. Is it done?" His deep voice rumbled with an undercurrent of threat, ready to take on any enemy that crossed him.

"Your Majesty," Faline bowed her head slightly and dragged Nellie over to the king. "It is a boy," she whispered. "He is still alive."

Shock and outrage lined his face, though his eyes were wide with fear. "What did that devil do to her?"

"It was not him," she said. "The baby is not warlock. He looks more like a Fae and elf mix. The queen could not bear to kill him, now that everything we thought we knew is uncertain."

"Fae?" the king asked. "How is that possible?"

Faline shook her head but Nellie knew. She better understood the type of pain and panic Faria had gone through these past few months. While everyone was busy preparing for war, Nellie had to endure on her own in their absence. How cruel they had been to her!

Nellie cleared her throat. "Your Majesty," she bowed to him. "I believe I know how that baby looks Fae."

"Speak. Quickly." Shouts echoed from outside followed by the warning of the war horn. Darroc had returned.

"Hunter," Nellie spat out. "He is Val. I believe that baby is Hunter's."

King Dennison stared at her. Then he nodded and ran outside, shouting orders as he went. Troops fell in line behind him, just as the drums started, echoing off the stone walls.

"I'm sorry, Faline," Nellie said, turning to her. "I only just put it together now. I hadn't spoken to her in so long…"

Faline shook her head. "That might have mattered before, so we could prepare differently, but it makes no difference now. You must run."

"What? I'm the secret weapon. This is what we have been preparing for." There was no way Nellie was leaving, not when the war drums' echo in the hall vibrated into her core. Every instinct she had now was to stay. To protect what was hers.

"Faria ran with the child. Amira demanded it. He will come for her. You must protect her!"

Nellie closed her eyes, steeling herself for what might come to pass. "What can I do?"

"Guide her when the time comes. You will know how. Hurry now!" Faline hugged her tight. "I will see you again, in this life or beyond. Go!"

Holding back tears with the thought of never seeing her adoptive mother again, Nellie ran through chaos of soldiers yelling and lining up outside, readying their weapons. A scream tore through the air, setting birds in flight.

Darroc.

Nellie shifted into a wolf and ran into the trees, following Faria's scent. She hardly noticed what flew past her. The forest was alive in its own way as if it, too, were preparing for battle. Animals skittered back and forth, and the moon seemed brighter, guiding Nellie's way.

She followed Faria's trail to the edge of a large clearing and halted. Hunter was there as well. If Nellie could find them so quickly then certainly so could Darroc. She changed back into herself but before she could run to them, a darkness blanketed the forest. Quiet, chilling, darkness.

She was too late. Darroc was there.

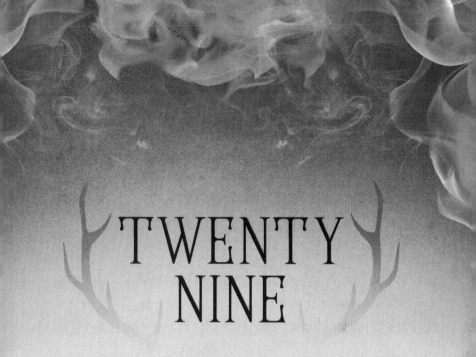

TWENTY NINE

FARIA

A Val child. There was no mistaking it. The first Val to be born in nearly one thousand years.

Faria didn't put much stock in the Fates or the Prophecy, but she did wonder if everyone had it wrong. If perhaps her son was the Chosen and she was just the conduit.

"I didn't think it was possible for me to have children," Hunter said. "In my entire lifetime, centuries, I never impregnated anyone. I just didn't think I could."

"Let's not put the image of you with others in my head at this moment," Faria whispered, half joking. "We need to get somewhere safe."

"We need to pick a name." Hunter stood, clutching the babe to his chest.

Faria chuckled. "I think that's the least of our…" her voice trailed off, a memory prickling at the back of her mind. She had the strangest sense of déjà vu and knew something terrible was going to happen. She searched the sky, the trees, what lay in the shadows beyond. An image of a burnt forest appeared, and she turned in a circle, wondering where the danger would come from.

"Ander," she whispered, realization striking as the name came back to her. "His name is Ander."

Hunter smiled. "I like that. Ander Agostonna has a nice ring to it. Perhaps when we have more time, I shall tell you my family name and we can incorporate it somehow."

Faria didn't respond, too distracted by the panic boiling. "I dreamed this," she said. "Hunter, I dreamed this. We need to get out of here."

They sensed Darroc before he made his appearance. Hunter gave the baby back to Faria and in the same movement, whipped daggers into the night. He said words in another language, something she didn't know, but it made the weapons sharper and move faster, undoubtedly directly toward their target.

A fireball tore through the forest but Faria was quicker than it. Clutching Ander to her chest, she leapt out of the way as the fireball slammed into the tree behind her, setting it ablaze.

The flames quickly spread into a circle encasing them, but it was not the same type of fire as when Hunter and she were together. The night that changed Fate's design.

This fire was black, deadly, and it instantly burned around them. Darroc was destroying their special glen, the place that held some of Faria's happiest memories. He was killing it just as surely as he was about to kill them.

"You took what is mine, wife." His voice was like oil, greasing into every part of her.

"They are not yours," Hunter growled into the night. "They will never be yours."

Darroc stepped through the trees. He was unlike anything Faria had ever seen before. His skin was purple and scaly, his eyes red with madness. Claws extended from his hands where fingers should have been, and impossibly long canines descended from his mouth. This was his true form. How did she not sense it the entire time? How could she think that being with him would do anything for her people?

It was doomed before it even began.

"My magic is in him," Darroc said. "He is mine. I do not need your princess any longer." His claws ground together, creating sparks and another fireball appeared before him. He was so powerful, so strong. Deadly. They could never win this war.

I cannot win this.

The fireball ripped through the air as Hunter ran toward it, as if to shield them from its burning death. What was he doing? That was suicide.

Faria clutched the air in front of her and imagined choking the life out of the black fire. The flames sputtered long enough for Hunter to fling it back at Darroc.

Hunter took weapon after weapon from his body, ranging from

throwing stars to two metallic balls meant to choke its target. No matter what he did, he was unable to keep Darroc down for long.

"Faria, you must run." His voice strained with the effort he expended. "Please, protect our son. Take him."

Darroc snarled at that. "Your son?" His eyes settled on Faria, where she saw her own death reflecting back at her. "Now I understand why you smelled of another male at our wedding. You dare sully what was mine?"

His canines slurred his speech and he seemed to grow another foot taller, his scales ripping from his skin. A blast from her left disoriented Faria enough to lose control of her magic. Another blast slammed her to the ground and her hold on Ander slipped. She had just enough control to tuck him into the roots of a tree before falling hard on her side.

The ground shook as something exploded, dirt and debris shooting into the air.

A ringing sound played in Faria's ears, her eyes blurred against the heat of the fire and the sting of the smoke.

She tried calling to her own flame but she couldn't concentrate past the pain in her ribs or the throbbing of her head. She called out Hunter's name, or she thought she did. Everything was a blur of black and red. She was dimly aware of the taste of blood in her mouth.

Somewhere, a baby screamed, but that couldn't be right. Her baby was safe. She made sure he was safe before she fell.

She couldn't remember. Nothing made sense. Nothing... there was nothing but darkness.

THE SCENT OF FIRE AND burnt ash seared her senses as she bit through the pain coursing through her wrecked body. The world was silent.

She was alone.

Seconds passed as her Fae-blessed senses returned to her broken elven form. Sound, then feeling. Her body burned from the blast every inhale pierced her sides. She must have cracked a few ribs. Slowly, her eyes peeked open just a sliver at first, expecting some sort of light to trickle through the canopy of trees. The blood moon, she remembered, prevented it. The forest was dark, and cold, and she was utterly alone.

Faria's hand itched with the burning of repairing skin and as she brushed the hair way from her eyes, she realized two things at once; Ander was no longer next to her, and Hunter was gone.

She breathed deeply and, ignoring the pain in her side, dove into her well of power, willing its forces to help strengthen her. Goosebumps shot down her arms and nausea threatened her as the power rose too quickly — higher and higher, until a violet light shot out her hands, only to be swallowed by the darkness surrounding her.

She looked for any signs of life, but that monster's strange magic had destroyed everything. Where there was once a rushing vitality in the Forest of the Dawn, now there was nothing.

Leather boots crunched on dead leaves and broken twigs beneath her as she tried to rise, but she fell to her knees, still too weak to stand. Panic set in.

Her eyes adjusted to her surroundings, and she was grateful for the low-light vision elves were gifted with. She found herself in her secret glen. Once filled with bright energy and love, it was now a graveyard of dark magic.

Scorched earth surrounded her, all traces of grass and flora crisped. It extended to the trees, their usual rich tones of gold and brown replaced with scorched black. Their branches held upright in a silent scream and the smell of charred decay permeated everything.

"Ander?" Her voice cracked in the silence of the dense night. No response. "Ander, please, are you there?"

Nothing returned her plea. He was gone.

Bile seared her throat, leaving the tang of denial creeping in its path.

Find Ander. Find Ander.

She swallowed down the panic threatening to overtake her, counting to ten to clear her head. Panic led to mistakes.

She steadied herself and leapt to her feet, taking stock of the injuries that remained. Her advanced healing had taken care of most of them.

She had only started to run for a moment before she stumbled over something hard a few yards away.

Something solid that didn't belong there.

Her knees skinned against rocks in the path, and suddenly her face was inches away from a male body. It took her eyes a moment to adjust, or maybe she just didn't want to believe what she saw. She didn't want to think that his neck was broken in an impossible way, or that his skin was burnt straight to the bone, or that his body laid lifeless before her. But staring into those glassy green eyes confirmed what she so desperately tried to reject.

He was dead.

No, no, no, no, no. This cannot be right, please gods this cannot be right.

The pit in her stomach expanded through her heart and overwhelming grief joined her panic. She screamed into the night until her lungs gave out, though she knew it would do no good. She dug her knees farther into the torn earth and pounded the cold ground, willing it to crack under her anguish. Time stood still as tears flowed down her cheeks.

She could not allow herself time to grieve, not when Darroc was still a threat to her people. Not when their son was missing.

Faria pulled herself together enough to reach out to Ander through the *innulum*, the bond elven parents had with their young. She wasn't sure with him being part Val if it would still work.

There, like a light swallowed by the dark, a tiny pinprick of life beckoned to her, its faint warmth resonating in the void. He was still alive.

Relief flooded her body as Faria picked up the bow and quiver that had fallen beside Hunter. Patting the ground for any fallen arrows, she felt something familiar. A black dagger. The Val weapon she questioned him about months ago, the one he hadn't had an answer for. Holding back tears, Faria reached around Hunter and felt for more weapons. She knew where he hid them all. Some were lost in the fight, but the throwing daggers he kept in his gauntlets and boots were still there, four in total.

Casting one last look at her true mate, Faria ran to find her son, following the imprint his essence left behind.

THIRTY

FARIA

It might have been hours or only minutes that she walked. Time slipped away from her as she formed a plan. All Faria knew was that the *innulum* led in the direction of the incessant humming she always heard in this part of the forest. She realized it belonged to the Gate of All Realms and if that was where Darroc took her son, she would follow.

The closer she got to the Gate, the more her body vibrated with its energy. It felt as though ants were crawling along her skin. It made her tremble and want to turn back, but it was just around the next bend through the copse of trees.

Before she could take another step, the earth quaked, its thunderous rumbles echoing through the Forest of the Dawn. She threw out her arms to keep her balance, the shaking so fierce it rattled her bones. Her body screamed in protest, having barely recovered from giving birth and then Darroc's attack. Her teeth clacked in her skull as she waited for the moment to pass, fearing what it meant.

A faint purple light glowed around her. Emanating from her core, it flared to life, blasting through the trees and the land beyond. It shattered into a million pieces and disappeared. A gut-wrenching pain rippled through her. Faria felt as though she were dying, that her very blood was ripping her apart inch by inch. She fell to the ground, trying to hold herself together. It blinded her, threatening to split her head open.

"Mother," Faria gasped into the night. She bent over, clutching her stomach as bile rose. This was the moment the queen had warned Faria about. She had said that Faria would know when it happened. When the protection she placed on her would end.

When she Faded from this life.

Screams tore through the air. Of pain. Of battle.

The war had begun.

Faria felt a hand on her shoulder and through her blurred vision she saw a girl. She looked familiar. Tan skin, freckles, the most brilliant hazel eyes shining through the night. Faria thought she must have been there as her protector, her savior, ready to guide her into the beyond.

"Fifi, we must go, now!"

Fifi? "Who are you?" Faria gasped the words out around the pain, around the hopelessness that surrounded her.

"Come, hurry!" The girl helped Faria stand upright and started running, pulling her to the Gate.

"Nellie?" Faria asked, clarity finally dawning on her. "Is that you?"

Animals screamed through the night, unlike any Faria had ever heard. Like something evil, forbidden. Like they didn't belong there.

Like they should have never been created.

"It's Darroc's army. His creatures." Nellie's voice shook with fear. "They will find us. Quickly, through the Gate."

"But my people, they need me."

"Your *son* needs you. You cannot end this while Darroc still has him. Come, now."

"I am queen now," Faria said, its truth ringing hollowly in her ears. "My mother. She is—"

"Dead. Yes. Please, Faria. This is how we protect them."

"By leaving them?"

Growls interrupted them and strange barks echoed in the trees. Something—many somethings—ran toward them.

"Now!"

Nellie pushed her through the Gate and ran after her. They were suspended in the air, the vibration ripping through her molecules.

Faria silently prayed to the three goddesses and all the gods in every realm that it would lead her to her son.

Dropping back to the ground, they appeared to be in a clearing, not unlike the one they just left. But instead of growls, Faria heard the faint sound of mental clanging, like weapons at the ready. She could not see what made the sound.

"Oh," Nellie whispered, horrified. "Oh, no."

"What?" Faria said, looking around, trying to make sense of where they were. Dense forest surrounded them but beyond that, her elven hearing picked up something more. Noises clashed. She fought to distinguish what she heard. Voices? Music? Blaring horns? The scents she tried to breathe in were so unfamiliar, nothing like Anestra.

A shift in the trees alerted them to change. She scented around her but could not tell what was there.

Animals stalked from the darkness into the clearing, forming a circle around them. Nellie shook beside her, the stench of her fear turning the air sour.

"What is it, Nellie?" Faria asked. She had to have known who they were, or she wouldn't have reacted so strongly.

"My clan."

"Your what?" Faria asked. She couldn't take any more truths that needed to be revealed. It was too much.

"My clan," Nellie said again.

"What does that mean?" Faria gritted her teeth. No one was who they said they were. Nothing was what it seemed. How many more secrets and lies must she endure? "Where are we?"

Nellie swallowed before grasping Faria's hand, her sweaty palm struggling to keep hold.

"Earth. We are in the Human Realm. On Earth."

EPILOGUE

Time has no meaning for him. He might have been unconscious for days for all he knows. There is nothing but darkness and waiting. No sight, no noise, no taste. It feels as though he is floating. It is only the third time this has happened to him. Each time it feels a little different, takes a little longer to recover.

The scent of decayed earth strikes him first, followed by a tortured scream that tears through the air. Still, he has to wait longer for his skin to regrow and vision to restore before he can get to her.

It is an excruciatingly long time before he sees shadows, then shapes, until finally he can decipher what is in front of him.

"Faria!" He tries to scream but his vocal cords are not yet repaired.

It will be too late. By the time he can follow her, save her, protect her, she will be gone.

There is still so much she doesn't know. Dangers that hide in the many realms, waiting for her. Creatures that will follow and find her.

She doesn't know that he cannot die.

He is alive.

ACKNOWLEDGEMENTS

The story of Faria Agostonna has been on an incredible journey, and there are so many people I have the honor to thank for getting her on page and into the hands of readers. It would be impossible to list every person involved, so if you find your name is not on this list, please accept my sincerest thank you.

I will first extend my gratitude to Melissa Hart, my thesis professor who took the time to not only read my story when it was nothing but bones, but provided valuable insight into turning that skeleton into something tangible and lasting.

Many thanks to my editors, Amaryah Orenstein and Quinn Nichols. Amaryah—your ability to find every gaping plot hole is absolute magic. This book would never have turned out this way without your insight. Quinn—thank you for your absolute attention to detail, support, and dedication to making sure my words were the absolute best they can be. This story would not have been anywhere near as successful without you. In fact, this story would not have been published at all without you! Thank you so very much!

To my Beta Readers! You guys kept me going every time I thought about throwing in the towel. Kayla Maurais, Ryssa Collin, Anakha Ashole, Lilian Sue, Jess Broman, Victoria A. Pietsch, and Nirmaliz Colón. The dream team! Each of you come from such different backgrounds and brought incredible insight. Thank you, thank you, thank you!

More than anything, I must extend my forever gratitude to my family. To my husband, Michael, who so selflessly took the reins of parenthood when I had to write and edit for hours on end. You supported all of my dreams, no matter how wacky. You helped me stay the course. You listened to my fears, my gripes, all of my woes. Thank you for your constant support and encouragement.

To my parents and siblings and their constant badgering. Thank you for repeatedly asking me when my book will come out. My mother deserves a special highlight for her endless cheerleading and pushing me to get off my behind and write. Thank you for the constant harassment.

Finally, to my son, Oliver, for giving me a reason to realize my dreams. I do this for you, my love, to show you that anything is possible if you believe.

ABOUT THE AUTHOR

 Emmie Hamilton is a writer, mother, and amateur candle maker. Her favorite pastime is creating worlds others wish they were born into. She received her MFA in Creative Writing from Southern New Hampshire University and has been previously published by Pure Slush Press and various non-fiction outlets. *Chosen to Fall* is her debut novel.

You can connect with her on Instagram @authoremmiehamilton or visit her website www.emmiehamilton.com for the latest publication information.

Made in the USA
Middletown, DE
18 May 2021